She Was Nobody's Trinket, Nobody's Toy....

"Poor Melly!" Sir Malcolm grasped both her hands. "When you return you will simply tell your aunt that you lost your way—or I shall tell her so! You were lost and fortunately encountered me, and I returned you safely to your aunt, who will be excessively relieved that you escaped grave peril."

Miss Bagshot was not so certain that Madame le Best would be the least bit grateful for the return of a scapegrace niece, but she was not inclined to quibble over so minor a point. "That's all well and good!" she responded bluntly. "So long as you remember that I do *not* intend to form a lasting passion for you, sir!"

Never before had Sir Malcolm encountered a damsel so adverse to lasting passions for himself. It was rather a pity, he reflected, as he studied the curve of her merry mouth. . . .

Other Cotillion Regency Romances

Published by POCKET BOOKS

BACHELOR'S FARE

GAIL CLARK

A COTILLION REGENCY ROMANCE
PUBLISHED BY POCKET BOOKS NEW YORK

Another *Original* publication of POCKET BOOKS

POCKET BOOKS, a Simon & Schuster division of
GULF & WESTERN CORPORATION
1230 Avenue of the Americas, New York, N.Y. 10020

ISBN: 0-671-41276-0

First Pocket Books printing June, 1981

10 9 8 7 6 5 4 3 2 1

COTILLION, POCKET and colophon are trademarks
of Simon & Schuster.

Printed in the U.S.A.

BACHELOR'S FARE

Chapter One

"I do not *think* I care for London," remarked Lady Davenham, as with a frown upon her flawless brow she surveyed the town house drawing room, "although it has been so long since we were last here that I do not perfectly recall. Certainly I do *not* care for the way this house has been kept up. I'll wager the holland covers were taken off the furniture only moments before we arrived. It is in sad need of polishing." She approached one of the ancestral portraits which hung upon the light-green-papered walls, stood on tiptoes to run a disrespectful finger along the frame. "Dust, just as I expected! Vivien, something must be done."

Lord Davenham turned away from the window where he stood, and gazed somewhat vaguely at his wife. Her attitude was indicative of awaited comment. "Guano," he supplied.

"Guano?" Lady Davenham glanced quickly at her finger. "Sometimes I wonder where you take your notions, Vivien; it is merely dust. Not that one wishes to find dust in one's drawing room; there is no excuse for it, even when one *has* been rusticating in the country for nigh on a year—still, dust is greatly preferable to bats." She transferred her frowning attention from her fingertip to her spouse. "Why do you think we have bats in our drawing room?"

"Not in our drawing room, surely?" His lordship, a tall well-built man, responded with an abstracted air. "I'm sure I never said such a thing. By the by, I believe the results are very good. I cannot speak with similar assurance about the efficacy of sugar-baker's scum, or hog's hair, and I certainly do not approve of the transportation of Egyptian mummies to Liverpool, where they are ground down into bone meal."

The frown cleared from Lady Davenham's brow as if by magic. "You are speaking of fertilizer!" she said.

This flash of enlightenment earned her ladyship no praise. "What else *would* I be talking about?" his lordship inquired, disarmingly perplexed. "Coke of Holkham has the right of it: 'No fodder, no beasts; no beasts, no manure; no manure, no crops'! It is *you* who said there was guano in the drawing room."

"I did not! You were not listening to me again— which I do not scruple to tell you, Vivien, is one of your *less* endearing traits!" Lady Davenham joined her husband at the window. "Admit that you've not heard a word I said."

"Personally," mused his lordship, "I am inclined to agree that no fertilizer exists more effective than that provided in such abundance by the animal population. Still, much benefit has been derived from more exotic materials like lime and chalk, horn shavings and potash."

To this assertion, Lady Davenham did not trust herself to respond. Silence descended upon the drawing room, broken only by the ticking of the long-case clock.

Gradually, the Duke became aware that all was not well with his Duchess; the Duke was not unintelligent, despite his habitual abstraction. "Poor Thea! I shall drive you distracted one day," he confessed, with the whimsy that was his saving grace. "You are very good to tolerate my air-dreaming. What was it you wished to say?"

With a gesture of her expressive hands, Lady Davenham dismissed her husband's gratitude. "Pooh! I'll warrant you were thinking about spading and raking and seeding and whatever else one does to a garden in the springtime. Excellent! While I am busy with our cousin, you will have something with which to occupy yourself. Just fancy, Vivien—after so many years we shall soon be reunited with Malcolm. What adventures he will have to tell us! I wonder if we will find him changed."

Lord Davenham had returned his attention to the window through which he had been observing his gardens below. Thea's pause clearly called for comment. "Watering and pruning," he observed.

Lady Davenham, whose attention was *not* on the gardens of Davenant House, paused in her contemplation of the neglected drawing room. *"What* have watering and pruning to do with Malcolm?" she inquired, a trace of irritation in her tone.

"Dashed if *I* know!" His lordship's own tones were a trifle strained. "I thought you had just asked me what else it is one does to a garden in the spring."

Lady Davenham forebore to point out that she already knew a great deal more than she wished to know about gardening—as she forebore from wreaking havoc on her husband's flowerbeds to discover if he was capable of strong emotion, a matter about which Thea had begun to cherish doubts. "It is you who are talking about gardens," she reproved. "Not I! I was wondering if we would find our cousin altered by his adventures— not that the *on-dits* which have circulated in his absence would encourage anyone in that hope. I would not especially *wish* Malcolm to reform—it was always a special treat to see him when he was sent up to us in the country when his poor papa despaired over him. No one ever dreamed up such larks as Malcolm—no, or was so much *fun!"*

Lord Davenham had an aggravating habit of attending to the portions of a conversation that one preferred he wouldn't, as he immediately displayed. "I do not think Malcolm has ceased to have 'fun,' as you call it," he remarked wryly. "Rumor has it that he was nicknamed Le Roué by the Princess Borghese. Do you know, Thea, while standing here I believe I have evolved a scheme by which to improve the system of irrigation troughs. Tell me what you think."

What Lady Davenham thought, and it was not the first time she had done so, was that there existed a wide disparity between her husband's outward appearance and his inner self. All the Davenants were wildly romantic looking, with unruly black curls, flashing dark eyes set beneath flyaway brows, adventurous noses, and sensual mouths; in times more suited to their bold natures, they had been buccaneers, robber barons, skilled courtiers. Yet here stood the current head of the clan, serene, elusive, and vague, plotting his annual assault upon his flowerbeds. In the person of Lord Davenham, Lady Davenham thought unkindly, the swashbuckling Davenant blood ran thin.

"I *think,*" she said, when the Duke had ceased to speak, "that you are trying to pull the wool over my eyes! It will not serve, Vivien; recall that I have known you all my life. You think that if you ignore unpleasant things they will eventually go away—or be dealt with by me, which is much the same thing. And while I understand that some people believe me to be of a managing disposition, I do *not* understand why you should recall Malcolm with disfavor!"

Thea had not ceased her housewifely tour of their environment, passing censurious fingers over windowsills, poking suspiciously at the furniture, shaking the curtains in search of dust. Dust she had found in plenty, judging by the smudge presently existent on the tip of her adventurous nose—Thea was a Davenant by birth as well as marriage, and very like the family in appearance, regret as she did the fact. As the Duke watched, she stooped and peered under the carpet. "Just as I suspected!" sighed Thea. "Tea leaves."

"Beneath the Brussels carpet?" inquired her whimsical spouse, arching one dark brow. "My dear, that *is* very bad."

"Not beneath the carpet, on it; they must be spread about and then swept up with a hard brush. That is how it should be cleaned." Thea straightened. "Not that I intend to bore you further with such stuff!"

"As I have been boring you." Though Lord Davenham's tone was kindly, his expression was unreadable. "I *have* been listening, Thea. You have decided Malcolm is incapable of managing his own affairs."

No Davenant, not even one who deprecated her heritage, emerged from the nursery without an instinctive understanding of worldly things. "I am certain Malcolm manages his *affaires* very nicely," responded Thea. "You were not *boring* me precisely, Vivien. Gracious! You are the Duke of Davenham, the head of the family; your preoccupation with estate matters may be forgiven you, I think. I am quite prepared to do so— providing you give me a reason why you do *not* wish Malcolm to come home!"

Conversation being a trifle difficult to maintain with a lady in constant motion, Lord Davenham detached himself from the window and strolled about the drawing room in his energetic wife's wake. He wandered amid small tables, circumventing several heart-backed chairs. Finding himself entangled with a straight-leg sofa, he arranged himself comfortably thereupon. "I remember Malcolm differently from the way you do, my dear—perhaps because I was eldest. Still *am* eldest, in point of fact! You seem to have forgotten Malcolm's habit of allowing others to stand the punishment for his deviltry."

This, from the vague and elusive Lord Davenham, was a very long and lucidly expressed viewpoint. Puzzling over her husband's unusual attention to the here-and-now, Lady Davenham seated herself opposite him on a carved-and-gilt settee. "You are severe!" she protested. "You may also be a little envious. Malcolm could sow his wild oats, but since you were the eldest you have always known that it was your duty to marry young and secure the succession, as *I* have always known I would be your wife. Perhaps it may seem somewhat unfair—not to *me,* as I've no inclination toward adventure!—but necessary to ensure that the line would not die out."

Lord Davenham contemplated the wonderfully shiny boot which he had propped upon one leather-breeched knee. "The line may yet," he remarked.

Reminded of their mutual failure to produce the heirs that had been the reason for their marriage, ensuring that the next generation of adventurous Davenants were at least partially legitimate, Lady Davenham also regarded her husband's gleaming boot. "Is *that* why you dislike to talk of Malcolm?" Thea gasped. "Because he is next in line? But you are a mere two-and-thirty, Vivien. Surely it will not come to *that.*" And then she glanced up from the Duke's footwear to discover a disturbing light in his dark eyes. Lady Davenham had not espied that expression since preparations for the journey had begun. Lord Davenham's habitual abstraction did not usually extend to the marriage-bed. "Vivien—" she murmured, her heart beating faster in her breast.

The expression in his lordship's eye grew even more intense. "*Primula vulgaris,*" he remarked. "Heartsease. Candytuft."

"*Primula vulgaris?*" echoed Lady Davenham. "How *can* you speak so to me, Vivien? I am your wife!"

"You are also absurd!" responded his lordship, clasping his hands around his knee. "I may be a trifle absentminded, but I have not forgot who *you* are, my dear! I don't know why you claim I have. Have I not been talking to you this past half-hour?"

If the Duke had not forgotten her existence, reflected the Duchess, it was because she made it her object to remind him at least once each day. "Sometimes you can be abominably provoking, Vivien! You do it on purpose, I think. All the same, to call me vulgar is to go too far."

Sternly accused, Lord Davenham studied his wife. Enthusiasm for life in general animated Lady Davenham, and an intense curiosity—especially about the details of other people's lives, which she was prone to try and rearrange. "Managing, perhaps; meddlesome, definitely; but *not* vulgar!" he protested. "Can it be, Thea, that you are hearing things?"

Carefully, Lady Davenham folded her expressive hands in her lap. "I distinctly heard you say '*primula vulgaris*,' Vivien."

"*Primula vulgaris!*" Lord Davenham laughed outright. "Not *you,* Thea! Bedding out!"

Bedding *out?* Though Davenants inclined toward such endeavors, conducting their liaisons with verve and élan amid great notoriety, Lady Davenham had thought her husband aloof from such escapades. Could it be that it was not only his wife's embraces that Vivien enjoyed? "Gracious God!" she uttered faintly, shocked to discover how grievously her judgment had erred. "How can you think of—I mean, you haven't got an heir!"

What *primula vulgaris* and heartsease had to do with his lack of offspring, Lord Davenham had no clue. Puzzled, he looked closer at his wife. She was in exceptional looks, he noted. Her cheeks were pink, and she seemed to be positively fascinated by his footwear.

His boots *were* worthy of attention, decided his lordship, but surely they had not caused Thea to behave so strangely. She was the perfect wife, managing the details of everyday life with the minimum of fuss. Yet here she was, if not precisely making a kick-up, at least looking distinctly miffed. Lord Davenham could not approve of Thea being made unhappy. He applied his not-inconsiderable intellect to recalling precisely what had been said.

Bedding out? Could Thea have mistaken—but she had always been shy to indicate her wishes—could a simple trip to London release a lady from what her husband privately thought of as the results of a large dose of propriety at a very impressionable age? Vivien could visualize Miss Marlypole, the dragon of a governess who was doubtless responsible for his wife's passive acceptance of the intimate side of married life. That Thea enjoyed their private moments, Vivien was aware. His only regret was that she never, by any gesture, suggested such moments herself.

Yet had she not just done so, no matter how circuitous the manner? A more animated gentleman than Lord Davenham might have clicked his heels together and shouted hosannahs to the skies. Vivien merely made a steeple of his fingertips, in which posture he looked very much like a pensive buccaneer. "You amaze me, Thea! Never in all the years of our acquaintance have you suggested such a thing. Not that it would have been proper to suggest it before the knot was tied, though *I* wouldn't have minded—but I am delighted with your suggestion, no matter what its inspiration. Shall we retire abovestairs?"

Lady Davenham, grappling with the concept of her husband as a thwarted adventurer, was earning a headache for her efforts. Consequently, she did not grasp the thrust of his conversation, nor understand why he should suddenly suggest that they retire. "Whatever *for?*" she crossly inquired.

Alas for Lord Davenham's hopes, so abruptly dashed. Not for the first time he consigned a certain governess to writhe in eternal flames. "Have it your own way, my dear; I thought you *wished* to retire. If you do not, I wish you would not hint at it." He let fall the hand which he had extended toward her. "I will not tease you further! Instead you must tell me if you agree that *primula vulgaris* and candytuft and heartsease will add sufficient liveliness to the flowerbeds."

"Flowerbeds!" Lady Davenham was aghast at the

misunderstanding. Never, during five years of marriage, and a lifetime of acquaintance, had Thea thought of retiring with Vivien abovestairs in the middle of the day. Now that the notion did present itself, she could not banish it from mind.

Well, and why *should* she banish it? Thea was not quite so passive by nature as her husband thought her; but she felt too uncertain of herself to force her presence on him. Yet was not the purpose of this marriage the getting of offspring? Shyly, she glanced at her spouse.

He was looking not at her, but into a far corner, and the brooding expression on his strongly marked features made Thea catch her breath. "Dibbles and beetles. Pick-axes and rolling stones and caterpillar shears," uttered his lordship into the silence. And then: "Beg pardon, my dear? Did you speak?"

Lady Davenham had definitely spoken, but it would not have been seemly to repeat her exasperated remark. Experience should have long ago taught her, she decided, that when a Davenham's demeanor was most romantic, his thoughts were most mundane. Vivien might look as if he contemplated catching her up in his arms and bearing her in triumph to the connubial chamber, but he had in reality probably been passing through a mental inventory of his potting shed.

Potting sheds! Modesty forbade Thea suggest her husband's interest might be more fruitfully focused on herself. Abruptly she rose from the settee. "Malcolm is approaching thirty. It is time he fixed his affections. Everyone will be mad for him—everyone always *has* been, and though he may have changed since our last meeting, I doubt it is as much as all *that*. Do you remember, Vivien, when he sent us the performing bear? How angry everyone was with him, especially the owner of the beast! But how exciting Malcolm made everything seem, even when it was *not*. And how *flat* everything seemed after he had left, even though nothing had really changed." Rather wistfully, she smiled.

"Which leads me to the conclusion that one should take one's excitement in small doses, if at all."

Had his concentration not been largely directed toward transporting his thoughts from abovestairs into his gardens, Lord Davenham might have deduced any number of surprising conclusions from his wife's remarks. But upon Lord Davenham's impeccably clad shoulders many responsibilities rested, and Thea did not require his assistance in carrying on a discussion, of necessity having learned to converse quite adequately with herself.

Thea moved to stare unappreciatively at her reflection in the pier glass opposite the fireplace. Mirrored in the glass was the feminine version of the dashing Davenhams: dark eyes and flyaway brows, adventurous nose and sensual mouth set in a perfect oval face crowned with riotous thick curls. Her neck was slender and graceful, and as for the rest of her—well, nature had intended Thea to be voluptuous, and though she might drape herself from neck to fingertip to toe (in this instance, an excessively prim carriage dress of white poplin with a deep blonde flounce), and dine for days on bread and water, she still could not disguise that fact.

Irritably, Thea smoothed her hair. Try as she did to repress those curls, drawing them back into a braided circle, their rebellious nature would not be quelled. Already errant tendrils had escaped to cluster softly upon temples and brow. And why the deuce, she wondered, hadn't Vivien told her she had a smudge?

Rubbing her dusty nose against her sleeve, Thea abandoned the glass. "I do not expect you to do the pretty, Vivien, at least not beyond attending to the observances of civility," she ironically remarked. Not for an instant did Lady Davenham imagine that the Duke could be persuaded, whatever her expectations, to bestir himself. "I know you don't enjoy the social whirl. And I shall not be a penny the worse of it, because I *do,* so you need not worry that I shall be fatiguing myself to death!"

So pregnant was her ladyship's pause that Lord Davenham roused from his preoccupation with his garden, which was a much more soothing subject for cogitation than the sudden aversion his wife seemed to have taken to himself. Had she not expressed a dislike of excitement? Perhaps she did not mean it. Still, he must not embarrass her with unwelcome overtures.

She was looking at him in a somewhat hostile manner, Lord Davenham noted. "Of course!" he said.

"Of course *what?*" Lady Davenham acerbically inquired.

"Of course whatever it was you asked me, my dear." Vivien disentangled himself from the sofa and drifted back to the window. "I do not wish to be disagreeable. Tell me, do you *truly* like those rhododendrons? I am of two minds."

A stranger listening to his amiable prattling might think Lord Davenham had no mind at all. Lady Davenham was not so easily deceived. "I do not understand you, Vivien," she remarked, narrowing her fine eyes. "Did I not know better, I would think you didn't *like* our cousin."

"Ah, but you *do* know better, do you not?" With an expert flick of his wrist, Lord Davenham opened his snuffbox, sampled its contents, made clear his intention to let a tedious subject drop.

Lady Davenham rested her lovely hands on the curve of a heart-backed chair and eyed her enigmatic spouse. *Would* she be disappointed in her dashing cousin Malcolm? It might be better if she were.

Chapter Two

The notion that he might disappoint his cousin Thea—
or any other female on the face of God's green earth
—had never entered Sir Malcolm Calveley's head. A
very handsome head it was, the Davenant family features set off nicely by sun-bronzed skin, and curly side
whiskers, and dark hair worn long around the ears.
Upon those dark curls currently rested a high-crowned
beaver hat, and around Sir Malcolm's enviable shoulders was a silk-lined Polish greatcoat with lapels and
cuffs of Russian lambskin.

Not inappropriately, it was of that country Sir Malcolm was speaking. "Barbarous, I do assure you!" he
avowed. "But fascinating, all the same. One must admire a people prepared to set their whole countryside
alight in preference to welcoming the Corsican. Oh, yes,
I was there! I have traveled from Moscow to Antwerp,
from Lisbon to Toulouse."

So fascinated was the coachman by the revelations
of the passenger who shared his box—a seat most frequently occupied by young bloods interested in horse-

flesh, not well-traveled swells—that he turned his attention briefly from the road. "Cor!" he admiringly said.

Sir Malcolm, who had all his life been accorded admiration from unlikely sources, instinctively recognized a spirit whose thirst for adventure had never been quenched. "And in Germany and Portugal, as well!" Sir Malcolm continued. "I was in Vienna for the Congress. Vienna is my favorite of all cities. She is like a woman no longer in her prime, fighting valiantly against the ravages of time, bittersweet with the knowledge of mortality, determined to be gay."

Philosophical digressions were not the sort of fare served up to him by the young bloods who ordinarily shared his seat, and the coachman was not certain he cared for such an exotic repast. In an effort to turn the conversation into more familiar channels, he said, "Ho! A woman, eh?"

No gentleman so cosmopolitan as Sir Malcolm could fail to recognize an invitation to exchange confidences. But Sir Malcolm did not repay the ladies who looked upon him with favor by discussing them with every chance-met acquaintance. And since almost all his adventures involved ladies who had favored him, this chivalry somewhat dampened his conversational style.

But the coachman awaited his reply. "Many women!" he obliged. Fondly, Sir Malcolm recalled several of those ladies, with whom his acquaintance had been, if brief, intense. Then he gratified the coachman with an explanation of how he had occupied himself during the Hundred Days when Napoleon had grown dissatisfied with being Emperor of Elba, and had returned to France, only to meet his final defeat on the battlefield of Waterloo. "And now," he concluded at length, "I have returned home."

If the young bloods who vied for the honor of sharing his seat were more prone to talk of "blazing hours" and "bits of blood," the coachman still had a very good idea of life among the nobs. "Responsibilities!" he wisely observed.

"Responsibilities?" Sir Malcolm looked amused. "Oh, no. Responsibilities are not for such as I, my friend. Let us say, rather, that it is curiosity which brought me home." Then he lapsed into silence, still wearing that half-smile.

As smiles went, it was not one which encouraged further presumption, decided the coachman, concentrating on his team. A great bit of an oddity was this well-breeched swell. He had an easy way about him, but the coachman would wager his many-caped coat that behind those careless manners lay a temper quick as a spring trap. He did not think he wished to know what had prompted his passenger's queer little smile.

Sir Malcolm was not the only passenger on the Dover-to-London stage; the stage, brightly painted and inscribed with the name of its proprietor, as well as the principal towns it served, carried several passengers inside, and several more outside. Bundles and packages were piled high on the roof, luggage stowed in the boots. They were making, thought the coachman, very good time. He glanced at his companion, and dared put forth an opinion that the roads in England were far superior to any found in France.

"And English horseflesh, too!" responded Sir Malcolm, gazing in a knowledgeable manner upon the specimens before him. "Cleveland bays, are they not?" And he gave his opinion of the traditional six-horse hitch. Gratified to discover that his passenger was not so very much of an oddity as to fail to appreciate that noblest of all beasts, the coachman presented his own viewpoint, and very soon all the outside passengers were engaged in a lively discussion of elegant tits, neck-or-nothing riders and spanking turnouts. A convivial soul, the coachman did not immediately perceive that it was not his opinion to which the others deferred; when he *did* realize that his place had been usurped by the passenger with whom he had generously shared his box, he grew seriously disturbed—so very disturbed, in fact, that he dropped his hands and gave even his wheelers their heads.

The team dashed along at full gallop, earning shouts of encouragement from the outside passengers, clinging like monkeys to their precarious perches, and shrieks of dismay from those within. The coachman thought that the swell beside him was sure to be stricken with envy at his skill and daring. Thought, but could not be certain. It was as he turned his head to ascertain whether or not Sir Malcolm admired him that disaster struck.

As a matter of record, Sir Malcolm did *not* admire the coachman. He would fail to admire anyone who landed his horses, vehicle, and passengers all in a ditch. Cursing colorfully in several languages, Sir Malcolm struggled to extricate himself from the very prickly bush into which he'd been thrown. "Hopgood!" he roared, an expression not of intention, but a demand for the assistance of his valet.

That diminutive individual emerged from the ditch to gaze with disprobation upon the hectic scene. The other passengers were no less vocal than Sir Malcolm, and the coachman was equally strident in his own defense.

Hopgood had a very adequate grasp of foreign tongues, and more than a hypothetical knowledge of his master's temper. He immediately lent his efforts toward removing Sir Malcolm from the prickly bush. "Oh, sir! Your coat!" he mourned. "I knew this would happen, indeed I did, when you told me we was to leave the Continent. If you'll take my advice as shouldn't give it, sir, you'll let me arrange that we should return straightaway to France!"

Sir Malcolm suffered leaves and twigs to be brushed from his Polish greatcoat, and tender adjustments made to his tightly fitting coat of superfine. "I have no wish to return straightaway to France," he retorted. "Perhaps you are not aware, Hopgood, that you have been grumbling since we left Calais."

Of course Hopgood was aware of the nature of his own comments; additionally, he was aware that his master's temper was wearing thin. "Beg pardon, sir, I'm sure!" he responded, simultaneously tut-tutting over the indignities dealt to Sir Malcolm's high-crowned beaver hat.

Sir Malcolm gazed upon his fellow travelers, emerging from the ditch. There appeared to have been few serious injuries suffered, judging from the spirited manner in which they were discussing hanging the coachman from the nearest adequate tree limb. It was an emotional scene.

No gentleman of Sir Malcolm's restless nature was a stranger to emotional scenes; experience had given him deep-rooted dislike of them. Snatching his high-crowned beaver hat away from Hopgood's solicitous care, he clapped it on his head and said, "We passed through a village a few miles back. Doubtless someone there can provide us with assistance."

Hopgood looked agonized. "Oh, sir! You do not mean to *walk!* Your boots, sir!"

Sir Malcolm surveyed those items, as if contemplating putting them to use in conjunction with a certain portion of his valet's anatomy. "Yes, sir! As you wish, sir! *Immediately,* sir!" hastily amended Hopgood. He darted back to the coach, took firm grasp of their luggage, and trailed Sir Malcolm down the road

Sir Malcolm strolled along the roadway, his thoughts directionless. It was his habit to live wholly for the moment, a custom that stood him in good stead with the gentle sex. His thoughts currently turned toward that gentle sex, as they often did. In this instance he was not, however, musing upon the various endearing habits of ladybirds and lightskirts, bits o' muslin and birds of paradise, nor of ladies of high station, nor even the Princess Borghese. Instead, he was thinking of his cousin Thea, the only female of beauty with whom Malcolm had never been tempted to dally, perhaps because he liked her so well.

Bachelor's Fare

A strange sound intruded into Sir Malcolm's musing, as if some hound labored for breath at his heels.
Puzzled, he turned his head. After him staggered Hopgood, laden with luggage. "Jackanapes!" observed Sir
Malcolm bluntly, as he forcibly relieved his valet of the
heaviest portmanteau. "Why didn't you leave these
things with the carriage, man? Never mind! Here is the
village." A few rustic cheerless buildings nestled amid
the trees.

Sir Malcolm unerringly directed his footsteps toward
the public house, Hopgood close on his heels. On the
threshold of a large, badly furnished room he paused,
than the sudden aversion his wife seemed to have taken
fire attempted feebly to survive. "Oh, sir!" said Hopgood, peering around him. "This is *not* what we are
accustomed to. Do come away!"

His warning came too late. Angry voices had caught
Sir Malcolm's attention. Looking martyred, Hopgood
set down the luggage.

A buxom serving-wench was engaged in an exchange
of vituperations with her employer, the owner of this
far-from-select establishment. Even as Hopgood set
down the luggage, and Sir Malcolm turned to discover
the cause of the commotion the proprietor gave the girl
a heavy slap. "Oh, I say!" protested Malcolm, who
among his not-innumerable virtues counted a genuine
reverence for womankind.

Not surprisingly, this mild protest earned only scorn
from its target. "The devil fly away with ye!" responded
that worthy, not of a disposition to grovel before gentry,
stumbling over his own awkward feet. To further
demonstrate his republican principles, he slapped the
serving-wench again. "Pot-walloper! Mugwump!" she
shrieked in response. He once more raised his heavy
hand, but before that hand could descend, Sir Malcolm
had grasped the man's shoulder.

"Oh, sir!" moaned Hopgood.

The light of battle gleamed in the barrel-chested
individual's eyes. "Think ye're a proper man with yer

24

fists, is it? We'll see about *that!*" And in very short time he *did* see, if not the precise blow which felled him, stars instead—strategy described enthusiastically by Hopgood, totally forgetting his place, as a nice bit of cross-and-jostle work, with a muzzler to finish it, as dandy an instance of serving up home-brewed as he'd ever seen.

The serving-wench gazed with some awe upon the gentleman. "Lawks!" said she, taking in for the first time the full impact of the stranger, an impact not the least bit lessened by the dust that smudged his great-coat, or the dent in his high-crowned hat, or the scratches on his sun-bronzed cheek. "Milord, you've been hurt. Let me tend to it."

"It is nothing." As was his habit with every female who crossed his path, Sir Malcolm leisurely inspected the girl. She was not a bad-looking lass, he decided. As was his habit when confronted by a pretty woman, he smiled. "Nothing to signify."

Such was the quality of Sir Malcolm's smile that the serving-girl forgot even her stinging cheeks. "Oh, please, milord!" she sighed. " 'Tis the least I can do."

Sir Malcolm glanced from the girl to his host, who would from all indications remain supine for some time yet. Nor would the coach soon be equipped to resume its journey. Undecided, he glanced once more at the girl, and recognized in her eager face another thirst for adventure that remained unslaked.

Sir Malcolm possessed great compassion for frustrated adventurers. He bestowed a look so kindly that it very nearly caused the girl to swoon. Hopgood tut-tutted, catching his master's attention. "The coach," murmured Sir Malcolm. "See to it."

It was not just scratches which the girl wished to tend, the valet thought gloomily, and set out in search of several stout-hearted villagers, and a wheelwright for good measure. While Sir Malcolm toasted his toes before the feeble fire, waited on hand and foot, Hopgood was as usual expected to deal with the more practical details of Malcolm's life.

Hopgood sighed. Sir Malcolm's weakness for the gentle sex would land them in the suds; he felt it in his bones.

Chapter Three

In Oxford Street, in London, stood a fashionable milliner's shop, a polished angular building with gilt letters over the window, which discreetly spelled out: "Mme. le Best."

Beyond that plateglass window—displaying such examples of the milliner's art as a delicate cap of fancifully embroidered mull trimmed with tucks and lace; a trim folding bag of beige moiré; a fragile fan of pierced horn leaves—the milliner's showroom lay, and behind the showroom her atelier. This workroom was cluttered beyond imagining with pattern books and pins and paper, scissors and tapes, needles and thread. Bolts of fabric were piled upon the shelves which lined the walls, and snippets of satin and lace, ribbons and bows were everywhere. In this chamber labored the seamstresses in Madame le Best's employ.

Madame was not happy with her hirelings, an opinion which she was not reluctant to express. "*Imbéciles!*" she scolded. "*Crétines!* The work proceeds *à pas de tortue* —at the pace of a snail!" The seamstresses put forth no argument, but exchanged commiserative glances and bent industriously to their tasks.

Madame le Best did not note their glances, being engaged instead in contemplation of her image in a large rectangular dressing glass. A woman of middle years with a shrewd, suspicious face, Madame was a walking advertisement for her own art. Her high-waisted gown of pale blue poplin boasted a vandyked skirt, and a triple vandyke ruff. On her faded hair she wore a cap of satin inlet trimmed with three rows of lace and a rose on top, fastened under her sharp chin with a garnet brooch.

Behind her the atelier had grown so silent that an alert ear could hear needles passing through cloth. Satisfied with her efforts, and having nigh exhausted her scant knowledge of the French tongue, Madame moved to the doorway. There she paused and raised one admonishing finger. *"Regardez!"* she said darkly, and withdrew into her showroom. A source of pride to its proprietress, this elegant chamber was done up in the Chinese style, with wallpaper that made free, even indiscriminate, imaginative use of dragons and pagodas and mandarins, its furnishings japanned and painted with exotic scenes, or fashioned of imitation bamboo.

If there was a certain smugness in her observation of her showroom, a degree of arrogance in the instructions she issued to the seamstresses, these small conceits may perhaps be forgiven Madame le Best; by dint of careful planning, and considerable hard work, Madame's feet were firmly planted on the ladder to success. Fashionable ladies flocked to her showroom in ever-increasing numbers. Nothing could halt her advance now, she thought with satisfaction, just as a young woman stepped into the showroom—a circumstance that would later lead Madame le Best to reflect bitterly upon the folly of tempting fate.

"Voyons!" muttered Madame, upon first espying the intruder. "And what is it you're wanting, Miss? If it's employment you're after, you've come to the wrong

door. *Tout même,* you might as well answer me some questions. You can sew a neat seam? Embroider? Net? Tat? Only the best will do for this establishment."

There was some justification for Madame's assumption that she beheld a damsel in search of employment, though a startled expression appeared in the girl's big brown eyes. Those eyes were the dominant feature in an enchanting little elfish face, additionally blessed with merry lips, and dimples. From beneath her bonnet peeped blonde curls. *"Ma foi!"* added Madame. "Have you nothing to say for yourself?"

Astonishingly, the damsel responded with great good humor to this rebuke. "Bless my heart!" she chuckled, setting down the large straw basket which she'd been clutching to her chest. "It *is* you, Aunt Helen! I didn't recognize you, got up so fine. Quite a start it gave me when I saw the name above the window—I couldn't puzzle out how some foreigner came to be doing business at my Aunt Helen's address! I was quite in a pucker about it, too! For I have traveled all the way from Brighton, and spent my last bit of money, and had you *not* been here—well, it don't bear thinking on!"

What didn't bear thinking on, grimly reflected Madame le Best, was the presence of this very unfashionably clad damsel in her showroom. She stepped into the entrance passage and closed the front door, then dealt similarly with the door between showroom and atelier. Then she gestured toward a chair japanned in gold and black.

Looking pensive, her visitor dropped carelessly onto it. "Le Best? Is that your name, Aunt Helen? Because if it *is,* I don't know why you was always called Bagshot, like the rest of us, because you was my papa's sister, and should have had the same name."

Madame le Best realized how gravely her complacency had tempted fate. She sank abruptly into an opposite chair. "You will not again mention That Man in my hearing!" she snapped. Her niece's lips parted. "Melly, hold your tongue!"

Briefly, Melly looked adorably puzzled, as if uncertain whether or not her aunt wished her to actually perform this feat. Then the bewilderment cleared from her brow. "You've changed your name!" she crowed. "If that don't beat all!"

Anxiously, Madame le Best glanced at the door to the atelier. It remained firmly closed. She turned to her niece. *"Why* did you leave Brighton, Miss? Surely you have not been turned out of yet *another* place?" Melly's guilty look was all the answer needed. "I should wash my hands of you!"

"You are deuced uncivil, Aunt Helen!" retorted that damsel, on a sigh. "Are you fretting lest I let the cat out of the bag? I am perfectly capable of keeping secrets, Aunt Helen, even when I don't know why I *should!"* Her lips trembled. "You'll be wondering why I came to you, I expect. You see, I was in a bit of a pickle, Aunt Helen, and there was no one else!"

So woeful a demeanor, such lachrymose tones had been designed expressly to tug at one's heartstrings, suspected Madame le Best. "You are *always* in a pickle, Melly!" she retorted. "And you must not call me Aunt Helen, but Aunt Heloise."

"Heloise?" Melly looked intrigued.

Before her niece could digress into speculation upon her change of estate, Madame le Best hastily spoke: "I went to no small trouble to get you that last recommendation, against my better judgment, and I warned you what would happen if you got up to your tricks! Perhaps the situation may yet be saved. You had better tell me about it."

A tear appeared in Melly's brown eye, to be followed in quick succession by several others which trickled down her cheeks. "It was the Hussars!" she sobbed.

The Hussars? Madame le Best was reminded that her niece was a trifle bird-witted. This opinion she aired. "I've known you from the cradle, Miss!" she added sternly. "Even if I *wasn't* on terms with your mama— may she rest in peace—as result of her foolishness over

That Man. So you needn't be trying to play off your tricks!"

In a very businesslike manner, Melly dashed away her tears. "You always *were* the most complete hand, Aunt Hel—Heloise! I shan't be a bit of bother, truly; just give me an attic where I may sleep and I will work my fingers to the bone." As if in proof of her assertion, she wriggled those digits. "You know I am a nacky seamstress; you taught me yourself!"

By experience rendered immune to tears and cajolery alike, stratagems common among the seamstresses in her own employ, Madame continued to look severe. "What *about t*he Hussars, Miss?" she insisted.

A kind-hearted girl, who hated to cause disappointment, Melly foresaw that in this instance she could not live up to her ambition of spreading sunshine throughout the world—and for a damsel of nineteen, Melly had already spread a great deal of sunshine, if not throughout the world precisely, at least among those masculine citizens who had been fortunate enough to cross her path. It was precisely for that reason that she found it so difficult to hold down a position. "They looked so very handsome in their uniforms!" she sighed. "Full-dress regimentals with pretty yellow boots!"

Madame le Best, pondering the perverse fate that had, at the moment of her triumph, inflicted upon her a niece prone to fall into pickles, suffered a moment's disorientation as result of that damsel's confessed preference for the military. Then she recalled that the Tenth Light Dragoons were on home service in Brighton. It was a fact, she suspected, that she should have recalled earlier. "You have been cutting a lark again," she deduced. "Will you never learn to impose a check upon your spirits, Melly? I don't know what is to become of you if you go on in this way."

Had she been of a more reflective nature, Melly might have derived a certain disappointment from her aunt's failure to appreciate her efforts to spread happiness and good cheer. But Melly was not familiar with rumination. "You always *was* one to kick up a dust over trifles!" Melly soothed. "I promise you it ain't anything so dreadful, Aunt Helen—Heloise! It was just a matter of Captain Birmingham missing parade on my account, and I still say it was very shabby of Lady Birmingham to cut up so stiff about it, as if I'd deliberately stuck the needle in my thumb!"

By these confidences, Madame's foreboding was not stilled. *"Did* you do it on purpose? The truth, Miss, if you please!"

But Melly, as befit a damsel bent upon bringing merriment into a dreary world, was disinclined toward truthtelling. Truth, in her experience, was less apt to inspire a smile than a scowl. It was her object to remove the scowl from her aunt's brow.

"As if I'd do such a thing!" she responded, dimpling. "You sound just like Lady Birmingham! I'll wager she wished *she'd* thought of it! Because Captain Birmingham was ever so solicitous when he saw the blood— and it's no use your asking why the Captain had gone into the sewing room instead of to the parade ground, where he belonged, like she did, because I'm sure I don't know!"

"So you were turned off."

"Oh, no! Not then!" Melly's philosophy of truthtelling was simple: admit only what might otherwise be learned. *"That* occurred after Captain Birmingham had taken me to dine with his regiment in the mess hall, to make up for the horrid things Lady Birmingham said." She heaved a great sigh. "Such a rowdy-do over nothing! I don't know what she thought could happen with all those people around—rather, I *do* know, because she said—but . . ."

"Never mind!" Madame interrupted. "I don't care to hear the rest!"

"I wouldn't have, anyway!" Melly added virtuously, momentarily encouraging Madame le Best's hopes that her own high-minded principles had been passed on to her niece. Alas for Madame's peace of mind. Melly then added: "I didn't like him half well enough for that sort of thing. At any event, Captain Birmingham was raked over the coals for neglecting the drill, and *I* was turned off without a character. Again! And so I have come here to you, so that you may tell me what I must do next."

What Madame le Best contemplated bidding her niece do did not accord with either high-mindedness or principles. "Since Brighton did not do for you, we must think of something else."

"Bless my heart! I did not *dis*like Brighton!" Melly was pleased to set forth at least one assertion with perfect truth. "It was great fun and I liked it very well, Aunt Hel—— Perhaps I should just call you Aunt Hell! But Lady Birmingham didn't like *me!*"

Madame le Best clearly understood how that dislike could be inspired. Melly was precisely the sort of giddy young female whom any quiet and modest—and in the case of Lady Birmingham, homely—female must instinctively distrust. Madame had a tendency to distrust Melly herself.

Melly watched her aunt, feeling rather like a prisoner at the bar, awaiting the judge's verdict. It was a sensation with which Melly was not unfamiliar, though thus far no true practitioner of law had been called upon to evaluate her scrapes. They would probably have been more lenient, thought Melly glumly. Doubtless, her Aunt Helen would pack her off somewhere as far away from London as could be found. Melly sighed. It wasn't her fault that her Creator had made her so highly susceptible.

As Madame le Best perambulated around the perimeter of her showroom, seeking a resolution to the problem posed her by her niece, she heard Melly sigh. Though Madame was ambitious, she was not devoid of feeling. Covertly, she studied the child. Child? Melly was nineteen, and so very flighty and mischievous in demeanor that any gentleman who espied her must stop and stare. For her own sake, she should be married, Madame thought.

"Melly!" she said.

That damsel looked up from an issue of *La Belle Assemblée,* through which she had been leafing with a resultant envy that made her feel half-sick.

Her aunt was looking cross, Melly thought. "I'm in the basket again, ain't I?" she sighed, letting the book drop. "I am very sorry! I do not *mean* to get into trouble, you know!" Tears filled her big brown eyes anew.

Almost Madame le Best's determination to discover some permanent solution for her niece failed her; she looked away from Melly's bright face. "Very well!" she said, quickly, before she could change her mind. "I have been thinking of engaging an assistant to help me in the showroom. You may have the position, Melly, providing I have *your* promise that you will do only as I tell you and keep a still tongue in your head!" The child could hardly get up to her usual mischief whilst dwelling under her aunt's thumb.

It was fortunate for Madame's spiritual well-being that she had bent to retrieve *La Belle Assemblée* from the floor, where Melly had let it fall, and thus was spared observing the excitement that blazed in Melly's eyes. "Thank you, Aunt Hel!" murmured Melly, with her most sincere and virtuous expression. "I will try *very* hard to be good!"

Chapter Four

"A nice bit of cross-and-jostle work, with a muzzler to finish it!" avowed Sir Malcolm, looking rueful. "I've a very handy bunch of fives, I promise you! Even my victim, when he awakened from his slumbers, was of the opinion I gave a good account of myself. In proof of his lack of hard feelings, he brought forth some excellent ale."

Lady Davenham's side ached with suppressed merriment. "And what of the serving-wench?" she inquired.

"Ah, the serving-wench! She sampled the ale, also— not for the first time, I suspect!" Sir Malcolm innocently replied.

"Rogue!" said Lady Davenham, appreciatively. "You haven't altered in the least, Cousin. Your behavior *still* merits the most severe reproof." She paused to sip ratafia from a crystal glass.

Perhaps he had not changed during his travels abroad, thought Malcolm, but he fancied his cousins had. With the shrewd attention of the connoisseur, he contemplated Lady Davenham, clad in a habit-shirt with high frilled neck, and three-flounced skirt fashioned from colored sprig. He had forgotten Thea was so voluptuous, and so prim. Then he glanced at Vivien, standing at the window, gazing serenely down upon his gardens. As always, it was impossible to guess what dwelt behind that aloof façade.

Alerted by the silence to the fact that the conversation had lagged, Lord Davenham turned a vague eye on the participants. "Puncheons. *Jardinières,*" he said.

"Puncheons?" echoed Sir Malcolm. "What the deuce?"

"Tubs on wheels which can be trundled through the garden to distribute water," explained Thea, looking glum.

"And *jardinières?*" persisted Sir Malcolm.

Lady Davenham drained and set aside her glass. "The terracotta tubs in which Vivien grows his fruit trees. At this time of the year they are brought outside. They spend the winter within doors, you see, where stoves are used to protect them from the cold." Her tone was distinctly ironic. "Charcoal, Cousin, is far preferable to wood! Gardening is Vivien's passion, Malcolm—if you can conceive of Vivien being passionate about anything, which I concede is difficult! Now, if you please, I would rather hear about *your* exploits!"

Sir Malcolm looked from Lord Davenham, whose serene attention was once more directed outside, to Lady Davenham, who was tapping her expressive fingers on the scrolled endpieces of the straight-legged sofa where she sat. There were few nuances of the game of hearts with which Sir Malcolm was not familiar. This marriage between his cousins had room for improvement, he thought.

"About my passions?" he murmured wickedly. "Shame, Dorothea! You have just got through chiding me about my shocking misadventures, and now you ask to hear *more* of them. I have already told you about my journey here, and of my travels on the Continent. That's all dull stuff for me, my Thea; I was *there*. I would much rather hear what you have been doing during our separation." He smiled. "Much as *you* may like to hear it, *I* do not especially enjoy talking about the fleshpots!"

Lady Davenham toyed with a curl which had escaped its severe braid to nestle on her cheek. "Le Roué," she responded. "You were ever an unobliging wretch! I am not a . . . a prattle-bag; you may trust me to treat your disclosures in confidence. *Not* that I wish to hear about your conquests among opera dancers and demi-reps!" Her expression was speculative. "Have you never considered contracting a marriage, Cousin? You must realize you are a bachelor of the first stare. At thirty it is time your affections became fixed."

Why Lady Davenham should seek to persuade him to enter into an estate for which she herself exhibited little enthusiasm, Sir Malcolm had not the most distant guess. "Though I may not enjoy *talking* about the fleshpots, neither do I intend *quitting* them! You may not reform me, Thea," he responded, with his forbidding half-smile.

Thea was not unacquainted with her cousin's temper, which his expression gave her good reason to recall. "Oh!" she said abruptly. "I did not mean to presume, Malcolm. It is just that I have got in the habit of arranging things. You will forgive me?"

In his window, Lord Davenham stirred. "Not fleshpots!" he was heard to mutter. "*Jardinières!* Terracotta tubs!"

To this interruption, Lady Davenham and Sir Malcolm wisely paid no heed. "It is you who must forgive me!" he protested, sitting down beside her on the sofa and taking her hands. "I should not have ripped up at you in that odious fashion. My manners have not improved during my travels, I fear!"

"Pooh!" Her cousin had lost none of his charm, reflected Thea, gazing not into his sun-bronzed face, but upon their clasped hands. "I do not stand on ceremony with you, Malcolm; you were right to deliver me a setdown. I *did* presume. But it was not idle curiosity!

Everything is an adventure for you, even carriage accidents. I think I must be envious."

Had all the population of his homeland been stricken with a thirst for adventure? wondered Sir Malcolm, dismayed. One man, however sympathetic, could accomplish only so much. Lord Davenham remarked from the window, "A Gothic ruin!"

"Oh!" Lady Davenham's dark eyes flashed. "How *can* you speak so to me, Vivien? I am only five-and-twenty! And though I may not be a diamond of the first water, neither am I an *antidote!*"

"An antidote?" his lordship echoed, looking puzzled. "I'm sure I never said antidote. It must have been Malcolm, which is not especially kind of him, after you went to all the trouble of opening the house on his account."

"On *my* account?" interjected Sir Malcolm, feeling as if he had wandered by accident into Bedlam, and was privy to an exchange between two of the inmates.

"Of course!" Thea's indignant attention was still focused on her spouse. "We are seldom in town, Malcolm. Vivien is wholly dedicated to the improvement of the estate. We now have improved strains of sheep and cattle, and *all* the houses have been rebuilt. Vivien takes his position as head of the family very seriously."

A less likely figurehead for the adventurous Davenants was difficult to imagine, thought Sir Malcolm, eyeing the current Duke, whose perplexed countenance had been withdrawn from the window and turned instead toward his Duchess. It occurred to Sir Malcolm that even so amiable a gentleman as Vivien might not care to see another man clasping his wife. Malcolm was not without experience concerning jealous husbands. He released Thea's hands. "Oh-ho!" said his lordship, so suddenly that Malcolm suppressed an instinctive guilty start. "I wan't referring to you, but to the garden, my dear!"

Lady Davenham was feeling less charitably inclined

than usual toward her aggravating spouse. "What *about* the garden?" she irritably inquired.

"And you say *I* do not listen!" Lord Davenham quirked a whimsical brow. "In this instance, at least, the shoe is on the other foot—and very pretty feet they are! You *are* a diamond of the first water, my dear. I have always thought so." He turned back to the window. "A Gothic ruin might look nice set among the rhododendrons, I think."

In a somewhat dispirited manner, Lady Davenham contemplated her fireplace. "The gardens of Davenant House already contain a lake, and several picturesque vistas enhanced by weeping willows from China and tulip-poplars from America," she explained to Sir Malcolm. "Not to mention the rustic shelter fashioned from tree branches and roots. And all this is in *addition* to the rhododendrons, magnolias, and, of course, the fruit trees!"

"Apples and apricots and cherries!" supplied his lordship helpfully.

Certainly Vivien was no jealous husband, decided Malcolm; the Duke would doubtless be more incensed by trespass upon his garden than upon his wife. Again, he clasped Thea's hands. "I begin to understand why you wished to hear of *my* adventures!" he said softly. "Poor Thea! You have had a dull time of it."

Guiltily, Lady Davenham flushed. "Oh, no!" she protested, without any great conviction. "I must applaud Vivien's dedication. He considers that he only holds the property in trust, and that it is his responsibility to pass it on in the best possible condition to his sons." Not that there would *be* any sons, she added silently, did not her husband devote to more practical matters some of the dedication deployed in his potting shed.

Lord Davenham stirred, glanced at the doorway, smiled. "The patter of little feet!" he very aptly observed.

"Little feet?" Again, Sir Malcolm abruptly released Lady Davenham. "I hadn't heard!"

"There's nothing *to* hear." Thea flexed her fingers, still warm from his grasp. "Vivien refers to Nimrod—oh, yes, the wretched beast is still alive, though he must be all of sixteen."

In accompaniment to these unkind remarks, there appeared in the doorway of the drawing room a long-eared, low-bellied, bandy-legged, sad-eyed, dew-lapped hound of liverish disposition and hue. Immediately, his sad eyes fixed on Lady Davenham. Snarling, he bared his remaining teeth. So stiffly did he move across the polished floor that his audience could almost hear the hound's ancient joints creak. When Nimrod at last gained his objective, and collapsed with a final wheeze across Lord Davenham's highly polished boots, his lordship and his lady and Sir Malcolm heaved a collective sigh of relief.

"All these improvements must be deuced expensive," remarked Sir Malcolm, for want of a more brilliant thought. The Duke left a bit to be desired as a conversationalist.

"I suppose so," replied his lordship, vaguely. "Tell me, Malcolm, what do *you* think of a Gothic ruin? I am inclined toward the picturesque school of gardening." He looked pensive. "Although I will concede Thea is correct in predicting that a Chinese pagoda might look somewhat incongruous in a classical setting."

What Gothic ruins and Chinese temples had to do with the expense of maintaining estates, Sir Malcolm was not certain; in search of enlightenment, he turned to his lordship's wife. Enlightenment, however, was in short supply that day. Thea had remembered that, in lieu of offspring, Malcolm stood to inherit. No wonder he was interested in Vivien's estates—*too* interested, she thought.

Deftly, Thea changed the subject. "You will be anxious to take up the threads of your old acquaintances," she announced. "To put in appearances at White's and Tattersall's and Gentleman Jackson's. Then there are the opera, Covent Garden, and Almack's to visit!" She smiled. "It has been a long time since I engaged in such a round of frivolity. I have been looking forward to your return, Cousin, ever since you first wrote us of your decision."

Sir Malcolm was appalled to learn of the plans made by Lady Davenham on his behalf, few of which appealed; Sir Malcolm had intended to comport himself in a fashion much less decorous and restrained. "You will stay here with us, naturally," continued Thea, interpreting her cousin's silence as consent. Rather shyly, she touched his sleeve. "Forgive me if I seem impertinent, but do you . . . have you . . . that is, are you heartwhole?"

Heartwhole? What sort of question was that for a lady to ask of a gentleman? Sir Malcolm opened his mouth to deliver a sharp rake-down. Then he realized that Thea would not ask such a question without good cause. Yet what cause could exist for such a query? He could think of only one. "Upon my word!" he said.

Happily unaware that her cousin had decided she still cherished a *tendre* for him, Lady Davenham continued: "I am happy to hear that! Oh, Malcolm, we shall have such *fun!*"

Fun? Perhaps Thea was more adventurously inclined than Malcolm had thought. But Thea had a husband, he reminded himself, and though Vivien might be elusive and vague, he was not negligible. "I am afraid we shall *not*, my Thea," Malcolm prudently said.

"You will wish to make your own plans, I credit." Thea sought to mask her disappointment. "I should have known you would. It is my own fault for being presumptuous."

No small part of Sir Malcolm's charm derived from his dislike of causing a lady distress, and as his cousin was his favorite among all the ladies by whose friendship he had been blessed, he performed an abrupt *volte-face,* and nobly fibbed. "You misunderstand. I meant I could not oblige you in your desire to go to Almack's. I have not the *entrée.*"

"Oh, if *that's* all!" Lady Davenham was startled by the quick revival of her spirits. "I daresay it would have been very dull, anyway. It *is* good to have you with us again, Malcolm. Vivien would tell you so himself, were he not preoccupied with Gothic ruins." Satirically, she eyed her spouse.

"*Not* you, my dear!" said his lordship, thus addressed, rousing in turn Nimrod, who snarled at this disrespectful treatment of his ancient and arthritic bones. Lord Davenham bent to scratch the hound's drooping ears. "I thought I told you that."

Lady Davenham regarded her spouse with no small degree of exasperation. Theirs had been an arranged marriage; she had known what to expect—but sometimes Thea wished she might spark some reaction other than the somewhat absentminded affection Vivien doled out impartially between her and Nimrod. "I was explaining to Malcolm that he is welcome to take up residence in Davenant House until more permanent arrangements can be made."

More permanent arrangements? silently queried Malcolm, disliking the implications that he would remain in London for so long. "An excellent notion!" applauded his lordship. "Then Malcolm may view the garden firsthand." Here Sir Malcolm conceded defeat, and, on the pretext of fetching his valet and luggage, left his cousin's house.

Lady Davenham continued to regard her spouse, with less exasperation now than puzzlement. She recalled her conviction that Vivien was less than enthusiastic about Malcolm's return. It seemed she'd been correct. Or perhaps she'd imagined the sardonic gleam in her husband's eye.

Definitely, she had *not* imagined that gleam; it was still there. Lady Davenham felt curiously compelled to defend herself. "Malcolm will settle on an eligible female; I will see to that! Vivien, you must perceive that he will be the darling of the *ton*."

As befit the eldest of a family of adventurers, Lord

Davenham's perceptions, on the rare occasions when brought to focus on the here-and-now, were marvelously acute. "I do not imagine," he gently remarked, "that it will be the *beau monde* our cousin wishes to embrace. But that's no bread-and-butter of mine! You must do with Malcolm as you wish."

"Thank you!" responded Thea, further nettled by this display of husbandly indifference. "I shall!"

Upon hearing his wife's acerbic tone, Lord Davenham displayed surprise. "Did I sound uncaring, my dear? I did not mean to. I *meant* that I wish you would do whatever makes you happiest."

Dare she tell him what at this moment would make her happiest? Lady Davenham had sorely suffered her husband's neglect of late. Thea rose from the sofa, shyly approached her spouse, who had once more assumed his daydreaming attitude. "Absentminded Vivien!" she murmured. "Sometimes I am tempted to *throttle* you, you wretch!"

Lord Davenham was not so sunk in air-dreams that he failed to note that his wife stood very close, wore a rueful blush. Could it be that she—? But no. He had already made that mistake once. If Thea was looking unusually desirable, it was as result of Malcolm's teasing compliments.

"Throttle?" echoed his lordship vaguely. "Oh no, my dear! It is much better to *squash* the little wretches, by break of day, or after a rain, when they come out of the earth to feed. It is good of you to bend your mind to the task—doubtless you are aware I have had to rise before daybreak to deal with the problem—but I don't think it is *possible* to throttle a snail."

So simply was his lordship's absence from the ancestral four-post bedstead, during one of the several hours when her ladyship would have preferred to have him present, explained. Her ladyship's lips moved. "Did you say something, my dear?" inquired his lordship, whose hearing—when he so chose—was remarkably acute.

But her ladyship could not air sentiments less befitting to a Duchess than a guttersnipe. "I have become accustomed to your vagueness," she responded. "Sometimes it amazes me to realize how little I know of what you *really* think."

To this far-from-subtle suggestion that he might bare his soul, Lord Davenham responded with a quizzical expression. "Feeling hipped, my dear?" he solicitously inquired. "Never mind! Tomorrow you shall help me mix white hellbore and the root of palma christi, barley meal and egg and milk into a paste with which we will rout the moles. Did you protest? You must not! White hellbore, etcetera, is a great deal more humane than thrusting a wooden stake into the creature's barrow, and then assaulting the moving earth with a spade, as my gardener is prone to do—yes, and a great deal less demeritous to the garden, too! Do you not agree?"

There was no rejoinder. Lest she succumb to the impulse to deal with her husband as the gardener dealt with moles, Lady Davenham had fled.

Chapter Five

While Mistress Melly Bagshot schemed to remove herself from yet another pickle, and Lord and Lady Davenham with the assistance of their cousin Malcolm teetered on the brink of one, the Chief Magistrate of Bow Street Public Office was confronted with difficulties of his own. With these difficulties he was acquainting one of his Runners, a dapper little individual whose balding pate was embellished by a scant fringe of black hair, and whose stout figure was enlivened by a carmine satin waistcoat embroidered with gold butterflies.

"Blood-and-Thunder!" he echoed, upon the cessation of the Chief Magistrate's confidences. "Aye, guv'nor, that's bad news. I thought we'd heard the end of that rascal all those years ago when he sloped off."

Sir John gazed from beneath his heavy brows at the bare and malodorous chamber which had served as his office for so long, then down at the scarred desk where he sat. "If he *did* slope off. There was speculation at the time that our cracksman was some neck-or-nothing young blood of the Fancy in whom the gull-gropers had got their talons fast, who'd resorted to burglary to relieve his pecuniary embarrassments. *I* don't know. But you almost caught up with our nimble-footed cracksman. When I caught wind of this rumor that Blood-and-Thunder has returned to England, I thought I should inquire your opinion, Crump."

The Runner filled his pipe in a leisurely manner. He was not unaware of the irony in his superior's tone. Crump had not shown to good advantage in the case of Blood-and-Thunder, as evidenced by the villain's escape.

"Lord love you, guv'nor," he said genially, as he concluded the complicated ritual which resulted in the lighting of his pungent pipe. "You must have your little joke! Even if it's true that Blood-and-Thunder has come home—and I misdoubt that very much, because there was no flies on *that* lad!—what could *I* tell you after so long? There was a most rigid and searching inquiry conducted at the time."

The Chief Magistrate reached into a drawer of his battered desk and withdrew a sheaf of papers. "So there was—conducted by yourself. It was you who named him Blood-and-Thunder, Crump, as result of his alleged fondness for that filthy drink." Without overt enthusiasm, he contemplated the Runner, with whom he was seldom in charity. This was not one of those rare occasions. "Sometimes I take leave to wonder if it was not *your* fondness for that same drink that resulted in the investigation leading up the garden path—as result of which the Home Secretary had some *very* pungent remarks to make about the efficiency of Bow Street, as you may well recall."

"Aye, guv'nor." Crump himself would have greatly benefited from a sampling of Blood-and-Thunder at this moment, or perhaps that combination of warm porter and moist sugar, gin and nutmeg, known as a dog's nose. Unhappily, he gazed through the dirty window at a nearby tavern, where, following intervals such as these, a cove's spirits might be revived. Not that Sir

John, though by nature testy, was usually as grumpy as a bear with a sore paw. It was all the result of that accursed Parliamentary investigation the previous year, when the Select Committee had delved deeply into the goings-on at Bow Street and various other public offices, and certain scandals had been brought disastrously to light. Ever since, a great many people of importance had taken a lively interest in matters that didn't concern them in the least. What was the world coming to? wondered Crump. The Committee had even abolished the watchmen's boxes in the wards, so convenient for a little doze, and so tempting to bosky young bucks who delighted in the long-established tradition of boxing the watch.

"Have you suddenly been stricken mute?" inquired Sir John, whose grumpiness had not been soothed by observance of Crump standing at his window and staring like a moon-calf at the tavern across the street. "I asked for your conclusions. Can it be that you have none?"

"Aye." Crump spoke around the stem of his pipe. "I have some." However, it would hardly be diplomatic to accuse his superior of being in a right rare tweak, and little more so to accuse his superior of subscribing to tempests in teapots. "It's a queer business."

Sir John slammed shut his desk drawer with a most unnecessary violence. "Is that all you can say? That it is *queer*? I will go further: it is *deuced* queer, Crump! And lacking the rascal's description, I can hardly cause it to be inserted in the *Bow Street Hue and Cry and Police Gazette*. I *have* arranged for details of various of the stolen items to be circulated again, but I doubt any of them will surface after so long—especially if he's been living abroad."

Ruminatively, Crump chewed on his pipe stem. " 'Twas my opinion at the time, guv'nor, that our Blood-and-Thunder *wasn't* a swell."

"You don't relieve me!" snapped Sir John. "If it is

47

your conclusion that he *wasn't,* Crump, then probably he *was*—or is! Devil take it, can't you recall anything that may be of use?"

The Runner's bright blue gaze was less genial than usual. Carefully, he removed his pipe from his mouth. "If I could recall anything of that nature, guv'nor," he responded stiffly, "I'm sure I would *say.*"

No mollifying words were immediately forthcoming from Sir John, rubbing his weary brow. Not for the first time, Crump toyed with the notion of devoting himself wholly to private inquiry work. As a Runner he was permitted to undertake such commission for anyone who could afford the fee; as a private detective he could devote all his time to such commissions, without being distracted by the poorly paid duties of a Runner, and without being subject to a Chief Magistrate.

Sir John dropped his hands to the scarred desktop. "I received a visit this morning," he announced, "from a group of women reformers led by the Quakeress Elizabeth Fry. What they wanted I am not certain, nor why they brought their business to *me.* As near as I could gather, they think Bible-reading in the prisons will put an end to vice. No sooner did I persuade the ladies that I could not help them than I was alerted that the Regent has received a snuffbox set with diamonds, in which were written pertinent verses from Ezekiel about wicked princes whose days have come. The Regent trusts that Bow Street will ensure that his days have *not.* Then I heard this rumor about Blood-and-Thunder. What I am trying to say is that I *do* want your opinion, Crump." Only silence greeted this admission. "Oh, very well! I will concede that you are *not* ordinarily cow-handed."

Crump recalled his most recent private commission, which had been to prohibit anything being stolen from the premises of a gentleman during a fancy dress ball. He had done his job very well; the gentleman's home had been kept safe from the degradations of pickpockets and thieves—but during the festivities the gentleman's wife had seen fit to elope with her dancing master, a development for which the gentleman had seen fit to blame Crump, and to accuse him of negligence, and to consequently withhold his reward.

He was not yet ready to devote himself to private commissions, decided Crump. "Lord love you, guv'nor, *I* know I'm not cow-handed!" he said benignly, demonstrating that the Chief Magistrate's somewhat grudging apology had not gone wide of its target. "But all I can recall about Blood-and-Thunder is that he had some connection with a milliner. *Which* milliner and *what* connection, I never found out! She could have been his mother, or his sister, or his ladybird; there's no way of telling now. At any rate, we needn't worry about it till we know it's certain he *has* come back."

"Need we not?" Sir John raised his heavy brows. "May I recall to you the Parliamentary inquiry we have just—barely!—survived? And that a member of our own Foot Patrol was convicted of conspiring very lucratively with a well-known thief? The Committee concluded that a severe system of police would be inconsistent with the liberties of the people—but how long will that decision stand if we are hit with another plague of burglaries, especially if they are enacted by a rascal who eluded us long ago? And if a true police force is implemented, Crump, *both* you and I will be out of a place! You begin to grasp the urgency of the matter, I think."

What Crump grasped was the fact that he might well be soon obliged to concentrate wholly on private inquiry work. "I doubt there's reward money in it," Sir John added, setting the seat on his Runner's distress. "Unless, which is unlikely, you can still catch him with some of the stolen goods. I am not assigning you to this old case. Instead, I am asking a favor of you, Crump. I want you to learn the truth of this rumor. I hope you will indulge me in this whim."

Crump emptied out his pipe on the windowsill and shoved it into his pocket. "No reward money," he gloomily echoed. "You're mighty certain, guv'nor, that Blood-and-Thunder *has* returned."

"I am." Sir John's tone was no more cheerful. "I am not so lucky that the rumor may be false. We dare not risk ignoring it, Crump. And any investigation you conduct must be on the *qui vive,* lest everyone from the Secretary of State down to the beadle of St. Bride's learns that Blood-and-Thunder is out and about again. Don't forget that the rascal is a very slippery customer; he's already wriggled off your hook once."

That circumstance, Crump was unlikely to forget. "There's a precious lot of milliners in London," he remarked.

"So there are." By his subordinate's observation, and obvious chagrin, Sir John was ignobly cheered. "You will be kept busy, Crump."

Crump preferred to be kept busy in other manners, like the private commission which he had on very good authority was about to be offered him, concerning a claim to an extinct title, and along with it dormant funds. The fee for such an undertaking would keep him for several months in tobacco and waistcoats. Since application for such work was made through Sir John, Crump dared not set up his superior's back.

He cleared his throat. "A precious lot of milliners!" he repeated. "Seems to me, guv'nor, that we both know someone very suited to such work."

The Chief Magistrate looked briefly wistful, before his eyebrows beetled into a deep scowl. "No! Absolutely not! Under no circumstances is she to be involved in this, Crump. We cannot afford to find ourselves in the middle of a three-ring circus display."

It was true that the party whom he had mentioned was prone to make monkeys of the denizens of Bow Street, and Crump reluctantly abandoned his scheme. "If I was to undertake this little whim of yours, guv'nor," he delicately inquired, "would it mean I *wouldn't* be available for a private commission, was one to present itself?"

The Chief Magistrate was not an unfair man, merely one on whom the responsibilities of his office had taken a deep toll. No one knew better than Sir John the inadequacy of his Runners' official salaries; even the additional money provided them by government rewards seldom totaled more than an annual £30. Consequently, and against his better judgment, he said, "If your services are requested, I won't stand in your way—providing you can convince me that you are making progress on my business. Does that answer your question, Crump?"

"Aye, guv'nor, it does." Crump was already halfway out the door. Once outside, he proceeded more slowly down the stairway and out into the street. Of habit, his footsteps carried him to the tavern viewed so clearly from the window above.

It was an old building, constructed partially of powdered flaking brick, its drab walls bearing ancient advertisements for soap, cure-all pills and physics, combs and pomades and snuff. Crump sat down at a table, prepared to seek a degree of solace in beefsteak and oyster sauce, washed down with stout. Despite the impression he'd given his Chief Magistrate, the Runner had no intention of tramping from milliner to milliner in search of one who had a relative or lover a great deal more enterprising than was prudent. The number of such shops in the city was staggering, females of every station being constitutionally unable to endure existence without access to folderols and furbelows. Crump had visited a few milliners himself, result of his acquaintance with a dollymop with a fondness for laces and bows.

For a few moments, Crump's thoughts lingered upon that little dollymop. During their last encounter she had pined for stockings of fashionable silk, nonsense his pocketbook could not stand. The Runner shook his head. There must be some means by which he could discover whether this rumor regarding Blood-and-Thunder had any basis, and at the same time allow himself sufficient freedom to pursue the private commissions which enabled him to enjoy his pipe tobacco and his eye-catching waistcoats—aye, and his little dollymop. Hard on the heels of that thought, Crump's least favorite among all the Bow Street personnel stepped into the tavern, a young man of nondescript features, anxious expression, and an irremedial habit of tripping over his own feet.

Samson Puddiphat! Crump grimaced so severely that the owner of the tavern wondered if the Runner had taken a sudden dislike to his beefsteak and oyster sauce. Then the Runner's features assumed their usual genial expression, and he gestured expansively with his fork.

In response to that gesture, Puddiphat made his way to Crump's table, after disengaging himself from a table that had put itself in his way. "Pleased to see you, Mr. Crump!" he enthused.

"Aye, I'm pleased about it myself, laddie." Puddiphat's eternal desire to please was one of the several things that most annoyed him, thought Crump, gesturing toward a chair. "Rest yourself."

Looking very gratified, Puddiphat did so, with careful attention to the saber which he wore with his greatcoat. These items constituted only part of the uniform of the Bow Street Horse Patrol. In addition, Puddiphat wore blue trousers, white leather gloves, boots with steel spurs, and a scarlet waistcoat. It was a costume that looked excellent on horseback, during the dark hours of the night when Puddiphat and his fellows patroled the roads leading into London. Crump was not impressed, however, with the appearance of the uniform in a tavern in midday. But Puddiphat was never seen in any other garb. More than once Crump had uncharitably wished Puddiphat might do himself an injury with the saber he always wore.

Confidentially, he leaned forward. Looking even more gratified, Puddiphat followed suit. "Tell me, laddie," Crump murmured, "do you still have a hankering to better yourself?" It was no special secret that Puddiphat yearned to exchange his saber for a Runner's Occurrence Book.

Chapter Six

Milliners were also very much on the minds of Lady Davenham and her cousin, Sir Malcolm Calveley, who stood outside the shop of one such artist, located in busy Oxford Street. "You need not come in with me, Malcolm, truly!" insisted Lady Davenham, giving her escort a little shove. "It will not take me long, I assure you! I know exactly what I want."

Sir Malcolm cast a knowledgable eye over Thea's walking dress of white cambric muslin, worn with a chip straw bonnet and a green sarcenet pelisse. "I know you do, and that is why I intend to accompany you! I am obliging you by attending this rout you have planned—"

"Wretch! It is in your honor!" interrupted Lady Davenham. "If you are thinking someone will recall that old tittle-tattle about why you left England, I wish you would not; a thousand other scandals have come and gone since then!"

"—and in return you must oblige me by attending to my good advice in the matter of your dress," continued Sir Malcolm, ignoring her protest. "Allow me to give you the benefit of my vast experience in this, Cousin, and I shall cease to feel guilty that I have up-rooted you from your bucolic setting." She did not appear convinced. Craftily, he added: "Unless you *wish* to display yourself to all of fashionable London looking like a dowd."

A dowd? Lady Davenham frowned at her reflection in the shop's plateglass window. Certainly she did not wish to look a dowd. Nor did she wish, as was all too easy with her generous figure, to look like Haymarket-ware. This desire, she explained to her cousin. "Fiddle!" he retorted, and whisked her through the door.

Inside the elegantly appointed showroom, Sir Malcolm paused to take stock. Several stylish ladies were engaged in inspection of a swansdown muff divided in-to compartments by bands of white satin, and compar-ing its attractions with those of a muff of Barbary goat-skin. Mediating the discussion was a sharp-faced, mid-dle-aged female wearing a gown of lilac merino with a scalloped hem, half-boots of plum-colored kid but-toned on one side, and a cornette of colored satin trimmed with blonde. Sir Malcolm had not exaggerated his knowledge of feminine fashion. Immediately, he recognized a milliner. Inexorably drawing his cousin with him, he approached Madame le Best.

Madame was not without experience of her own. *"Pardon!"* she said to the chattering ladies, as she de-tached herself. Monsieur was no stranger to such estab-lishments as hers, she thought, and inquired what serv-ice she might provide.

"We are come on behalf of my cousin, Lady Daven-ham," Sir Malcolm responded; since Madame le Best was no pretty lass, he was merely polite. Feeling a trifle giddy, Madame gazed upon Monsieur's alleged cousin, whose expression was at once rebellious and chagrined. "Lady Davenham is in need of a gown for a rout. I have a special sort of gown in mind for the occasion. You were recommended as one who could provide a garment such as I require."

"As *you* require?" interjected Lady Davenham, who was not of a mind to stand meekly by while arrangements were made on her behalf. "What of *my* requirements, pray?"

Sir Malcolm turned on her ladyship the full impact of his smile. "Do you not want to be all the crack, my Thea? Certainly you do, if only to please me!"

Too well did Lady Davenham recall her cousin's habit of having his own way. "It doesn't sound very comfortable," she responded skeptically.

"Comfort! *Voyons!*" interjected Madame le Best. Monsieur's cousin, was this lady? Madame thought not. But it was not her habit to inquire into the relationships between her customers and their gentleman friends. Lady Davenham's costume, she dismissed as provincial. The figure within that costume was less easily overlooked. "Milady is very near perfection," the milliner murmured. *"Très magnifique!"*

Sir Malcolm also gazed upon his cousin, who did not appear to appreciate the compliment. "A diamond of the first water!" he solemnly agreed. "I have it on good authority. She would be even more *magnifique* if you could convince her to abandon her corsets! Yes, *I* know as well as you they're not the fashion, but you must persuade *her* of that. And while you are at it, you must also persuade her that she will appear to excellent advantage in the gown I wish her to wear, because if she does *not* wear it, I will suffer so keen a disappointment that I will be unable to attend her rout!"

Lady Davenham was not best pleased to be reminded of the underhanded methods by which her dashing cousin contrived to have his own way. "Wretch!" she muttered, as she walked to the table set between japanned chairs and buried her flaming cheeks in the most recent edition of *The Ladies' Monthly Magazine.* Sir Malcolm went on to describe the requisite garment in exact detail, without the least evidence of remorse for having put his companion out of countenance.

Madame le Best was not surprised to find Monsieur

knowledgeable; she had recognized an expert on matters sartorial as soon as she set eyes on his slate-gray coat and yellowish-brown vest of matelassé fabric, blue-gray breeches, and Hessian boots. Monsieur had spared no expense to provide himself with the best. Nor, from the gown he was describing, did he intend to stint on his cousin—cousin? Lady love! "Milady is very fortunate," Madame remarked.

Sir Malcolm recalled the latest encounter between milady and her husband, during which Vivien had waxed enthusiastic about his determination to invent a reaping machine. To date his lordship's efforts in that line had not been successful, although he had managed to avoid the more nightmarish repercussions of his attempts to couple horse traction with a system of moving knives. "Milady is not so fortunate as you may think," he replied. "I will be frank with you, Madame le Best: milady seeks to attract the attention of, er, a certain gentleman who fails to, ah, appreciate her better qualities."

"Oh, *là!*" murmured Madame, rolling her eyes heavenward: Here was as farfetched a tale as she'd heard in many days. Few gentlemen would be sufficiently shortsighted as to fail to appreciate milady's 'better qualities,' no matter how provincial her attire; and Madame wouldn't wager a brass farthing that Monsieur cared a fig for any gentleman but himself. Brass farthings put Madame in mind of payment. She mentioned a sum. Monsieur did not protest, didn't even quiver an eyelid. Monsieur must be very wealthy, deduced Madame. Enthusiastically, she embarked upon a discussion of the relative merits of cord and braids and bands of self-material as trimmings for milady's gown.

Lady Davenham, meantime, had grown heartily bored of *The Ladies' Monthly Magazine,* had turned her attention instead to a bonnet modeled on a classic helmet, and a beaver creation fashioned after a man's top hat. She still was not certain how her cousin had persuaded her to visit this fashionable shop. Thea was perfectly content with her own dressmaker, uninspired though that good woman's efforts might be. To drape herself about in the highest kick of fashion—or to *un*drape herself, as the fashion was—was only to call attention to herself. Yet she did not want to be a dowd, either, especially on the occasion when she reintroduced her dashing cousin to the *ton*. Malcolm was accustomed to the company of sophisticated, worldly females—*very* sophisticated and worldly, if one believed the *on-dits* about the Princess Borghese. Thea supposed she could endure being made fashionable, at least for one night.

So perfectly did a sigh punctuate her thoughts at that moment that Lady Davenham briefly believed she had herself expelled breath. Then she realized she had not. She glanced away from the beaver hat to discover that a mischievous-looking damsel had perched upon the nearby japanned chair. The girl wore a plain calico morning dress. Her eyes were big and brown, and her blonde curls were dressed in full ringlets on either side of her enchanting face.

"It *is* a nacky bonnet, ain't it?" she sighed anew. "Or maybe I should more properly call it a hat, or a capote, or a toque! For the life of me I can't recollect the difference, not that I think it matters one whit!" She giggled, and looked guilty, and clapped her hands to her lips. "There I go, jawing on again, after my aunt said I must *not!* But a person gets deuced dreary talking to herself! Beg pardon if I've said something I shouldn't, I'm sure! My name is Melly Bagshot, ma'am."

"And I am Lady Davenham," responded Thea, smiling at the deplorable manners of this beguiling minx. "Madame le Best is your aunt?" It was only an idle query, but all Melly required to launch into a spirited explanation of her hotfoot departure from Brighton, complete with details concerning Captain and Lady Birmingham, pricked thumbs and missed parades and dinners in the regimental mess hall. "Gracious!" Thea said faintly, when Melly paused for breath.

"Oh, I am sadly bird-witted!" confided that damsel,

unrepentant. "I only get out of one pickle to tumble into another, and Aunt Hel ain't at all happy about it, I can promise! But that's the way it *is* with me. There's wild blood in the Bagshots."

"Bagshot?" echoed Lady Davenham. "Is your aunt's name not le Best?"

Melly grimaced. "Oh, it is! My aunt's French! She lost all during the Revolution—or her family did! *My* family, that is! We have come down in the world, you see! You may trust my Aunt Hel to turn you out in prime style, ma'am! But bless my soul, here I am jawing on, just like I said I *shouldn't*. Please don't tell my aunt that I've been misbehaving, or she'll *never* let me set foot out of this blasted shop!"

Thea was enough of a Davenant to recognize a damsel prone to larks and frolic, and to understand how such a damsel must deplore being restrained. With no little sympathy, Thea glanced at Madame le Best. Melly cautiously followed suit. Her attention was immediately caught by the gentleman with whom Madame conversed. "Bless my heart!" she said.

Lady Davenham could not help but be amused by the admiration on her companion's elfish features; it was an expression she had glimpsed on numerous female faces of late. "The gentleman is my cousin, Sir Malcolm Calveley," she kindly explained. "He has recently returned to England after several years abroad." Whether Malcolm had benefited from that sojourn, Thea was still not prepared to say.

Lady Davenham's cousin? Melly thought not. In her experience, gentlemen did not usually accompany their cousins to milliners' shops. She eyed her companion with new respect. Then Melly looked once more at Sir Malcolm. There was a gentleman who would well understand a girl's little weaknesses, she thought; it would have been the sunniest of all days had he fallen in *her* way. "It's almost more than flesh and blood can stand!" she sighed.

That sigh interfered greatly with Madame le Best's

concentration, interrupted in mid-speech her dissertation upon the relative advantages and disadvantages of Indian and Chinese and French gauze. No sooner did she pause than Sir Malcolm grasped the opportunity to beckon to his cousin. As he did so, he noticed the damsel seated next to her. As was his habit, he smiled.

"Monsieur has described to me exactly the gown milady requires," Madame le Best enthused, as Lady Davenham approached. "Monsieur exerts himself to bring milady into fashion. Milady is very fortunate to have a—ah!—cousin so *sympathique*—and very wise to allow him to guide her in setting herself up in the latest mode!"

"The latest mode?" echoed Thea, doubtfully. "I don't think—"

"Do you not trust me, my Thea?" inquired Sir Malcolm, withdrawing his attention from the pretty damsel who had responded with a roguish glance to his appreciative smile. *There* was no frustrated thirst for adventure, he reflected, with amusement. "You will take the shine out of every other female at your rout."

"*Oui,*" agreed Madame le Best, with what she fancied was a Gallic gesture. "It is assured!"

Lady Davenham reminded herself that Malcolm's appearance at her rout was the first step toward settling him with an eligible wife, and that Malcolm had threatened *not* to appear unless he obliged him concerning this matter of a gown. "Have it your own way, Malcolm!" she said, resigned, as she permitted Madame le Best to guide her toward the atelier. "You generally do!"

Generally he achieved his object with a great deal less effort, Sir Malcolm reflected, as the milliner disappeared with Thea into the workroom, there to subject her to a stern lecture upon the underpinnings most flattering to the current mode—a long chemise of linen, reaching well below the knees; light flexible stays; a cotton petticoat in warm weather and fine flannel in the cold, and then the gown or slip; or, if one was *very* daring, nothing but tights—and, in general, to give her ladyship a world of good and wholly unappreciated advice.

As his cousin was initiated into the mysteries of the atelier, Sir Malcolm surveyed the showroom, a small abstracted frown on his sun-bronzed brow. No dislike for furnishings in the Chinese taste prompted that indication of dissatisfaction; after life abroad, he was finding England very tame. If only Lord Davenham's attention might be diverted from his garden to his wife, then his wife's attention might be diverted from Sir Malcolm, who consequently would be free to pursue his own preferred diversions, among which were not *levées* and *soirées* and routs.

As Sir Malcolm frowned upon the showroom, Melly in turn contemplated him, from the corner of the chamber where she had withdrawn in hope of placating her aunt. Sir Malcolm was positively cudgeling his brain, she decided, else he would have long since become aware that a very merry pair of eyes peered at him over the top of a volume of *The Gallery of Fashion*. Melly didn't think Sir Malcolm was generally oblivious to such things. A resourceful lass, she closed the book and callously let it drop, conduct that would have appalled her aunt, who had carefully collected each of the monthly issues of *The Gallery,* and who was very proud to possess the entire nine volumes, containing in all two hundred fifty-one hand-colored aquatints.

"What the *deuce?*" inquired Sir Malcolm, startled by the noise of the falling book. Setting aside the puzzle of whether or not Thea still nourished a *tendre* for him, and the resultant puzzle of whether or not he had to consider her sensibilities—Sir Malcolm always considered the sensibilities of the ladies who on his behalf had been stricken by Cupid's darts—he turned to discover the distraction's source.

By a mock-bamboo bookcase stood a girl, and at her feet a book. She had clasped her hands to her breast in an attempt to look dismayed—an attempt wholly set at naught by the dimples in her cheeks and the twinkle in her big brown eyes. Sir Malcolm, result of long experience, immediately recognized a lure cast out. Gallantly, he bowed, and with a bewitching smile restored the damsel's book.

"Why, bless my soul!" giggled Melly, with fluttering eyelashes and an arch glance. As Sir Malcolm parted his lips to respond in kind, a stern voice issued from the atelier.

"*Eh, bien!*" said that voice. "Monsieur, *regardez!*"

"If that ain't just my luck!" Melly sighed.

In Madame's hand were several sketches, and on her face a darkling look. She nudged Lady Davenham, whose doubtful attitude was doubtless result of Monsieur's conversation with Madame's own scapegrace niece. "*Allons!* We shall make Monsieur's eyes pop right out of his head."

Roused by Madame's sharp elbow from speculation upon the cause of her cousin's sudden interest in her wardrobe, and appalled by Madame's misinterpretation of that interest, Lady Davenham gasped: "But I do not *want*—"

"*Zut!*" hissed Madame, vowing to award Melly a proper trimming immediately after the showroom was cleared of customers. "Of course you do."

Malcolm rejoined them then, scrutinized Madame's sketches. Covertly, Thea stared at him. *Could* the milliner be correct in her assumptions? Lady Davenham honestly did not know.

Chapter Seven

Despite Lady Davenham's assurances that old *on-dits* would remain buried, Lord Davenham was even then discovering that the ancient scandal concerning Sir Malcolm Calveley had arisen moldering from its crypt. *"What* old tittle-tattle?" he inquired, somewhat plaintively, of the gentleman who sought to acquaint him with that distasteful fact. "I thought we were talking of growing plants without using soil, by feeding them on solutions of water and mineral salts. Are you *quite* sure you're of sound mind, my dear James?"

"As right as a trivet!" responded his lordship's companion, a bluff and plain-spoken country squire. "Everybody is talking about it. I thought I should drop a hint or two. Never have I known such a person as you are for keeping yourself well wrapped in lamb's wool!"

The perplexity that had appeared on Lord Davenham's serenely handsome features, as result of his friend's allusion to Sir Malcolm Calveley's reprehensible history, magically cleared away. "Yes, let us talk of wool!" he responded enthusiastically. "Will you attend Coke's clippings this July? What improvements the man has brought about in his flocks and harvests! I am promised for the Woburn sheep-shearings, under the auspices of Bedford, also. Tell me, James, which breed do *you* favor? Romney Marsh or Border Leicester?" He looked contemplative. "I have decided to revive the use of black-spotted Jacob sheep as ornamental lawn-mowers in my parks. It was such a charming custom. Legend has it that they first arrived in Britain after the defeat of the Armada—swimming ashore from the shattered galleons, you know!"

"What I *know* is that you are attempting to pull the wool over *my* eyes." The squire had been acquainted with Lord Davenham for the larger portion of his life-time, and therefore knew that his lordship's evasive manner stemmed from a sensitive nature and an innate desire for privacy. "I will not let you do so. It is ridiculous, in a man of your rank, to seclude yourself like a hermit—yes, and dangerous."

"A hermit, James?" Hermits did not ordinarily pos-sess wives rumored to be running wild over other gen-tlemen, Lord Davenham reflected, as he responded to his friend's ominous predictions with a gentle smile. "I am not so secluded as all that. Have we not just de-parted the spacious auditorium of the Royal Institution of London, where we listened to an erudite speculation upon the nature and propagation of light? Am I not even now walking with you down Fleet Street, en route to the Temple, on some legal errand of your own? You may note, James, that I have *not* inquired into the nature of that business."

"And you wish I would be similarly restrained," de-duced the squire, a short and portly individual with complexion of a ruddy outdoors hue, and a tempera-ment that did not shilly-shally around a point. "I'm sorry I must disappoint you. If you won't think of your-self, Vivien, at least think of your wife!"

"My wife?" This advice caused a disquieting gleam to appear in his lordship's eye. "You would do much better to stick to sheep, James! Or if you do not care for sheep, there are always turnips. Townsend recommends them highly as winter feed."

No one who did not love his lordship would ever attempt to engage him in a personal conversation, so much did he dislike them, but the squire knew where his duty lay. A man with an interest in land management equal to Lord Davenham's own, James would much rather have conversed about such practical matters as sheep-shearings and crops. However, Vivien was in a spot of trouble, and he must be made to see that it would not be simply wished away.

Rudely, the squire expressed an adverse opinion of Lord Townsend's turnips. Having thus secured Lord Davenham's amazed attention, he continued inexorably. "You may as well listen to me and have it over with, Vivien; I shan't be silenced on this head! People are very curious about Calveley's sudden return to England —almost as curious as they were about his departure. You can't stop their speculations by burying your head in the sand."

"Sand?" His lordship gazed vaguely downward as if he expected to find himself knee-deep in that substance. Perhaps James did not perfectly comprehend that a change of subject was prudent? His lordship dropped a gentle hint. "James, have you ever considered having your swamps drained? It should have been done long ago. I suspect your agent isn't doing his job properly."

"The devil with my agent!" snapped the squire, determined to be distracted neither by Lord Davenham's digressions nor the importunations of the countless street-sellers who thronged the ancient thoroughfare. "Consider, Vivien: Le Roué! The Princess Borghese!"

Lord Davenham did consider, wearing a faint frown. His old friend had the tenacity of a bulldog. "You are speaking of my cousin," he observed, "although I fail to see what Malcolm has to do with draining your swamp. Unless you are thinking *he* would make a better agent? My dear James, that settles it. You are *not* of sound mind!"

"Not my swamp!" persevered the squire, with an exasperated glance. "No, nor my agent! It is Calveley I wish to discuss."

Looking slightly shamefaced, like a street urchin caught out in some rude act, Lord Davenham bought some steaming chestnuts from a street-seller and popped several into his mouth. "I know you wish to discuss my cousin, James, but I do *not!* In point of fact, I do not want to even *think* about Malcolm." Before the squire could voice further objections, his lordship embarked upon a brilliant refutation of the theories they had just heard concerning the nature and propagation of light.

For some time the squire listened without murmuring either acquiescence or protest, merely munching in a ruminative manner upon his lordship's chestnuts. When they arrived at the old Middle Temple gate, built by Inigo Jones from a design by Sir Christopher Wren, he deemed it time to interrupt the pleasantries. "I don't blame you for not wanting to think of Calveley; it's deuced annoying to have to concern yourself with this sort of twaddle when there are so many more *important* things going on. But you must! Consider the succession." Lord Davenham's frown reminded his friend not only that the subject of Lady Davenham was taboo; but also that, though slow to anger, Vivien was very handy with his fists. There was in his lordship's stillness a hint that anger was not far off. "Dash it, Vivien!" James said plaintively. "You should know that it's folly to give a mettlesome filly her head!"

Lord Davenham did not immediately answer, being wholly occupied with reminding himself that he could not indulge his impulses to roundly snub friends who presumed—at least not if they wanted to maintain those friendships. Vivien wished to keep the squire's friendship every bit as much as he wished to avoid a discussion of his wife. Perhaps if he refused to answer James's questions, James would cease to ask them?

With a mighty conversational hop, Lord Davenham progressed from the propagation of light to animal husbandry. "I am not especially concerned," he allowed, "with the improvement of horseflesh. Sheep, however, are an altogether different matter; I take particular pride in the wool of my merino flock. Persuade that lazy agent of yours to have the swamps drained and you may raise your own flock."

Though not an especially patient man, the squire was astute, and he knew that the ice on which he trod was very thin. He had expressed his concern. If Vivien chose to divulge confidences, which seemed highly unlikely, it would be in his own good time. "I don't care to raise sheep!" James responded irritably, as they walked down the Middle Temple Lane.

Relieved that his friend had at last ceased to badger him, Lord Davenham brandished the umbrella—green, lined with yellow—that he carried not as any concession to fashion, but because the grayness of the day hinted strongly at impending rain. "If you do not wish to raise sheep, then why did you introduce the subject?" he very reasonably inquired. "Cattle will do just as well—but you must make up your own mind!"

"Thank you!" the squire responded ironically. By this time the gentlemen had passed the Brick Court where Oliver Goldsmith once lodged, and ahead of them lay the Middle Temple Hall, where Shakespeare had long ago presented his first performance of *Twelfth Night* in the presence of Queen Elizabeth. Beyond the Hall, the Temple garden stretched. "You are roasting me again. You know I don't want to raise cattle, either. In point of fact, I don't even want to drain my swamp!"

"No?" His lordship gravitated toward the gardens, narrowly avoiding collision with a barrister hurrying along the peaceful pathway, clutching at his flapping gown and gray wig. Then he turned quizzically to his friend. "I daresay you know your own business best.

As you think *I* do not. You are determined to issue me dire warnings, even though I assure you there is no need to trouble yourself."

"I am that." Eager to take advantage of this sudden receptive mood, James still sought a tactful phrasing for his next remark. "I am very much afraid that Lady Davenham—that is, a certain amount of notoriety surrounds Calveley—dash it, Vivien! She's been *coquetting* with him!"

"Coquetting?" Lord Davenham could hardly take offense at a remark he had practically invited. Wondering what had inspired his passing madness, Lord Davenham gazed upon his green and yellow-lined umbrella. "I very much fear you are suffering from maggots, James."

"Maggots?" The squire reminded himself that no gentleman, even a gentleman so unworldly as Lord Davenham, must relish learning that his wife was openly intriguing with another man. Naturally, Vivien would attempt to change the subject. What had they been talking about? "In my swamp?"

"No," responded his lordship gently, "in your brain. Reassure yourself, James; Thea has coquetted with no one in all her life. Indeed, it is Thea you should talk to about these *on-dits* which so concern you. She has the disposition to meddle, not I."

Obviously, the problem must be approached from another angle, decided the squire. He moved a prudent distance from his lordship's umbrella before repeating: "It's a fool who allows a mettlesome filly too much rein."

Whimsically, Lord Davenham regarded his friend. "What is this obsession you have today with fillies, James? I did not know you were in the petticoat line!"

Exasperated, the squire scowled at his friend. "I'm not!" he snapped.

"You relieve me." Lord Davenham bent and plucked a rose, inhaled of its fragrance, tucked the flower into the top buttonhole of his vest. "Relieve me on another matter, James! If I thought you were referring to my wife in so singular a manner, I should be obliged to accuse you of impertinence, which neither of us would care for." He smiled. "And in any event, I doubt Thea would like to be kept on a short rein."

It was Lord Davenham who was singular, decided the squire. What signified Lady Davenham's dislike? A man was master of his own home, surely, and all who resided therein. At least most men were, James amended. In the Davenham household, from all appearances, the established order might well have been overthrown. He hastened to catch up with his friend, who during his reflections had strolled away down a garden path.

"Vivien!" he wheezed, and clutched at the Duke's arm. "People also recall that old rumor that Lady Davenham would marry Calveley instead of you—it was *more* than a rumor; wagers were laid on it in the clubs! I know that for fact, because I put my own name in White's betting book." Recalled by his friend's quizzical glance to the callousness of this observation, the squire turned ruddier yet. "I wagered that she'd have *you*, of course! The point is that people remember that sort of gossip, and now Calveley no sooner returns than he begins to pay Lady Davenham attentions that are a little pointed. I'm not saying there's anything to it, mind, but it *looks* bad!"

"Looks bad?" Lord Davenham reached out and ruffled the squire's whiskers, seemingly under the impression that the wheezing noises issued from his arthritic hound. "Nonsense, James!"

Ignorance was bliss, reflected the squire; it was a philosophy to which Lord Davenham obviously ascribed. "Have you not the least concern for the prospect?" James wearily inquired.

The prospect which most interested Lord Davenham was that of escaping the concerned queries of his old friend. Vivien gazed about him, with the guilty air of one whose attention had strayed. "The prospect? It is very pleasant—*so* pleasant that had I been aware of it,

I might have considered becoming a barrister at law—
had my position allowed such a thing, that is! It is very
peaceful here, as befits a place where the rights of
sanctuary are still observed—and I confess to an ignoble pleasure in the thought that even the Lord Mayor
must leave his robes outside when he ventures into this
community." He dug the ferrule of his umbrella into
the soil of a flowerbed. "Beg pardon, James! Did you
speak?"

The squire had indeed spoken, and those muttered
words had been no praise of Lord Davenham's evasive-
ness. "I appreciate the delicacy of your position, Vivien.
Calveley is your heir. You can hardly take your wife to
task for associating with him."

"I cannot?" His lordship rotated the ferrule of his
umbrella to and fro. "I do not wish to argue with you,
James, but it seems to me that I may take my wife to
task for anything I please."

At least a step in the proper direction had been
achieved. The squire rendered devout thanksgiving.
"Then you will wish to intimate to Lady Davenham
that you cannot approve her association with profligate
men," he suggested delicately.

"On the contrary, James; I wish to do no such
thing." Lord Davenham was inspired by the results of
his umbrella's application to drop down on one knee.
"Thea wouldn't like it."

"Really, Vivien!" The squire was aggravated almost
beyond belief. "It is not for me to tell you how to deal
with your family, but I warn you that if you do not
make *some* effort to remedy this situation, it will grow
abominably out of hand. Or perhaps you do not *care*
if your family is made an object of notoriety!"

"Not at all," responded his lordship, who was now
digging with his quizzing-glass, and every evidence of
pleasure, in the flowerbed. "I don't pay much attention
to such things, you know. If Thea doesn't mind being
talked about, why should I? At any event, the Davenants always *are*."

Faced with such obduracy, the squire retracted his prematurely offered thanks. "I will say no more. 'Tis you who must bear the consequences of your folly. I only hope those consequences may not be such as force even you to come down out of the clouds!"

This admission of defeat attracted Lord Davenham's attention as prophecies of disaster had not. "You are very good to concern yourself with me, James!" he said gently. "But you need not. Thea has taken Malcolm in hand with a notion of settling him respectably—and though I doubt she will be successful, it would be wrong of me to interfere. As for Malcolm, he may stand next in line, but I haven't stuck my spoon in the wall yet. Nor do I plan to do so in the near future. Now, James, are you satisfied?"

The squire was far from satisfied, but he refrained from saying so; already he had tried his old friend's civility too hard. "Why *did* Calveley leave England, and with such unseemly haste?" he inquired abruptly. "For all the tittle-tattle, no one seems to know."

Lord Davenham's interest was not held. He picked up a handful of soil and studied it through his quizzing-glass. As he did so, he said vaguely, "It distresses me beyond description to disappoint you, James, but I have never paid particular attention to Malcolm's pecca-dilloes."

The squire was not deceived by this offhand manner —or so he thought. "Hah! You don't like the fellow above half."

Lord Davenham rose and dropped the dirt back into the flowerbed. "You really would be wise to study the different types of soil, James," he said. "I could tell you all sorts of interesting things from the sample I just inspected."

"I'll take your word for it!" the squire responded hastily, glancing at the violated flowerbed. "And *nothing* you can say will persuade me you have a fondness for Calveley—no, or that you trust him an inch! You're not half so absent-minded as you make yourself out to be a great portion of the time—and *why* you chose to do so is beyond my ken!"

Lord Davenham responded to this outburst with a thoughtful look. Ever-hopeful, the squire paused. Perhaps he might yet explain his queer conduct to an old friend?

Clearly comment was called for, decided his lordship. But he could not explain his actions to himself, let alone to his companion. Did she wish to leave him, a man could not bind a woman to him, even his own wife. He could only hope that she would decide she wished to stay. Yet to try and influence her to do so seemed somehow unfair.

That James would scoff at this quixotic attitude, Lord Davenham realized. "Ants," he supplied. "I wonder if I should tell the keeper of these gardens of my favorite remedy—if one burns empty snail shells with Storax wood and throws the ashes on the ant hill, the little inhabitants will presently be obliged to remove themselves. What do you recommend, James?" The squire grimaced, grunted, stamped angrily away.

Lord Davenham exhibited no dismay as result of his friend's desertion. Nor did he follow the squire out of the Temple gardens. Instead, Vivien opened his yellow-lined umbrella against the drizzle that had begun to fall, and strolled for a time among the red and white rose bushes, looking very pensive, and a little amused.

Chapter Eight

Much as Miss Melly Bagshot might have admired Lord Davenham's fashionable yellow-lined green umbrella, that item would have been of little practical benefit. More than inclement weather bothered Melly. Her aunt's determined efforts to curb her natural high spirits had afflicted Melly with what is best described as a drizzle of the soul.

At least the weather matched her mood, she thought, glancing up from the netted miser's purse to which she was applying henna beads in a paisley cone pattern. The world appeared dismal and gray through the plate-glass window of her aunt's shop. Not that Melly would have minded a certain inclemency of weather, if only she could have escaped her aunt's watchful eye. Even now that piercing eye was fixed on her, as its owner alternately cajoled her customers and chastised the seamstresses busily working in the atelier.

Suddenly the bleak vista was greatly enlivened by the advent of a leather-hatted man, clad in a blue great-coat and a scarlet vest. He was studying his reflection in the glass, decided Melly, as she watched him grimace at himself. Intrigued, she set down her work. The leather-hatted individual removed himself from the window and reappeared on the threshold of the showroom. There he halted. The saber that he wore over his blue greatcoat was lodged in the doorjamb.

"Bless my soul!" murmured Melly, as she avidly drank in the details of the newcomer's raiment, which additionally included leather stock, blue trousers, Wellington boots with steel spurs, and white gloves. Though this fellow could hardly compare with such gentlemen as Sir Malcolm Calveley, who need only step into a room to set a girl's heart aflutter, and who doubtless had never got stuck in a doorway in all his life, the newcomer was a fellow, nonetheless. Melly advanced.

His hair was brown, his figure unremarkable, his countenance earnest, anxious, and a trifle foolish—though it may have been his predicament which made him look that way. Without preliminaries Melly reached out, grasped the saber, and extricated it from the doorway. The saber's owner untwisted his neck, and ended his resemblance to a dog chasing its own tail. His gaze fell upon Melly. He froze open-mouthed, as if turned suddenly to stone.

Melly was not unfamiliar with the newcomer's bizarre behavior, a frequent affliction which smote young men on first sight of herself. "Hallo!" she said, and smiled. "That's a nacky rig you're wearing, sir! It looks like a uniform. I have a partiality for the military, you know!"

In response to these confidences, the newcomer made a supreme effort to recollect his scattered wits. Alas for good intentions; he could not reclaim what he never possessed. However, he did manage to sweep off his leather hat without decapitating himself with the saber. "S-Samson!" he responded. "Samson Puddiphat!"

"What a pretty name!" Melly fluttered her eyelashes and sighed.

Her companion looked blank. *"Puddiphat?"* he inquired.

A less determined lass might have faltered at this moment. Melly merely grasped hold of the sleeve of his blue greatcoat and urged him to enter the showroom. "No: Samson!" she replied. "Samson is a very pretty name. *Are* you a military man, Samson?"

This question was one which had never before been presented to Puddiphat; it set him at a loss. *Could* a chap in the hire of Bow Street be considered a military man? It was a pretty puzzle, decided Puddiphat, after prolonged attempts at cogitation. He would have to remember to ask the opinion of Mr. Crump.

It then occurred to Puddiphat that the young lady was observing him with a degree of impatience. This was not an unusual reaction from people engaged in conversation with Puddiphat. *Why* people became impatient with him, Puddiphat was not certain; he tried hard to please. With an idea of explaining this to the young lady, he opened his mouth. To encourage him, Melly smiled. By the impact of that gesture, Puddiphat was once more deprived of speech.

Madame le Best was not unaware of the newcomer, as she was not unaware that her scapegrace niece was once more casting out lures. Recognizing in Puddiphat's besabered person an emissary of officialdom, Madame left her seamstresses to their own devices, and her customers to a heated discussion of Hungarian and Polish frogged decorations, Greek and Egyptian motifs. "Oh, *la vache!*" she muttered, recalling her niece's weakness for a uniform. "And what do *you* want?"

Inarticulate at the best of times, Puddiphat made no attempt to explain that what he wanted was the mischievous-looking damsel who still held fast to the sleeve of his greatcoat. With a monumental application of willpower, he wrenched his gaze away from the damsel's elfin face and stared instead at the sharp-featured female. She was looking unfriendly. This reaction to his presence did not surprise Puddiphat; in his recently gleaned experience, emissaries of officialdom were not especially welcome in milliners' shops. Since meeting with Mr. Crump in the tavern located near the Bow Street Public Office, Puddiphat had seen the interior of a great many such shops. He had also amassed a great deal of unwanted information about such devices as Armenian Divorce Corsets and Bosom Shields and Invisible Petticoats.

This particular milliner was observing him in a very hostile manner, and even the mischievous-looking damsel seemed disappointed. Puddiphat concentrated very hard. "Looking for a milliner!" he announced.

"Enfin, we progress!" Madame adjusted her embroidered muslin cornette. "You have found a milliner, *n'est ce pas?"*

A milliner? After lengthy pondering, during which he sought desperately to ignore the provocative damsel who stood so close to him, Puddiphat grasped the import of this remark. Certainly he had found a milliner. "Bonnets!" he said, in proof of that fact.

"Bonnets?" Madame's voice was ironic. *"Voilà!* What would you prefer: a capote with a crown of puffs, a toque of eyelet embroiders—or perhaps a yellow straw hat tied with an organdie fichu?"

In an attempt to visualize himself thus decked out, Puddiphat wrinkled his brow. "A fichu!" giggled Melly then. "My aunt is bamboozling you, Samson, although it ain't exactly *kind!* She don't mean *you* should be wishful of wearing a bonnet—but perhaps you have a friend?"

Why the young lady was staring at him in that wide-eyed manner, Puddiphat could not imagine, and he wished she would not, because it made his head spin. He clutched at his chin, as if thereby he might anchor down his whirling thoughts. "Of course I have a friend! Any number of 'em! A fine figure they'd cut with fichus tied around their heads!"

"Piffle, Samson," soothed Melly, as Madame silently marveled at the rapidity with which her niece had arrived on a first-name basis. Casting out lures was as natural for the minx as drawing breath, decided Madame; scolding had no more effect on Melly than it would have had on Madame's japanned chairs. "A *lady* friend?"

"Or," inserted Madame, "a wife!"

Relieved to have finally achieved enlightenment, Puddiphat released his chin and smiled. "Don't mind admitting I was beginning to wonder if you weren't both dicked in the nob—or a trifle bosky!" he confessed. "Dashed if *I* know any chaps wishful of decking themselves out in ladies' bonnets!"

The great majority of Puddiphat's inane utterances were offset, in Melly's opinion, by his obvious wish to please. She was also aware that she was responsible for at least a portion of Puddiphat's inanities. It was a relief to discover she hadn't lost her touch. "What about your lady friends?" inquired Melly, fluttering her long lashes. "One of them would like a nacky bonnet, I'll wager!"

"Lady friends?" Puddiphat had made the mistake of looking straight at Melly, with the result that his faculties were again arrested.

Though Madame's customers could content themselves forever with heated discussions about rival decorations and motifs, they would not, without proper motivation, actually decide among those fashionable things. Madame was eager to supply that motivation and reap her consequent reward. However, she was even more eager to find some solution to the problem presented by her niece. *"Mon Dieu!"* she remarked. "Then it *wasn't* to purchase a bonnet for your lady friend—or your wife—that you came to my shop."

Here was a female who knew how to cut right to the heart of a matter, realized Puddiphat. He awarded her a grateful look. "No," he replied.

Madame le Best strove for patience. "If not bonnets, then *what?* We can show you reticules and purses, tippets of fur or eiderdown; slippers of satin or kid. *Non?* Perhaps some long gloves or mitts? A scarf in violet or poppy-red?"

Puddiphat interrupted this catalogue with a sudden gesture that caused Melly, mindful of the saber, to move hastily aside. "I see what it is!" he concluded wisely. "You think I want to *buy* something! Well, I don't!"

Madame contemplated the customers left unsuccored, the sales consequently unmade. *"Quel diable!* If you do not wish to buy, then why are you here?"

In Puddiphat's makeup, a sparsity of wit was compensated by an abundance of such admirable virtues as dogged dedication to his duty, a keen sense of responsibility, and perseverance that frequently stood him in good stead when other people's applications of brilliant logic went wide of the mark. These virtues did not always made him happy, as in this case, when Madame's remarks reminded him of all the milliners he had yet to interrogate. So fruitless had his investigations thus far proven that a less charitable soul than Puddiphat might have wondered if he'd been deliberately sent to chase wild geese.

Aware that Puddiphat's attention had wandered— one could hardly *fail* to achieve that awareness, since Puddiphat was currently frowning in a dreadful manner at the tip of his nose—Melly reached out and gave his arm a nip. Puddiphat started. Now it was Madame who moved hastily away from his saber. "My aunt wishes to know why you have come here, Samson!" Melly explained.

"Don't blame her!" Puddiphat responded. "Like to know it myself! Crump didn't give me the particulars of the business—if these *are* particulars, about which I have doubts! Thought Crump was the best of good fellows to give me the opportunity to better myself! *Now* I think it may've been a proper take-in." He looked unhappy. "A fellow don't *wish* to make a Jack-pudding of himself!"

"Bless my heart!" cried Melly, who was in fact as tender-hearted as she was prone to larks. "I'm sure you ain't such a thing!"

Puddiphat, who possessed grave reservations on that head, nonetheless recognized a good intention. He gazed upon the source of those good intentions, and was immediately entranced.

Madame le Best crossed her arms beneath her bosom, covered this day with green silk. *"Ah, ça!"* she murmured. "You expect to discover this opportunity here? Perhaps you would be so good as to explain."

Puddiphat was eager to do so; his dreams of advancement were so potent as to distract him even from Melly, that inspiration of dreams of quite a different kind. "A Redbreast!" he said, by way of introduction, indicating his scarlet waistcoat. "First in the Metropolis to wear a uniform! Patrol the roads leading into London, calling out 'Bow Street Patrol' to such carriages as pass by. Carry a pistol and a truncheon and a pair of handcuffs!" He delved into the recesses of his blue greatcoat and brought forth these items, which he proudly displayed.

"Do put those things away!" snapped Madame, glancing quickly at her customers. "What will people think?"

"The worst!" supplied Puddiphat, after giving the question serious thought. "Probably that you were being nicked as a result of pinching something. But it wouldn't likely be me as would arrest you. That sort of thing doesn't often come the way of the Foot Patrol—not even the Inspectors! But if I was to prove myself I might be made a Runner, and then I might very well be the one to arrest you, and have a fair chance at the reward money myself!" He smiled, content in the belief that he had rendered an excellent account.

His smile was so lacking in guile, so full of generous bonhomie, Madame refrained from boxing his ears. "So you wish to become a Bow Street Runner," she summarized, in the same breath as her niece expressed keen disapproval of Puddiphat's intention to clap Madame in jail. "Perhaps you might explain, young man, how you think you may do so in *my* shop!"

"Not *your* shop, exactly!" For a fellow who craved

acceptance, even affection, from his fellow creatures, Puddiphat was definitely in the wrong line of work. He harked back to his original explanation. "Looking for a milliner!"

"Oui!" Madame tapped the fingers of one hand, hard, against the elbow of her other arm. "And you have found one! What do you suggest is our next step?"

"Next step?" Puddiphat privately thought this conversation was going a great deal too fast. What did one normally do with a milliner, he wondered, aside from entrusting her with details of wardrobe?

One answer presented itself. "Moonshine!" squealed Puddiphat, and fell back a pace. Alas, this act brought his saber into disastrous proximity with the table strewn with fashion issues. With a crash, the table toppled. Puddiphat swung around to discover the source of the commotion. His saber connected with Madame's shins.

"Merde!" winced Madame, clutching the afflicted extremity. *"Crétin! Imbécile!* Tell me instantly what has brought you here—or, even better, leave!"

Agonized though he was to have earned such severe disapproval, Puddiphat did not shirk his responsibilities. "Beg pardon, ma'am! No offense intended, I'm sure. Thing is, I'm looking for a *special* milliner! One who has in the past come afoul of Bow Street—or who knows someone who did." He was painfully aware that this explanation was somewhat lacking in conciseness. "A gentleman acquaintance—maybe even a father or a husband—a rum customer, in short!"

Madame le Best was also victim of a pained awareness, centered in her shin. Distracted, she did not become aware of the reflective expression on Melly's elfin features until it was too late to forbid that impulsive damsel to speak.

"Mercy on me!" Melly sank back on her heels amid the scattered periodicals which she'd been crawling about the floor in an effort to collect. "Can it be you are looking for my papa? I wish you luck! My mama could never find him, and she searched for him for *years!*"

"Your papa?" Puddiphat gaped at Melly. "*Your* papa was a rum customer, Miss?"

"The rummest!" Melly cheerfully admitted, as she restored the magazines to the table, after setting it upright. "He ran off and left Mama and me when I was just a little thing. Not that Bow Street would care about *that,* though it made my mama very sad."

Certainly Bow Street was not interested in gentlemen who took French leave, the number of whom was no testimonial to the joys of the marital state; and Puddiphat's dedication to duty extended only so far. "You still *are* just a little thing, Miss!" he besottedly observed.

Madame le Best regained the use of her vocal cords, briefly rendered impotent by mention of Melly's reprehensible parent. "I will not have That Man's name spoken beneath my roof!" she snapped. "Melly, show this person to the door."

Chapter Nine

Davenant House was one of several late Stuart resi-
dences in Soho Square, once a center of gaiety, still a
respectable address. Built of rose-colored brick with
Portland stone parapets and window columns, the
house consisted of three floors above a basement, and
an attic beneath the steep tiled roof.

Through the plastered and pedimented doorway of
Davenant House passed the most sought-after lords
and ladies in the land this evening. Through the spacious stone-paved hallway they proceeded, up the
stone staircase with its wonderfully scrolled handrail,
along the upper hallway, into the drawing room. There
they tussled politely with one another for possession of
the straight-legged sofa, gilt settee and heart-backed
chairs, whispered avidly behind fan and gloves about
the scandalous history of the guest of honor, and tried
very hard to appear utterly bored.

"Drum and concave threshing," observed Lord
Davenham, who disliked large gatherings of people
almost as much as he disliked inquiries of a personal
sort, "enables machines worked by four men to turn

out a ton of threshed corn a day. A ton; imagine it! And when we learn to harness steam power to land implements, the output will be even more."

Lady Davenham was not noticeably impressed with this demonstration of her husband's preoccupation with the affairs of his estates; she cast him an exasperated glance. In response to this indication that his wife was heeding him, his lordship brushed back a lock of hair which had fallen forward onto his handsome brow, and smiled. "In my opinion, one of the most important of all inventions was Jethro Tull's seed drill, which was made up of parts of an organ, a wheel-barrow and a cider mill."

"Vivien, we have guests." Lady Davenham's tone was tart.

How could Thea think he had failed to note that, to him, unpalatable fact? With an expression of faint distaste, Lord Davenham glanced around his drawing room. Guests notwithstanding, he continued to expand upon seed drills.

Recipient of these observations, Lady Davenham temporarily conceded defeat. At least with her rout, she had scored a marked success. This evening would be talked of for at least a week, and accorded that highest of accolades, a dreadful squeeze. Yet Thea was experiencing none of the elation due a successful hostess for it was through no effort of hers that this *coup* had been accomplishd. These members of the *ton* who thronged Davenant House this night could not care less that the wooden floor had been polished with beeswax and turpentine, and the Brussels carpet subjected to damp tea leaves, and the furniture shined with a mixture of small beer and sulphuric acid treacle and ivory black. Doubtless these fashionable guests would not notice were guano in truth scattered about the chamber. Curiosity about Sir Malcolm Calveley had brought the *beau monde* to Davenant House.

Their curiosity was being well satisfied, she reflected; Malcolm was in his element, entertaining his rapt audience with descriptions of his travels, irreverent tales of Paris and the denizens of the Palais Royale. "Malcolm seems to be enjoying himself," she said aloud.

This remark had the effect of distracting Lord Davenham briefly from his preoccupation. "Malcolm always *does* enjoy himself," Vivien responded, "even when he *shouldn't*. Tell me, my dear, have you an opinion on the oxen-versus-horses controversy regarding the sowing of seed?" Thea did not answer. Under the impression that this lack of comment was result of ignorance, his lordship immediately set about repairing the gap in his wife's education.

As perhaps need not be here explained, Lady Davenham had not the slightest interest in farming, yet she felt too self-conscious to leave Vivien's side and mingle closer with their guests. No feelings of social inadequacy prompted this reaction, or sudden cessation of curiosity. It was all the fault of her dress. Thea glanced cautiously at her reflection in the gilt-framed glass set over the chimney shelf. Hastily, she looked away.

"My dear." Once more Lord Davenham demonstrated his uncanny ability to observe what one least preferred. "Your face is flushed. Perhaps you would enjoy some fresh air."

Was Vivien inviting her to stroll in the gardens, perhaps—Thea blushed deeper—even to engage in certain activities not enjoyed since prior to their departure from their country estates? Thea glanced shyly at her husband. How damnably attractive he wâs. Any woman must yearn to erase his distracted air. Stroll with Vivien in the gardens? The notion appealed very much, despite the fact that it was a damp, moonless, foggy night. Callously she abandoned her guests to their own amusements. "Oh, yes!" she said.

How animated Thea grew over his suggestion—*could* she want to stroll in the gardens? Vivien mused. He thought probably not. Now if it were Malcolm who issued the invitation—

Without further preamble, Lord Davenham threw

open the window by which they stood. "Very well! You would be very interested in seeing the seed drill work, Thea, and you may read all about it in Tull's *Horse-Hoeing Husbandry;* I will lend you the book."

So much for romance. Disgruntled, Lady Davenham considered shoving her spouse through the opened window. Great pleasure was to be derived from thusly imagining him planted in his own flowerbeds. So much, too, for Madame le Best's promise that Thea's new gown would make gentlemen's eyes start right out of their heads.

Madame's promise had not pertained to Vivien, Thea recalled. She looked at her cousin Malcolm, currently responding irreverently to an *on-dit* that, following the opening of Parliament, the Prince Regent's carriage window had been shot out. Did Malcolm take nothing seriously? she wondered. He caught her glance and smiled. Evening wear suited him, decided Thea. Malcolm looked very handsome in his frilled shirt and knee breeches and long-tailed coat. For that matter, so did Vivien. Fancy dress suited the Davenants—with the exception of herself.

It came to Lord Davenham's notice that his wife was exhibiting no measurable excitement in response to his generously offered reading list. He concentrated on his wife.

Thea was unhappily studying her reflection in the chimney glass. As Vivien watched, she surreptitiously tugged up her low-cut neckline. And so she should! privately thought his lordship, or at least temper nature's bounty with a discreetly arranged shawl. Not that his lordship had the least objection to said display, save that it made concentration on anything else deuced difficult. Gentlemen and scholar though he might be, Lord Davenham was also very much a Davenant. It was not ice water that coursed through his veins. "I wish you would stop fidgeting with your dress!" he therefore remarked. "It makes it deuced difficult to concentrate."

"It does?" Slightly cheered by this intimation that her new gown was not entirely without effect, Thea awarded her reflection another doubtful glance. Assuredly she did not look dowdy, she decided. She was less certain that she did not resemble Haymarket-ware.

Her gown was fashioned of light delicate cream-colored silk gauze embroidered with flower sprays, worn over a satin slip of bluish-pink. The bodice was cut very low over the shoulders, the neck in a deep V; the short sleeves were held up by a narrow satin band; the wide skirts were deeply flounced and trimmed with a profusion of open-work embroidery, in vandykes and scallops, alternating with puffings and pipings and insertions. In itself, the gown was an admirable display of Madame le Best's talents. On Lady Davenham, the gown became a showcase for bounty unequaled elsewhere in the room. Lord Davenham was not the only gentleman who had glanced with fascination upon Thea's décolletage. Thea was unaware of this, of course. Thea's awareness was blunted by her dissatisfaction with life in general, with herself, and especially with her dress.

With it she wore long gloves of white kid with ruching around the top, and round-toed evening shoes with rosettes. Her dark hair had been released from its severe braid to cascade in ringlets from the crown of her head to her neck. Set amid that profusion of curls was a pearl-studded bandeau. Around her neck was a string of perfectly matched pearls. "You have not answered me," she complained, turning from the glass. Lord Davenham's expression was contemplative. "And if you say one more word to me about seed plows, Vivien, I think I shall scream!"

Lord Davenham was too tactful to explain that his thoughts had fondly dwelt not upon seed plows, but instead his wife's lush person. "As you wish, my dear. What would you like to talk about?"

As is the usual way with people asked this question, Lady Davenham's response was blank. "Tell me,

Vivien," she said after a long pause. "Do you like this gown?"

What Lord Davenham would have liked to do with his wife's gown was immediately remove it, an impulse prompted by no consideration whatsoever of his responsibilities as head of the Davenant clan. "It's very nice, my dear!" he diplomatically said.

Whatever adjectives might be applied to her gown, "nice" was not among them, decided Thea, who had turned away from the mirror only to be confronted by her reflection in the window glass. "Shocking," perhaps; "indecent" or *"outrée"*—but definitely not "nice." "I mean, how do I *look?*" she asked.

"Oh, very fine!" Lord Davenham decided that even a clan so impervious to public opinion as the Davenants might be dismayed were its leader to comport himself like some prehistoric caveman. "A diamond of the first water, my dear, as I think I've said before."

Husbands were legendarily indifferent to their wives' attire, remembered Thea; but she fancied most husbands would have taken notice of *this* dress—would, in fact, have forbidden their wives to publicly wear such a gown. Thea half-wished *she* had been thusly browbeaten; without her corsets—indeed, with hardly any covering whatsoever on most of her upper body—she felt only half-dressed. If only Malcolm had not been so insistent! But he had made it very clear that if she did not wear the gown, he would not attend the rout. "I have the oddest suspicion that Malcolm is up to something," she remarked. "He has grown so secretive."

The cause of that furtiveness, thought Lord Davenham, was nothing more sinister than Malcolm's determination to thwart Thea's plans. But it was not Vivien's habit to cut up his wife's pleasure. "I would not tease myself about it," he said vaguely. "Malcolm was always involved in one escapade or another."

"Do not tease myself!" echoed Lady Davenham, indignant not because of her husband's indifference to their cousin so much as by his lack of reaction to her dress. At the least she would have liked to have a compliment, and even better would have been an invitation to rendezvous in the damp and misty garden—or elsewhere! "One may lead a horse to water," she muttered.

Horses? Lord Davenham was delighted by his wife's effort to introduce a topic of conversation less controversial than their dashing cousin, and her own bold gown. "I have an idea for a reaping machine to be pushed by a team of horses. . . ."

As Lady Davenham chafed her arms, she decided there was only one explanation for the lack of attention paid her by the masculine members of her family: she *had* become a dowd. Still, she didn't think it necessary that she be constantly reminded of that unpleasant fact. "There is nothing to choose between you and Malcolm!" she remarked. "I am quite out of charity with you both."

Why his wife might be out of charity with him, his lordship understood; he imagined she'd caught him showing more interest than was seemly in the charms displayed by her gown. Considering his wife's strict adherence to propriety, and her excessive modesty, it was miraculous that she'd worn such a gown at all. But why this annoyance with Malcolm? Had he dared similarly presume? Was this unusual gown result of his return? Despite his resolution to let Thea work out her own fate, speculation upon Malcolm's influence left Lord Davenham feeling somewhat uncharitable. "That would be very bad!" he said.

"*What* would be very bad?" inquired Thea, who had grown very melancholy as result of thinking she was an antidote. "It is very difficult to have a conversation with someone who does not pay attention!"

"I *am* paying attention!" responded his lordship; was he not consequently feeling very cross? "As I attended to James. You remember James? I encountered him recently at a meeting of the Royal Institution of

London—I *did* tell you, did I not, about the nature and propagation of light?"

If Lord Davenham's interest in propagation might be concentrated closer to home, mused his unhappy lady, the dukedom might not lack an heir. "Several times; pray do not repeat the lecture to me again. What has the Royal Institution to do with our cousin, pray?"

"Not the Institution, James. And you accuse *me* of not paying attention!" As he pondered this inequity, his lordship took snuff. "As is the way with things one would much rather not hear about, they're not easily forgotten once one *has*. Why *did* Malcolm leave England? Do you recall?"

"I do not think I ever knew." Lady Davenham wished she might chafe her chest as well as her arms; ladies clad in next to nothing should not stand next to open windows lest they succumb to terminal gooseflesh. "It was something to do with a woman, I thought."

"My dear, it *always* has to do with women, in Malcolm's case." Vivien's voice was amused.

Somewhat unfairly, Lady Davenham decided that her husband found her a figure of fun. She also decided that she did not appreciate his amusement at her expense. "Have you grown so bored with your reapers and threshers that you must now meddle in woman's work?" she inquired acerbically. "I am very used to manage for myself, you know. I do not require any assistance in getting Malcolm settled respectably. Look at him! As I predicted, he is the darling of the *ton*. Soon he will have the *entrée* everywhere." Thea thought of the Lady Patronesses of Almack's Assembly Rooms, who were unanimously starched-up. "Or almost!"

Although Lord Davenham's mood was hardly improved by the alacrity with which his wife leaped to their cousin's defense, he was far too well bred to succumb to his churlish impulse to turn Thea over his knee. "You must do as you think best!" he responded vaguely.

"Thank you!" muttered Lady Davenham ungraciously. "I shall!" With this exchange of amenities, conversation between them faltered. Belatedly recalling her responsibilities as hostess, Thea looked around the drawing room. Some commotion appeared to be centered around the doorway. Even as Thea glanced in that direction, she heard a distant snarl.

A snarl? Surely Vivien's ill-tempered hound could not have escaped his chamber? Thea's faint hope was abruptly dashed as the throng prudently parted to let the hound pass. Dangling from the beast's mouth was a fragment of fashionable blue stockinet, which had until recently formed the pantaloons of a gentleman guest. Lady Davenham wished very hard that she might become invisible.

Lord Davenham was not moved by such petty considerations. His guests could be no more distressed by Nimrod's presence than his lordship was by theirs. Indeed, the wide swath which the dog cut through the drawing room put Vivien very strongly in mind of Moses parting the Red Sea. Serenely ignoring the indignant whispers attendant upon the arthritic hound's passage, Lord Davenham made encouraging remarks. At length Nimrod arrived, wheezing, at his lordship's feet. He collapsed upon Vivien's highly varnished shoes, and sneezed. Concerned, Vivien immediately closed the window.

"I like that!" observed Thea, with more than a touch of sarcasm in her voice. "I may stand here shivering for a half-hour in the cold and you are unaware—but let that wretched hound so much as sniffle and your solicitude knows no bounds. I conclude Nimrod stands higher in your estimation than I."

Despite a very strong temptation, Lord Davenham did not point out that Nimrod had not draped himself in garments expressly designed to distract a man's thoughts from such mundane considerations as opened windows and cold night air. "If you didn't want the window open, why did you say you *did?*" he inquired, picking up Nimrod and permitting the wheezing hound to nestle against his chest.

"I *didn't!*" snapped Lady Davenham, nettled at the sight of Nimrod enjoying a demonstration of the affection that she had failed to inspire. As if he sensed her displeasure, Nimrod bared his teeth. Abruptly, Lady Davenham decided that she would be more comfortable among her guests, despite the brevity of her gown.

"Mettlesome fillies!" explained Lord Davenham to his hound, as Lady Davenham walked away.

Chapter Ten

Though Lord and Lady Davenham had not especially enjoyed the rout held in their cousin's honor, Sir Malcolm had found the proceedings tolerably entertaining. Despite his ability to divert himself in any given situation, however, Sir Malcolm was not unaware that certain other members of his family were not similarly blessed. Indeed, that fact would have been difficult to overlook. As best Malcolm could remember—no easy feat, for it was well before the hour of noon, and he had the devil of a head—Thea had spent half the evening framed with Vivien in a window, and the other half flirting very determinedly with himself. At least Malcolm *thought* she had been flirting. *Tendre* or no, Thea's notions of amusement did not march with his own.

Nor, for that matter, did Vivien's. Malcolm had a very clear memory of the head of the adventurous Davenant clan, cradling the pestilential Nimrod against his chest, and murmuring beneath his breath about mettlesome fillies as with perfect aplomb he made considerable inroads on the champagne punch. Malcolm could only conclude from this bizarre behavior that Vivien was more of a Davenant than anyone had hitherto suspected. Difficult to credit Lord Davenham yearning after bits o' muslin and lightskirts—but there it was. Malcolm had it, as it were, straight from the horse's mouth. And none knew better than Malcolm the perils of adventurous instincts frustrated, as his own had been of late. In point of fact, it was exactly that circumstance which had brought him out at an hour when he would have been much more wisely still abed, suffering Hopgood's sovereign remedy for a throbbing skull. The cool air was exercising its own beneficial effect. Sir Malcolm looked around.

Wide and flagstoned Oxford Street was abustle, even at this early hour—which was not so early as Sir Malcolm imagined it; working folk had long since gone to their places, and the street peddlers had set up on their favorite corners, and apprentices had taken their shop shutters down, thus presenting to public view displays of silks and muslins, jewels and silver, china and fine glass. In these tempting arrays, Sir Malcolm had scant more interest than in his fellow pedestrians. He paused by a streetlamp enclosed in a crystal globe. How the deuce was he to divert Vivien's attention from his gardens to his wife, wondered Malcolm, and Thea's attention consequently from himself? Obviously, it would take more than a new dress. As if in search of inspiration, Sir Malcolm glanced once more along the length of Oxford Street. If inspiration did not beckon him, adventure did. This day it had disguised itself in the person of Mistress Melly Bagshot.

"Well, bless my soul!" observed that damsel, tripping gaily forward and taking a firm grip on Sir Malcolm's sleeve. "If this ain't the greatest piece of luck! I have been fretting myself to flinders cooped up in that shop, and now *finally* my aunt has sent me on an errand, and here *you* are, just as if you was *waiting* for me! Oh, I know you wasn't doing any such thing—not that my Aunt Hel would believe it! She kicked up *such* a dust when she thought I'd made a dead-set at you. Not that I *mean* to cast out lures, and so I told her, which put her in a dreadful tweak!" Having delivered herself of these artless confidences, Melly dimpled up at him.

Though his one previous encounter with her had not been lengthy, Sir Malcolm immediately recalled where he had met Miss Bagshot. So remarkable a feat of memory, in a gentleman suffering from the effects of a slight overindulgence the evening before, a gentleman moreover whose encounters with winsome lasses had been legion, partially explains his success with the opposite sex. Sir Malcolm never forgot a pretty face. And Melly's elfish features were prettier than most. "Fortune has smiled on me," he said.

"It *has?*" Melly opened wide her big brown eyes. "Fancy that! I wish Fortune might smile on me! I can tell you it ain't comfortable to stand on bad terms with someone when you're in their debt. Dashed if I know how a relation of mine turned out to be the highest of sticklers—not that there's any harm in the Bagshots, mind you, other than a little wild blood. But there I go, jawing on again! Tell me about your, er, cousin's party, sir. Were you there? Was it *very* grand?"

No member of the adventurous Davenant clan could claim unfamiliarity with wild blood, or fail to feel compassion for a damsel thus penned in by circumstance. "Oh, very grand!" replied Sir Malcolm, as he removed Melly's fingers from his sleeve and laid them on his arm. "You will enjoy hearing all about it while I escort you wherever you wish to go."

With a practiced flutter of her lashes, Melly greeted this gallantry, and with a dimpled smile. "Where I should *like* to go is back to Brighton, sir, and I do not think you could accomplish *that!* Although I daresay it is just as well, because my aunt would doubtless get on her high ropes was I to take French leave—my papa did so before me, you see! And without my aunt's assistance, I'll never get another place. You wouldn't know about such things, but one can't, not without references." She sighed. "And one don't get references when one has been turned off."

Whether due to the cool air or the delightful Miss Bagshot, Sir Malcolm's thoughts had begun to clarify. "*You* were turned off?" he inquired.

"Oh, yes! Several times!" Melly looked sad. "This *last* time was the worst, and mayhap I *don't* wish to return to Brighton after all, because was Lady Birmingham to get wind of it, she'd doubtless cut up prodigious stiff! Lady Birmingham can make a body *most* unhappy, as I should know, because I sewed for her. Bless my heart, if she wasn't such a curmudgeon, Captain Birmingham wouldn't have come into the sewing room, and I wouldn't have pricked my thumb, and now I wouldn't be out of a place!"

"Ah." In accordance with his philosophy of savoring whatever Fate placed upon his platter, Sir Malcolm was enjoying this particular repast very well. "I think I would like to hear more about this pricked thumb, Miss Bagshot."

By this display of interest, his companion's spirits were revived. "Do call me Melly!" she begged. "It's a trifle awkward for me to be a Bagshot when my aunt calls herself 'le Best,' not that I can fault her for changing her name because she's wishful of attracting the nobs! But you was asking me about Birmingham! Mercy on me, that *was* a dreadful pickle!" She giggled. "I am always in a pickle, sir!"

"Melly, you amaze me," murmured Sir Malcolm.

Upon hearing her name upon his lips, Melly flushed becomingly. "You are teasing me!" she protested. "I may be bird-witted—oh, yes! I admit it! But I know when I am being humbugged! You ain't the least surprised that I am in a pickle—no, nor should you be, because unless I miss my guess, you are often in a pickle yourself! Upon my word, I envy you; no one will try to impose a check upon *your* spirits, or forbid you outright to cut larks! But you was wishful of hearing about Birmingham!" She launched into a description of her adventures in Brighton. So very droll was her delivery, and so very accurate her rendering of Lady Birmingham's histrionics, that Sir Malcolm laughed outright, and informed Miss Bagshot that she should go upon the stage.

This kind suggestion, however, won Sir Malcolm the opposite of its object's thanks. Melly removed her hand from his arm and drew herself up to her full height, an impressive gesture, even though she was only five feet tall. "No, I should *not* go upon the stage, sir, and it ain't kind of you to suggest it! No offense, but I'll wager you know very well what happens to girls who tread the boards, and I mean to play my cards better than that. Bless my heart, I could remain a seamstress, and come to the same end."

The damsel protested too much, thought Sir Malcolm, an error of judgment which may be forgiven him only because no damsel quite like Melly had ever come his way. "You must not try and bamboozle *me*, Melly," he responded wickedly.

In response to this inference that she had already embarked upon the pathway that had led many an unwary damsel to a ruinous end, however much said damsel may have enjoyed the process, Melly gasped. "I will have you know, sir, that I do not tell taradiddles—or if I do, I ain't telling one *now!* I suppose you have gotten in the way of thinking you are quite at the top of the tree, and it ain't any wonder, because you need only walk into a room to set a girl's heart aflutter—but you don't know all there is to know about all of us yet!"

Obviously he did not, else he would not have unwittingly offered insult. Not quite certain how he had done so, Sir Malcolm put forth an apology. He was not thoroughly recovered, he decided, from the previous evening's overindulgences.

"Oh, pooh! I ain't one to bear a grudge!" Cheerfully, Melly reclaimed his arm. "You was going to tell me about your, er, cousin's party."

"My, er, cousin?" echoed Sir Malcolm, deftly maneuvering Miss Bagshot amid their fellow pedestrians. "I suspect it is you who now misjudge me, Melly. Lady Davenham *is* my cousin. And you would not have liked her rout."

"I would not?" With no small respect, Melly eyed her escort, who, in addition to being the most agreeable gentleman she had ever encountered, was speedily being revealed as also the most depraved.

"It was very dull," explained Sir Malcolm. "Except for those few moments when my cousin's arthritic hound assaulted a gentleman guest—my *other* cousin, that is: Lady Davenham's husband."

"Mercy!" murmured Melly, fascinated by this glimpse of the diversions enjoyed by the *ton*. "If that sort of thing ain't to your taste, why do you attend?"

Sir Malcolm, sufficiently recovered from his excesses to feel hungry, essayed into a baker's shop and procured a hot roll for himself, and for his companion a cherry tart. "I didn't wish to disappoint Thea. It was on my account that she and Vivien came to London and opened up the house—they reside in the country."

Melly had always known that the nobs lived by different standards than the lesser folk, but this hint at what those standards were caused her to stare openmouthed. "Doesn't this Vivien person *mind?*"

"Mind? No, why should he?" Sir Malcolm wondered if he might somehow make Vivien so jealous that he would be asked to depart Davenant House. "Although I'm sure he would rather have remained in the country. But Thea is given little enough opportunity to visit the Metropolis, and it would be cruel of me to curtail her enjoyment."

Perhaps, thought Melly, she was sufficiently bird-witted as to have failed to properly understand. "This Vivien person," she suggested, "ain't similarly enjoying himself."

"One never knows with Vivien," admitted Malcolm. "Fond as I am of my cousins, I will be the first to confess Vivien is a queer fish. Now eat your tart; there's a good girl!"

Sir Malcolm chose a strange way to show his fondness for this Vivien person, reflected Melly, as she obediently devoured her tart; perhaps the nobs thought it nothing to carry on with another man's wife. Sir Malcolm was a regular out-and-outer, in comparison to whom Captain Birmingham and all the other gentlemen of Melly's acquaintance had been mere novices in the gentle art of leading damsels astray. Not that Melly had been led astray yet. But it was just a matter of time, due to the wild blood of the Bagshots. Contemplating that inevitable day, Melly brushed pastry crumbs from her chin.

Happily unaware that Miss Bagshot suspected him of engaging in an especially adventurous *ménage à trois,* Sir Malcolm applied his pocket handkerchief to the evidences of cherry tart that still adorned her pretty face. An enchanting face it was, he thought, with its big brown eyes and dimples and delightful little nose: a face to put him strongly and disagreeably in mind of Lady Davenham's current mission. "My cousin," he remarked, "has decided it's time I take a wife. Her rout was for the purpose of reintroducing me to the *ton* so that I may choose an eligible candidate from among their ranks."

Melly was amazed by the degree of Lady Davenham's sophistication. What kind of female could dally with her lover beneath her husband's nose and at the same time scheme to marry him off? In such wise, what sort of man would dally with another man's wife under her husband's nose? And what sort of husband would tolerate all this dallying? Such nuances of behavior were beyond the scope of Melly's comprehension. However, she understood perfectly how it felt to have relatives who schemed.

"It's enough to put one smack in the pathetics!" she sighed. "*I* know! My aunt's wishful of getting me leg-shackled so that she may wash her hands of me. Oh, she don't admit it, but I know what she's about."

Upon Miss Bagshot's elfin features sat an expression so incongruously somber that Sir Malcolm laughed. "You do not wish to be leg-shackled, Melly?"

"No, sir, I do not." Melly looked severe. "But you must not be taking the wrong notion again, even if my blood *is* wild! When I toss my bonnet over the windmill, it will be because I have formed a lasting passion, and I do not mean to form a lasting passion for someone who will play fast and loose with me, or offer me false coin! A girl must think of her future, because no one else will if she *don't*. Not that I wish to speak out of place, like my aunt says I do, but you looked like you was wishful of saying something you *oughtn't!*"

Sir Malcolm's various adventures had engendered in him no jadedness, and no lack of the ability to derive amusement from the situations in which he found himself. He took a closer look at Miss Bagshot, who had just delivered so sharp—and so obviously reluctant—a setdown. Her pelisse was shabby, her bonnet out of date, her expression glum. "Come out of the mops! I am not going to offer you a slip on the shoulder, you absurd child."

Melly's big brown eyes flew to his face. "You ain't?"

"Certainly not! At least not on such short acquaintance. But you have not told me where you were going when I encountered you."

"Bless my soul!" Melly clapped a glove, which had not benefited from exposure to her cherry tart, to her mouth. "I clean forgot! My aunt will be as cross as crabs, not that it signifies, because she almost always *is!* I was going to the chandeler's shop for a half-ounce of coffee and a quartern of sugar, and it slipped my mind altogether, which just goes to show I'm every bit as bird-witted as Aunt Hel claims!" She looked around her, puzzled. "And I don't even know where we *are!*"

"Never mind, I do," soothed Sir Malcolm, who had paid more attention than his companion to the direction in which they strolled. "There is a shop just around the corner where you may execute your aunt's commissions—if you still wish to do so."

Bird-like Melly cocked her pretty head. "I never *did* wish to do so, but I wanted to get out of that blasted showroom. Now Aunt Hel will probably never let me out again because I have been gone so long! I daresay it don't sound so terrible to you, but you ain't penned up as if you was in jail!"

"Poor Melly!" Sir Malcolm grasped both her hands. "When you return you will simply tell your aunt that you lost your way—or I shall tell her so! You were lost and fortunately encountered me, and I returned you safely to your aunt, who will be excessively relieved that you escaped grave peril."

Miss Bagshot was not so certain that Madame le Best would be the least bit grateful for the return of a scapegrace niece, but she was not inclined to quibble over so minor a point. "That's all well and good!" she responded bluntly. "So long as you remember that I do *not* intend to form a lasting passion for you, sir!"

Never before had Sir Malcolm encountered a damsel so adverse to lasting passions for himself. It was rather a pity, he reflected, as he studied the curve of her merry mouth. "So be it! We shall be two fugitives from justice this afternoon, and have all manner of adventures while our jailers' backs are turned. And I shall not presume upon our friendship. How does that sound to you?"

Melly was somewhat disappointed that Sir Malcolm had not responded with just a little argument to her rebuff—not that she would have altered her position, but it would have been gratifying to be admired by so discerning a gentleman, far as he might be above her touch. "It's a bargain!" She giggled. "What will we do?"

"First we will go and get my carriage, and then I will show you London. After that, we shall see!" Miss Bagshot having expressed wholehearted approval of Sir Malcolm's plan of action, they resumed their progress

down the street, Sir Malcolm enlivening their perambulations with the more diverting details of his travels
from Lisbon to Toulouse, and Miss Bagshot responding
with an account of the arrival in Madame le Best's
shop of an emissary of Bow Street, which in retrospect
she thought good fun. Miss Bagshot's opinion of Bow
Street might have altered somewhat, had she happened
to glance behind her. Trailing down the street in her
wake, skulking behind lampposts and lurking in doorways, was none other than Samson Puddiphat.

Chapter Eleven

Behind the rosy bricks of Davenant House lay a garden. No ordinary garden was this, as might be expected of any realm where Lord Davenham's imagination ruled. Despite the limitations imposed on his endeavors by available space, his lordship had transformed a lily pond flanked with perennial flower borders into an irregularly shaped lake fed by a stream issuing from a grotto in the Elysian Fields. Romantic graveled pathways wound through those erstwhile fields, picturesque vistas enhanced by weeping willows from China and tulip-poplars from America, as well as a stone Colossus, a miniature bridge, temple, and old mill. Rhododendrons, magnolias, camellias, and laburnum added color to the shrubberies. Set artistically amongst these delights were fruit trees in terracotta *jardinières*.

Lady Davenham evinced no delight for the lovely vistas spread out before her. Her expression, as she trod along one of the graveled pathways, was not that of a lady whose thoughts held any appreciation of either beauty or romance. The flyaway Davenant brows slanted downward; the lovely lips were tight. Not even one curl escaped its severe confines this day to nestle on her brow. In summation, Lady Davenham had very much the aspect of someone whose temper had been sorely strained.

Nor was Lady Davenham's mood improved by her first glimpse of her spouse, on his knees, grubbing contentedly in his flowerbed. Nearby, Nimrod oversaw the proceedings from within a wicker basket. The hound saw Thea, and snarled. Lord Davenham glanced up and smiled.

"Hullo, my dear!" said he. "Have you come to keep me company? I am tending to my flowerbeds, as you see."

This was no time to uselessly wish that his lordship might someday be equally eager to tend to cultivation of a different order, Lady Davenham reminded herself, or to indulge in highly improper speculations upon dalliance as conducted in a potting shed. Ignoring Nimrod's sharply expressed disapproval, she moved closer to Vivien. "Bachelor's fare!" she said.

Why was Thea in a temper? Puzzled, Lord Davenham glanced from his flowerbeds to his wife. "No, no, my dear! Heartsease and candytuft! Low-growing perennials! I do not think there *is* a flower called bachelor's fare." He grasped a big-bellied copper watering pot.

Though she was ordinarily tolerant of her husband's love for growing things, Lady Davenham was this day in no mood for a discussion thereof. Frowning even more severely, she yanked away the watering pot. "Vivien, I am quite in a temper!" she explained.

"Oh?" Lord Davenham's own temper was not in the best frame, and not without good reason; as result of which he chose to be perverse. "Can it be that you do not *like* low-growing perennials?"

"The devil with perennials!" interjected Lady Davenham. "Vivien, it is most important that I talk with you!"

Carefully, as if to defend himself, Lord Davenham picked up a trowel. "We *are* talking!" he gently pointed out. "If you so dislike the perennials, I shall order them removed straightaway. What would you like put in their place?"

"Nothing!" snapped her ladyship. "Vivien, this is *serious!*"

"Piffle, my dear!" Having found it a trifle uncomfortable to engage in conversation with someone towering above his head, Lord Davenham arose from his knees. "It is not at all serious. I frequently order the flowers changed myself. The plants must frequently be rotated in order to maintain the bloom. We have a variety in the greenhouse. Come and choose the replacements yourself."

Lady Davenham drew a deep breath, which culminated in a sneeze—Thea had been prone to sneezes and sniffles since the evening of her rout. Other ladies who publicly displayed themselves in dresses comprised of next to nothing above the waist, she thought, earned more for their efforts than head colds. "Vivien, sometimes I think you are deliberately obtuse! I do not wish to speak to you of plants, but *Malcolm!*"

"Malcolm dislikes my ageratum and verbena?" queried Lord Davenham as he tucked the trowel under one arm, the better to brush dirt and grass off his hands and knees. "I didn't know he'd even been in the garden! Nor would I have expected him to know the difference between a French marigold and a snowdrop. But if he does not approve of the perennials, of course I will replace them. What would *he* prefer?"

Lady Davenham secured her husband's attention by the simple expedient of reaching up and firmly grasping his chin. In response to this assault upon his person, her husband blinked. Nimrod's protests were much more vocal, consisting of wheezes, yelps, and snarls.

"I do not wish to speak of gardens," Thea enunciated very clearly. "I want to talk about Malcolm. Our cousin isn't the least bit interested in gardens. He is *very* interested, however, in bachelor's fare, which is not a plant, but a term applied to bits o' muslin—and, in this instance, a chit from a milliner's shop."

"A milliner's shop?" echoed Lord Davenham, his lady having made speech possible by releasing his chin. "What was Malcolm doing in a milliner's shop?"

"Striking up an acquaintance, apparently!" retorted Thea.

"I wish you would not be so literal-minded," complained his lordship. "I mean, what *took* him there?"

"*I* did!" responded Thea ruefully, on another sneeze. "Although I would *not* have, had I foreseen this! Malcolm insisted on being present when I ordered the gown for our rout—indeed, he practically designed the garment himself. Our cousin, it would appear, has had no little familiarity with feminine attire. He threatened, if I refused to humor him in it, to forgo the rout."

How personal an interest Sir Malcolm had in Lady Davenham, Lord Denham was beginning to unhappily comprehend. Pondering how best to deal with this enlightenment, he drew his wife into a rustic shelter fashioned from tree roots and branches. Thea sank down on a wooden bench. "*How* am I to find a wife for Malcolm when he is larking about the metropolis with a . . . a dollymop on his arm?" she asked. "Any respectable female must be put off by the incurable irresponsibility of his conduct; no sooner do I introduce him to the *ton* than he flees the suitable ladies paraded before him in favor of a harum-scarum young woman who, if she isn't already no better than she should be, will doubtless soon be *worse!* Oh, yes, I have met her. She is a sad romp! And somehow knowing the chit makes it that much more difficult to bear."

Lord Davenham had, during these disclosures, moved Nimrod's wicker basket into the shelter and placed it in a patch of sunlight. His habitual ill temper temporarily appeased by this display of concern, the hound settled back to worry at the fragment of blue kerseymere from which he had refused to be parted ever since Thea's rout. "What has Malcolm *done* with this young female?" his lordship inquired, as he seated himself by Thea on the wooden bench.

"Heaven knows!" responded Thea gloomily. "One hesitates to venture a guess. Malcolm encountered her in Oxford Street, and nothing would satisfy him but that he must take her up in his carriage and point out to her the sights—London Bridge and the Tower, Carlton House and, for some inexplicable reason, Newgate! And *then* he took her to Astley's! To shower such distinguishing attentions on a dab of a girl—I vow I am *wholly* out of charity with the wretch!"

Lord Davenham kept private his opinion that attentions showered by his reckless cousin on a milliner were much more fitting than attentions bestowed upon Thea herself. As result of their cousin's new interest, Thea was naturally feeling a little out of sorts. "Dear me, how tiresome of Malcolm! He is incorrigibly fond of the ladies, I fear."

"And he is *not* a marvel of discretion!" responded Thea. "I mean—Astley's!"

In preference to his cousin Malcolm's indiscretions, Lord Davenham cogitated upon Astley's Royal Amphitheater, home of trick-riding and equestrian feats, situated in Westminster Bridge Road. "Did you wish to go to Astley's, my dear? You should have said so! I will be pleased to take you there myself. I have always enjoyed the clowns."

Upon the rustic garden shelter a brief silence descended, while Lady Davenham counted silently to one hundred—silence, that is, save for the sounds of Nimrod wheezing and drooling over his scrap of blue kerseymere—and Lord Davenham directed his thoughts to his own less personal concerns. Of these, he had many, as befit the head of a large and adventurous family. Lord Davenham had obligations to his tenants, to his households and his lands. There were matters of the estate to be considered, draining land and making roads, improvements in stock; and when all those items were dealt with, there was that question most pressing in the mind of any farming gentleman—the price of wheat.

Yet all these matters paled in significance beside the question of whether or not Vivien had somehow unwittingly alienated the affections of his wife. Lord Davenham knew he was not the most exciting of husbands, and that his thoughts dwelt all too often on the prosaic and mundane, but it was not easy to throw off an inbred sense of responsibility. More than Thea's dragonish governess should be consigned to eternal hellfire. The Duke added several of his own preceptors to the score.

It was too late now, however, to lament that he was in thrall to his own properties; as it was too late to develop a flair for swashbuckling romance. Lord Davenham could only hope his wife would eventually come to realize that during their years together they had shared experiences more important and enduring than whispered compliments and flirtatious glances. "Thea," he said.

"If you *dare* to speak to me of—of verbena or heartsease, Vivien, I may never speak to you again!" interrupted Lady Davenham, in tones so irritable that Nimrod elevated his dewlaps above the basket-rim and snarled. "I am concerned about our cousin's future— and so, as head of the family, should you be! It is our duty to see him settled respectably."

Since Lord Davenham had not intended to speak of his garden, had indeed spent the past several moments in contemplation not of his responsibilities, but of the recent erratic behavior of his wife, his own habitual good humor grew a trifle strained. "Perhaps Malcolm doesn't *wish* to be settled!" he suggested reasonably. "Marriage does not suit everyone, my dear—and Davenants less than most! It has me in quite a puzzle why you are so set on weaning Malcolm away from a life-style which suits him very well."

Thea wished he'd remained engrossed in his flower-beds. Not the inference that Malcolm would prefer to be fancy-free disturbed Thea; ambivalent as were her feelings toward her cousin, she recognized his inconstancy. However, the intimation that her own husband yearned to be equally inconstant caused her great distress. "Oh!" she gasped. "As if there were nothing wrong in—in foraging among the fleshpots!"

Lord Davenham who had just spent the greater portion of an evening watching his wife attempt to coquette with their cousin, thought that in her he beheld the pot calling the kettle black. But Vivien was not of a mean and little nature, and did not point this out. "I don't think there *is* anything wrong with the fleshpots!" he responded judiciously. "Providing one doesn't abdicate one's responsibilities in order to sample them. Tell me, did you take Malcolm to task over this young woman?"

"Her name is Melly." As result of her husband's confessed desire to himself forage among the fleshpots, Lady Davenham was deep in a fit of the blue devils. Scant wonder he displayed so little enthusiasm for marital intimacies of late, she decided: Vivien did not wish to be married to her at all. "And, yes, I spoke to Malcolm about the chit. He laughed and seemed not the least bit affected by my displeasure over his conduct. *All* the Davenants are incorrigible! It is enough to cast one into despair." Abruptly she rose from the bench.

Because it did not occur to Lord Davenham that his wife was prone to think of herself as a changeling thrust into the Davenant cradle, he naturally assumed that in this sweeping denunciation she included herself. Matters, he decided, had gone much further than he'd suspected. Obviously, more was at stake here than a simple matter of a tempting décolletage. "My poor Thea!" he said gently. "Is it so very bad?"

Having informed her he regretted their marriage, he now dared ask if she *minded!* Thea chose to let-him think she'd misinterpreted his remark. "Oh, no!" she responded ironically, giving Nimrod's basket a wide berth. "Malcolm merely hovers on the brink of a ruinous entanglement—for what that chit may lack in sense, I'll wager she makes up in guile! The next thing we know, Malcolm will have to leave the country *again,* and he has just got home." She made a dismissive gesture. "But I should not have troubled you with this. You have more important matters on your mind, like ants and snails."

It being very difficult to carry on a reasonable conversation with a lady whose back was turned, Lord Davenham also quitted the bench. *"Not* ants and snails: caterpillars!" he said. "One cuts tufts of them off the trees at the break of day—they hang gathered into knots through the cold of the night, you know."

Caterpillars! Her husband was so indifferent to her feelings that in one breath he revealed dissatisfaction with their marriage and in the next engaged in discussion of a particularly repellent variety of bug. Apparently, she stood even lower in Vivien's opinion than an insect. Thea could not decide whether she wished most to fling herself weeping upon Vivien's chest, or assault him with his trowel. In an attempt to control her emotions, she exited the rustic shelter.

Unaware that his lady contemplated committing mayhem upon his person, Lord Davenham followed her outside, in the process of which he exchanged his trowel for a pruning fork. "I do not mean to be unsympathetic!" he explained. "I am very sorry to see you thrown into such a pucker. Perhaps there is something I may do."

Certainly there was some manner in which his lordship might ease his wife's distress. Thea eyed the potting shed. Then she swung around to observe her spouse. Again it struck her how very handsome Vivien was, in the way of all the Davenants, with his unruly black curls and flashing dark eyes. Sometimes Thea thought Vivien was even more handsome than Malcolm, for where Malcolm's manner was bold and suggestive, Vivien was less easy to define. His very elusiveness was an intriguing trait. Confidences as rendered up by Lord Davenham were as diamonds offered by a lesser man.

Confidences did not appear to be forthcoming, alas. Watching her husband strip excess foliage from the rhododendron with his pruning knife, Lady Davenham yearned to brush back the dark locks which had tumbled forward on his brow. Would he welcome such a wifely gesture, were she bold enough to make it? Thea could not bring herself to find out. "I don't know what you *can* do!" she responded sadly, interpreting her husband's absent-minded assault upon his rhododendron as symbolic of his dissatisfaction with his wife.

Lady Davenham's spirits might have been elevated had she but realized that Lord Davenham imagined the rhododendron as his cousin, Malcolm, being pruned where it would do most good. Yet Vivien was fond of Thea, and could be no part of her unhappiness. "You have always said that you do not require my assistance, Thea," he said, more calmly than he felt. "That you are perfectly capable of managing for yourself. I have seen no reason to interfere with you, because I have had other matters with which to deal, and you have managed very well—until now! You must not accuse me of being ineffectual, my dear. I am not so preoccupied that I have failed to notice in which direction the wind blows."

"Oh?" Thea frowned. "Which way *does* the wind blow, pray?"

Having reduced the rhododendron to stubble, Lord Davenham set down his pruning knife. "I beg you will not insult my intelligence." With considerable effort, he produced his vague smile. "If you want Malcolm, I will contrive to extricate him from the clutches of

the milliner, because had you not been bethrothed to
to me from the cradle you would doubtless have had
Malcolm in the first place. But you must not expect me
to pretend to be deaf, mute, and blind."

In response to these gentle accusations, Lady Davenham's lips parted and her cheeks flushed. So pro-
found were her husband's misapprehensions that she
did not know where to begin to set him right. Nor was
she sure she *wished* to set him right, since even the conviction that she was overly fond of their dashing cousin
had failed to rouse his ire. Too, Thea was very truthful,
and she honestly did not know whether or not she still
nourished a *tendre*.

As she hesitated, the moment passed; Lord Davenham brushed past her and strode along the graveled
path. Thea picked up her skirts and hurried after him.
"Where are you going?" she gasped.

Did Thea fear for Malcolm's safety? Think that
Vivien would seek to relieve his spleen via a bout of
fisticuffs? Though the notion was not without appeal,
Lord Davenham was not so immature. Nor was he so
lacking in consideration as to cause his wife needless
distress—despite his urge to shake her until the teeth
rattled in her demonstrably empty head.

Lord Davenham stepped up his pace lest he succumb to this base impulse. Over his shoulder, he said:
"I am going to prepare for a meeting of the Horticultural Society, my dear! I read in the *Society's Transac-
tions* that a new shipment of plants from foreign lands
has recently arrived. I am anxious to speak with Knight
—the Society's president, you will recall! He has been
carrying out some unusual experiments with pineapples
and nectarines. But I am forgetting Nimrod!" He re-
traced his steps and picked up the wicker basket, giving his wife a wide berth.

Lady Davenham's supposed partiality for her dashing cousin Malcolm signified precious little to her
spouse. This new indifference was almost more than

Thea could bear. Muttering bitterly beneath her breath, she stalked into the house, and up the staircase, and into the connubial bedchamber. There she locked the door behind her, threw herself down on the bed and beat her fists against the mattress.

Chapter Twelve

Master Samson Puddiphat, though by temperament prohibited from indulging in hysterics, would heartily have sympathized with a lady so beset as to take recourse in assaulting her pillow. By the indirect inspiration of Lady Davenham's tantrum, Puddiphat was being similarly provoked. Miss Bagshot did not *mean* to be provoking, Puddiphat told himself, as he carefully maneuvered his saber through the showroom doorway.

"It's lucky for you my aunt ain't here!" said Melly, hands on her slim hips, swathed this morn in a patterned daytime silk. "Something to do with a presentation gown. I don't know where you've got this hubble-bubble notion that you should clap my aunt in jail, Samson. Her prices ain't *that* high!"

Puddiphat concentrated on a chair japanned in lilac and gold, lest further contemplation of Miss Bagshot's impatient and mischievous face deprive him anew of his powers of speech. *"Don't* want to slap your aunt in jail!" he protested.

"Oh." Looking very thoughtful, Melly stroked the

fabric of her gown, a high-waisted *robe en caleçons* with fitted bodice and skirt so narrow that walking was difficult, the product of Melly's own needle. Melly meant to cut a dash, if only behind her aunt's back. "Then you are looking for my—" She recalled her aunt's strictures on this subject. "—that man! I don't know why you think you'll find him *here*. Didn't I tell you he showed us a clean pair of heels?"

"*Did* he?" Cautiously, Puddiphat elevated his gaze from the floor to his white leather gloves. "By Jove! Poor little thing!"

"Poor little thing? *Papa?*" An astonished expression flickered across Melly's piquant features. "Bless my soul!"

"*Not* your papa!" Puddiphat glanced sharply at Miss Bagshot, then dragged his gaze away. "As you well know! It's not fitting, Miss, that you should try and hoodwink an officer of the law. There are severe penalties for such things—or if there aren't, there *should* be!"

"Mercy on me!" Melly sank down upon one of the japanned chairs. "It's *me* you wish to clap in jail! This is the worst pickle I have *ever* been in!"

So stricken was Puddiphat by this declaration that without awaiting invitation he dropped down onto another of the japanned chairs. Hastily, Melly dragged the magazine-laden table out of his saber's reach. *"Not* a pickle!" he protested. "I swear!"

"That's all *you* know about it!" Melly responded darkly. "My aunt wasn't half so grateful as Sir Malcolm said she'd be to have me back. Instead, she took quite a pet and accused me of telling clankers, when it wasn't me as told them, but *him!* I'm sure I might as well be in jail for all the freedom I'm allowed, so you may as well cease shilly-shallying and take me before the magistrates!"

Valiantly, Puddiphat sought to correct Miss Bagshot's misapprehensions. "Don't *want* to take you in! You haven't *done* anything!"

The young lady's sulky expression did not alter. "Tell my aunt that!" she snapped.

Puddiphat's memories of Madame le Best were not such that he wished to converse further with her on any topic, especially the conduct of her niece. Though Puddiphat was not precisely needle-witted, he was sufficiently acute to recognize a suspicious and dangerous character when he saw one. "A suspicious and dangerous character! Thought so at the time!" Miss Bagshot looked bewildered. He added: "Daresay you won't like it, but I followed you! The Tower! Carlton House! London Bridge! Newgate!"

By this proof that incarceration in her aunt's showroom had not yet robbed her of all her allure, Miss Bagshot's sulks were somewhat eased. "Pooh! It's no skin off *my* nose if you want to make a cake of yourself by following me about—you won't be the first to do so!" She smiled. "Nor the last, I hope!"

Anxious as he was to please, Puddiphat could not let this misconception pass. "As sure as check!" he offered, to spare his companion's feelings. "But I wasn't following *you!*"

"You *wasn't?*" Melly's eyes opened wide. "Fancy that! Were you on the trail of some desperate criminal, perhaps? I wish you had told me, Samson! Seeing Bow Street make an arrest would have been even more exciting than Astley's! Did you get your man?"

That apprehending desperate criminals was no large part of his duties, Puddiphat saw no reason to explain. "Don't know *what* he is!" Puddiphat confessed. "But I mean to find out!"

Perhaps because her own wits were not razor-sharp, Melly had a little difficulty puzzling out the meaning of his words. "It is Sir Malcolm you was following! He *said* we was fugitives from justice, but I didn't pay him any mind. Bless my heart! What's he *done?*"

"As to that, Miss, I'm not certain," Puddiphat unhappily confessed. "Tell you what! Your aunt's right to cut up stiff about your rubbing shoulders with such." It then occurred to him that this was hardly a diplomatic approach. "Don't blame you, of course! Hard on a high-spirited little thing like you to be cooped up! Thing is, Miss, you could help Bow Street."

"I *could?*" Miss Bagshot was not averse to a vision of herself as heroine of the hour, having spared London from the deprecations of a hardened criminal. *Then* her Aunt Hel would see the folly of condemning her to remain indoors. "Fancy that!"

Having exhausted all the visual potential of his white leather gloves, Puddiphat transferred his gaze to the Chinese wallpaper. "Tell me about this Sir Malcolm!" he invited.

Miss Bagshot understood that she was in a ticklish situation: she did not think Sir Malcolm Calveley would thank her for bringing him to the attention of Bow Street. However, as matters stood, she was not likely to encounter Sir Malcolm again. Amusing as had been the afternoon passed in his company, Melly could not deceive herself that it had resulted from anything but a whim. Sir Malcolm would have many whims, all involving females. Melly had simply been in the right place at the right time.

On the other hand, *did* Melly set Bow Street on to Sir Malcolm, he was very likely to seek her out again, if only to read her a dreadful scold. And if he did not seek her out, how was she to further his education? One could not base a friendship upon two encounters, especially the sort of friendship upon which one intended to persuade a gentleman to presume.

"Oh, he's dangerous enough!" Melly equivocated, recalling the manner in which feminine hearts fluttered when Sir Malcolm stepped into a room. "First my papa, then my aunt, then me—and now Sir Malcolm. I ain't perfectly clear in my mind why you wish to arrest anyone at all!"

Puddiphat removed his gaze from the Chinese wallpaper, which had made him very dizzy with its recurring motifs of dragons and pagodas and mandarins, and looked at Miss Bagshot. Melly dimpled. Puddiphat focused on his blue-clad knee, his head now properly a-spin. "Want to become a Runner!" he explained, after a lengthy pause punctuated only by snickers and giggles from the atelier, where the seamstresses were taking full advantage of their employer's absence. "Like Townsend and Sayer, Armstrong and Keys!" He thought of the Runner responsible for his newly learned familiarity with milliners' shops, who during their last encounter had called him a nodcock. "And Crump. For your information, Miss, Bow Street personnel *can't* be properly termed 'military men.' "

"What a pity!" sighed Melly. "I *do* have a weakness for military men. But your uniform is very nice, all the same, Samson. *Why* do you wish to become a Runner? Ain't it dangerous?"

"A fig for danger!" Seeking the proper degree of bravura, Puddiphat threw out his chest. Unfortunately, this action disturbed the balance of his saber, which flew straight up into the air, very nearly putting paid to the tip of its owner's nose. Grasping the weapon with both fists, he restored it to its former position. His anxious features were flushed.

Melly was a good-hearted girl, for all her little faults; she was not of the temperament that derives amusement from other people's woes. Too, Puddiphat's uniform *did* put her in mind of the military, for whom her professed fondness was a fact. Additionally, Melly wished to practice her wiles.

Gracefully, she removed herself from the japanned chair—or as gracefully as was possible for a young lady in a very narrow skirt. In order that Puddiphat might compose himself, she moved away. However, Puddiphat was inured by repetition to his little mishaps, and his pink cheeks were due more to exertion than to embarassment. "Reward money!" he explained. "It most often comes a Runner's way."

"Reward money?" Melly paused with a scarf of cream-colored sheer muslin, embroidered with drawn work and gold metal thread, draped elegantly around her shoulders. This piece of impudence would have greatly incensed Madame le Best, who had severely ordered her niece *not* to meddle with the shop's merchandise. "What *is* reward money, Samson?"

Puddiphat was very flattered by this indication of interest. Enthusiastically, he explained how Runners' slender incomes were augmented by a system of private fees and government rewards. "Thousands of pounds a year, I swear it! Which is a great deal better than riding about in the dark all night. Not that the Horse Patrol doesn't encounter danger, but I'd rather take my chances with desperate criminals than potholes!"

Thoughtfully, Melly exchanged the muslin scarf for one with leaves embroidered around the hem. "And if you was to apprehend a dangerous criminal, you'd receive a reward?"

"Don't see why I shouldn't!" If Puddiphat had failed to clearly explain government rewards and private fees, it was because he was not entirely clear on the details himself. "Tell you a secret! Think I'm on the trail of something *big!*"

Melly exchanged the second shawl for a turban of white satin with yellow French knots, which looked enchanting on her head. That head was abuzz with speculation. "And you mean to deal with it yourself?" she shrewdly guessed.

Puddiphat, who had discovered that he might gaze upon Miss Bagshot's slender back without impairment of his vocal abilities, shamelessly indulged himself. No hopeful puppy-like aspect had Puddiphat this day, but —due to the great dark circles around his eyes, the result of his nightly patrol of the roads into London and his daily forays among the city's milliners—the look of an anxious raccoon. "Eh? Oh! *Must* deal with it myself, Miss. If I breathe a word, one of the Runners will take over the case, and there goes my chance of advancement."

"As well," murmured Melly, setting aside the turban, "as the reward."

"It's not so much the reward money." Puddiphat sought to explain his freedom from mercenary considerations, no easy task with Miss Bagshot's big brown eyes fixed on his face. "It wouldn't make a difference even if there *wasn't* a reward."

"And so you wish to arrest Sir Malcolm," concluded Miss Bagshot, resuming her seat.

"Not exactly! Don't know yet if there's anything to arrest him *for!*" In his determination not to be misunderstood, Puddiphat leaned forward, an act which put his saber in disastrous proximity to the magazine-strewn table, as a result of which the table once more overturned. This time it was Puddiphat who tidied up the wreckage, Miss Bagshot's skirt being too narrow for such things.

If Melly's movements were inhibited, her imagination knew no confines. She was almost grateful to Puddiphat for the shambles he was making of the showroom —in his present crouched posture, the saber was even more dangerous, and had already overturned one of the japanned chairs—because it gave her the chance to reflect upon his startling statements. Sir Malcolm Calveley had attracted the interest of Bow Street? Melly decided she should not have been surprised. A gentleman capable of engaging in so torturous a relationship with his cousins—if they *were* his cousins—wouldn't stick at anything. Now it grew more imperative than ever that their friendship be cultivated, as opposed to being allowed to wither on the vine. Though she might not mean to toss her bonnet over the windmill for him, a girl couldn't help being curious about such a rogue—especially a girl in whose veins the wild Bagshot blood flowed.

Miss Bagshot's silence had not escaped Puddiphat's attention, nor her contemplative air; would-be Bow Street Runners must learn attention to detail. Puddiphat was very serious in his ambition, whiling away the scant leisure hours allotted to him between the Horse Patrol and milliners' shops with such improving tomes as Lavatar's four-volume *Physiognomical Fragments,* which dealt with the characteristics of various types of villains, determined through a careful study of the cadavers of executed felons. *So* serious, in fact, was Puddiphat that he did not overlook the possibility that Miss Bagshot was somehow implicated in Sir Malcolm Calveley's unknown crimes.

Her next words did little to dispel that impression. "Bless my soul!" sighed Melly. "I have been properly taken in. It ain't what I like, I promise you! Here I thought Sir Malcolm was a regular out-and-outer, and instead it turns out he's a desperate character! Yes, and very clever and artful in his ways. You won't do for him easily, Samson!" She looked almost cherubic. "At least not without *my* help.'"

"*Your* help, Miss?" repeated Puddiphat, by this unexpected reaction put totally off stride. "But you just got through saying Sir Malcolm Calveley was a regular out-and-outer! Heard you myself!"

By Puddiphat's powers of comprehension, Melly was not impressed. "I ain't denying I said it!" she retorted impatiently. "Yes, and meant it, too! But have it your own way! There's no flies on Sir Malcolm, as you'll shortly find out."

If Puddiphat was slow to grasp a situation, grasp it he eventually did; and comprehension of Melly's offer brought him up off his knees, in which posture the preceding exchange had been conducted, while he sought to retrieve the magazines. "You *would* help Bow Street?" he inquired.

From all indications, she would have to lead Bow Street by the hand, reflected Melly. She gestured Puddiphat to the other chair, with her most beguiling smile. "A girl must think of her future!" she said sadly. "If Sir Malcolm has been wicked, he deserves to be taken into custody by Bow Street—or by you! I'm sure I wouldn't wish to stand in the way of such a thing."

"Beg pardon, Miss!" If Puddiphat's wits were most often to be found begging, his instinct for mischief compensated him, especially when the outcome of that mischief would likely make him look a fool. "Seems to me you're wishful of doing exactly that! It's not *right* for a young woman to wish her, er—"

"Gentleman friend!" supplied Melly. "My gentleman friend, Puddiphat—or, better yet, acquaintance, for there ain't nothing at all between Sir Malcolm and myself!" Which was no more than the truth, even if Melly yearned that there might be.

Puddiphat continued to look suspicious. "To wish her gentleman friend clapped in irons! It's not fitting!"

"He is *not* my gentleman friend!" Melly patiently pointed out. "I just said so! But I can see you don't believe me! Think of it this way, Puddiphat: I do not *like* to think of Sir Malcolm penned up in jail—I know he will be unhappy, for *I* am unhappy, because my aunt keeps me as tightly locked up as if I was in quod! And there's no escape for me unless I can somehow figure how to come up with the Ready-and-Rhino, because my pockets are to let and I have no chance of finding respectable work without a reference—and I ain't ready for work that ain't respectable!" She sighed. "The only way out of this pickle is to help you apprehend Sir Malcolm so that you may share the reward money with me! You must not think I *like* the notion; I don't! But if one of us must languish behind bars, I'd much rather it was him than me!"

So startled was Puddiphat by these frank admissions that he stared straight into Melly's elfin face. She gazed beseechingly on him. As Puddiphat sought for speech, and Melly marshaled her further arguments, there appeared in the showroom doorway a whimsical dark-haired gentleman.

Chapter Thirteen

Puddiphat received no further assistance from Miss
Bagshot that day, save her firm escort to the door. Having dispatched the aspiring Runner, Melly turned to
curiously survey the newcomer, who wore pantaloons
and half-boots and a brass-buttoned blue coat. His attire did not especially interest Melly, elegant as it was.
Those strongly marked romantic features, the adventurous nose and unruly dark curls, flashing eyes and
flyaway brows, were strongly reminiscent of Sir Malcolm and his cousin Thea. Miss Bagshot was not so
bird-witted that she failed to realize that before her,
looking very whimsical, was no other than Lord Davenham.

No doubt, decided Melly, Lord Davenham was curious about the presence of an aspiring Runner in her
aunt's fashionable shop. Madame le Best would not
appreciate the loss of Lady Davenham's patronage did
his lordship take a pet. Not that his lordship looked like
he was prone to put his foot down firmly— "You will
be wondering about Puddiphat! I did myself! First I

thought he meant to arrest my papa, then my aunt, then Sir Malcolm, then myself—for trying to hoodwink Bow Street, which I *wasn't,* though I'm not sure it ain't a nacky notion! He needs to arrest *some*one so he may be made a Runner, you see."

"Ah." Lord Davenham's quizzical look increased. "I see that it would be very tempting to try and hoodwink Bow Street—just to find out if one *could.* Am I correct in assuming that I address Miss Bagshot?"

Impressed by his lordship's powers of deduction, Melly dropped a little curtsy, no easy feat in very narrow skirts. "My dear," murmured Vivien, "you are so very *young.*"

"Young, am I?" An endearingly indignant expression sat on Melly's elfin face. "Lady Birmingham didn't think so—no, or Captain Birmingham, either! Or I wouldn't have had to leave Brighton. Not that I am *sorry,* because London has turned out to be a great deal more larkish than I thought it would, even if my aunt does keep me locked up as if I was in jail—and when I think of how unfair I am being treated— Well! All I did is prick my thumb." She sighed. "You will tell me there's no use sniveling over spilt milk. But I *did* like Brighton—watching the fishing boats, and viewing the remains of old Saxon camps, and galloping on the Downs!"

Especially Miss Bagshot had liked the Tenth Hussars, concluded his lordship, who was not so lacking in adventurous spirit that he failed to recognize a sad romp. With some reluctance, he changed the subject. "I believe I wish to speak with your aunt."

"Aunt Hel?" Melly grasped Lord Davenham's sleeve and tugged him toward a japanned chair. "You didn't like the dress!"

"Dress?" Lord Davenham righted the chair, one of several items disarranged by Puddiphat's saber, and sat down. "You mean my wife's gown? It was very nice. Rather, I wished to speak to your aunt about a cousin of mine."

"Your cousin?" echoed Melly, perplexed.

"Sir Malcolm Calveley." When made aware of its existence, Vivien liked to clear up as much perplexity as he could. "I understand he has formed a rather close acquaintance with a milliner—your aunt, I assume."

"Aunt Hel!" Melly sat down so abruptly she almost missed her chair. "Bless my soul! For all her supposed highmindedness, Aunt Hel *is* a Bagshot! She rang a peal over *me* for giving her the slip when she is no better—yes, and accused me of telling clankers, too! It makes me mad as fire!"

"I think," Lord Davenham interrupted apologetically, "that I have made an error. You must forgive me for it; I am not in the habit of meddling. Doubtless my wife would have known in an instant that it was *you* whom my cousin took on an outing, and not your aunt."

"So would *you* know, sir," giggled Melly, "had you even seen my aunt! She ain't at all in Sir Malcolm's way. Took quite a pet, she did, even though he explained how it was he'd found me wandering lost through the streets." She looked anxious. "Oh, sir, you won't tell my aunt it was all a hum?"

"You have my word, Miss Bagshot," Lord Davenham solemnly promised.

"Then *that*'s all right!" Melly smiled again. "I do not mean to get into pickles; that's just the way it is with me! I am very susceptible to frolics and larks! Not that there is anything *wrong* with looking at the Tower or London Bridge or Newgate Prison—though now I have seen it I can understand very well how it would be very cruel of me to connive at sending your cousin to jail! As for Carlton House, I've already seen the Pavilion at Brighton, and nothing could be queerer than that. It was Astley's that I *truly* liked. I ain't seen such a thing before." Her dimples disappeared. "And after the way Aunt Hel cut up stiff, it ain't likely I will again!"

Sorry as Lord Davenham was to learn the mischievous Miss Bagshot possessed an unfeeling aunt, he was even more moved by another of her remarks. "Forgive me for interrupting, but you said something about sending my cousin to jail. I assume you meant my cousin, Malcolm. On what did you base your remark?"

His lordship certainly had a high-flying manner of speech, reflected Melly, who was deriving inordinate enjoyment from her first exposure to a Duke. "You ain't paying attention!" she scolded, once she had deciphered his remark. "I said Puddiphat was wishful of arresting someone, did I not? He's settled on Sir Malcolm as the most likely person to have done something that he should be arrested *for*. And I shouldn't wonder but what he's right! I'll wager there's very little Sir Malcolm would stick at."

Lord Davenham, contemplating his cousin's obsession with the fair sex, said, "I imagine not. Did this Puddiphat give you any hint of what he means to arrest Malcolm for?"

Melly tried very hard to remember just what Puddiphat had said, an exercise which caused a frown to mar the perfection of her brow. "He claimed Sir Malcolm was a dangerous and suspicious character, but he didn't say *how*. I see now that I should have tried to find out—but Puddiphat will be back, on that I'll lay odds, and so I still *can*."

"I would be very grateful for your assistance in this matter, Miss Bagshot." Lord Davenham had derived no little amusement from the spectacle of Melly engaged in deep thought. "It would not suit me to have my cousin made to stand his trial."

Although Miss Bagshot did not frequently engage in prolonged cogitation, she was very tenacious of those few ideas she had. "*How* grateful?" she asked bluntly. "Because Puddiphat has already promised that if I help him bring Sir Malcolm to justice he'll share the reward—or if he ain't exactly promised it yet, I'll see to it he soon *does*! You mustn't think I'm on the dangle for a fortune, sir, because I'm not. It's just that I don't wish to be leg-shackled, and I don't wish either to enter into a dishonorable occupation, but without a reference and without any money—well, if Aunt Hel was to turn me out, I'd *truly* be in a pickle, and there ain't any doubt in my mind that she eventually *will!*"

Nor was there any doubt in Lord Davenham's mind that Miss Bagshot would eventually embark merrily upon a career that was slightly less than honorable, and enjoy it immensely, but he could not fault her for awaiting her best shot. Nor did he fault her avarice. In addition to his characteristic whimsy, his lordship had a second saving grace: he seldom roused sufficiently from his habitual preoccupation to judge his fellowmen.

"Oh!" cried Melly, misinterpreting his lordship's silence. "You have taken me in disgust. I'm sure I'm very sorry for it, but a girl must think of her future, and there surely ain't no future for me here in Aunt Hel's shop. I don't want to be a milliner; I don't even want to sew! For that matter, I don't especially want to see Sir Malcolm clapped in jail, either, because I know what it's *like!*"

Lord Davenham stirred. "You misunderstood, Miss Bagshot. I think it would be an excellent idea were you to, er, humor this person from Bow Street—and then relate his remarks to me." He looked serene. "If you are very clever, you may earn a reward from *both* of us, my dear!"

Melly did think of it. "I thought you *didn't* wish your cousin to stand his trial!" she responded suspiciously. Then she recalled the dalliance that the Duke endured between his cousin and his wife. Scant surprise if he was a bit uncharitably inclined. "You poor man! You can't be blamed for wishing to see Sir Malcolm behind bars, so scaly has he behaved to you! But wouldn't it be simpler to just send him about his business? I know I am being *pushing,* but someone needs to drop a hint or two! All three of you are going on in a very bad way."

"We are?" His lordship brought forth a snuffbox. "I see nothing exceptionable in it."

"No?" Melly wondered if Lord Davenham was of entirely sound mind. "You must know your own business best, and *I* know when I've received a setdown! You are a very strange person, sir. Anyone else would be fit to murder Sir Malcolm—oh, *I* wouldn't! He'd suit *me* right down to the ground, but I ain't you. Or your wife!" Her elfin features were unhappy. "I suppose Lady Davenham is very cross with me, sir!"

Vivien inhaled, sneezed elegantly, and put away the snuffbox. "I suppose she must be. She called you 'bachelor's fare.' "

"Bachelor's fare!" echoed Melly indignantly. "Bless my heart! Still, I suppose I must swallow it with good grace, because naturally she was out of sorts. Did she send you here to scold me, sir? Because before you do, I'd like to point out that my aunt already *has,* even if she don't know the whole of it."

"It is not for me to scold you." Thoroughly amused by Miss Bagshot, Vivien gently smiled. "Instead, I wished to see you for myself. I do not blame my cousin for escorting you around London, Miss Bagshot! Any gentleman would have done the same."

By his lordship's gentle smile, Melly was not unimpressed. "Bless my soul!" she murmured. "Are *all* of you so handsome and well-set-up? Oh, I know I should not have said that, but you must know you *are!* And I am very sorry that Lady Davenham is cross with me. I did not *mean* to steal a march on her or cast her in the shade. The afternoon I spent with Sir Malcolm was the merest peccadillo—I was just in the right place at the right time. She needn't fear I'll make her play second fiddle!"

Intimation of how far matters had progressed between his cousin and his wife caused Lord Davenham to quirk a dark brow. "Second fiddle, Miss Bagshot?"

Melly clapped her hands to her lips. "I've done it again, ain't I? Put my foot smack in my mouth!"

"And a very pretty foot it is!" courteously responded Vivien. Clad in neat slippers, Miss Bagshot's feet peeked out from under the hem of her narrow skirt. "Don't put yourself in a pucker; I don't mind."

"No?" Wide-eyed, Melly dropped her hands to her lap. "Sir Malcolm *said* you didn't, but I thought he was cutting a wheedle! I must say you are being very *calm* about it, sir! *I*'d have their heads on a platter if my cousin and my wife was to plant the antlers on my forehead—not that I have a cousin and a wife, but you know what I mean!"

"Is that what they are doing?" Lord Davenham raised the second brow. "Egad! Surely there must be some more civilized manner of dealing with the situation. It sounds deuced distasteful, this removal of heads."

From long experience, Miss Bagshot knew when she was being teased. Gentlemen were prone to tease Melly, due perhaps to the infectious nature of her dimpled smile. "You are bamming me, sir," she said wisely. "I guess I've been pushing again. But it's plain you ain't no better able than a newborn babe to handle your own business. What you *should* do is pretend you ain't interested! That'll take the ticket every time." Came a pause, during which snickers and giggles issued from the atelier. "There! I've made you angry. But I *like* you, sir, and I like Lady Davenham, and Sir Malcolm, too. I suppose you'd think me bold as a brass-faced monkey if I was to offer to fix it up all right and tight! Because it's plain as the nose on my face that you ain't one to straighten out this tangle yourself! Sir."

So Miss Bagshot advised assumed indifference? Lord Davenham wondered if that was how his wife interpreted his lenience. By not so much as a twitch of his own adventurous Davenant nose did Vivien reveal annoyance at Miss Bagshot's declaration of his incapacity to manage his own affairs. "It is not for me to judge you bold, Miss Bagshot," he responded courteously. "You must do as you please."

"Oh, no, I mustn't!" said Melly archly. "Even I know better than that. My Aunt Hel would wash her hands of me altogether if I was to toss my bonnet over the windmill." She frowned. "Can it be, sir, that you *really* don't care?"

As has been previously demonstrated, Lord Davenham's mental processes were very acute; he understood immediately that Miss Bagshot sought to discover his sentiments concerning the Davenant *ménage à trois*. However, he did not feel inclined to make that confidence. Evasively, he gazed around the showroom. "I have never before been in a milliner's shop. Indeed, I am not even certain I know what a milliner does."

"You don't?" Melly was astounded that so downy a gentleman could, in this most important of areas, be so abysmally ignorant. "Why, a milliner trims dresses delivered to her by the dressmaker—perfects and embellishes them, you see! And she designs fichus and mantillas and delicate lace ruches and all sorts of things. It ain't child's play! And my aunt makes all manner of hats. There are lingere bonnets and turbans, capotes and caps and cornettes—it has taken me all this time to learn the difference between them, and I still ain't sure I know! But you are getting up! Are you leaving?"

"I fear I must, Miss Bagshot." Lord Davenham had indeed risen from his chair. "I am to speak at a meeting of the Horticultural Society, and I do not care to be late."

"Fancy that!" marveled Melly as she walked with him across the showroom floor. "The *what* Society, sir? What will you talk about?"

"The Horticultural Society, my dear." Lord Davenham paused in the doorway. "I have been doing experiments upon the science of growing plants without using soil. I call it hydroponics, from the Greek words *hudor* and *ponos*—waterworking. The plants are fed on solutions of water and mineral salts."

"Bless my heart!" Melly secretly pitied the poor plants. "And it actually *works?*"

"Oh, yes." Lord Davenham was amused by the ardent manner in which Miss Bagshot hung upon his words. "But you will not be interested in such things."

"That shows all *you* know!" responded Miss Bagshot, miffed. "I have always liked plants—yes, and had a knack for growing things! Once I even had my own little garden in amongst the cook's kitchen stuff, and grew some snowdrops and tulips. I would have liked to try my hand with magnolias and rhododendrons, but there just wasn't room." She cocked her pretty head to one side and smiled. "How can anyone *not* like plants, sir?"

This question Lord Davenham could not answer, though he suspected his wife might. "I wonder, Miss Bagshot," he murmured, "if you would care to attend the Horticultural Society meeting with me? You would find it very interesting, I think—unless your aunt would mind?"

Surely her aunt would not disapprove of so innocent an outing, thought Melly—and even if she did, what was one more pickle, after a lifetime of them? Had not Melly vowed to straighten out Lord Davenham's tangled relationships? What better way to start than with a large dose of sunshine?

"I should admire to!" cried Melly, her cheeks flushed with her excitement, in which she clutched and hugged Lord Davenham's arm—and for the record let it be stated that Lord Davenham evidenced not the slightest dislike of this trespass. "And on the way you may tell me what it is this Horti-what's-is Society *does!*"

"My dear," responded Lord Davenham, as he led Miss Bagshot out into the street, "I would be charmed."

Chapter Fourteen

Lady Davenham would have benefited from a large dose of sunshine; she was sunk in gloom, as became apparent to Sir Malcolm the instant he stepped across the threshold of her bookroom. Situated at the front of the first floor, this small chamber contained tall oak bookcases with rectangular glazed windows, a few chairs with high arched backs, silver sconces on the walls, and a kneehole writing desk. At this latter item was seated Thea, staring glumly at her household accounts. Nimrod was stretched out in a highly unattractive manner, snoozing on the hearth.

"Good morning, Cousin!" Sir Malcolm—resplendent in a loose floor-length *banjan,* fashioned of expensive silk and belted at the waist, slippers, and a tasseled cap —strolled farther into the room. "You wished to speak with me?"

Lady Davenham looked up from her accounts. "No!" she snapped. "But I think I must, since you are involved in this imbroglio as deeply as I." She pushed the chair back. "Sometimes, Malcolm, I vow I wish you had *not* come home!"

Sometimes Sir Malcolm experienced that same wish, due primarily to his cousin's unsolicited efforts on his behalf. To tell her so was out of the question, naturally. Sir Malcolm seated himself comfortably on one of the bookroom's several chairs—or as comfortably as was possible due to the chair's high arched back. "I did not mean that!" Thea broke into his thoughts. "This is a bad business. I am wholly overset."

Of what business had put Lady Davenham out of temper, Sir Malcolm—among whose virtues was no disinclination to heed gossip—had no doubt. "If you are referring to the recent meeting of the Horticultural Society—"

"The Horticultural Society!" Lady Davenham fairly shrieked. "Good God, Malcolm! If *you* begin boring on about verbena and ageratum, I shall—oh, I don't know *what* I shall do, but it will be something very drastic!"

Obviously, his cousin had not yet learned of the disruption of the Society's recent meeting, and Sir Malcolm did not feel obliged to disclose that disruption's source. From all accounts the members agreed that never had their august body enjoyed so stimulating an interval. Malcolm thought of the mischievous Miss Bagshot, and smiled. Then he thought of Miss Bagshot's escort.

What the devil was Vivien about? Malcolm mused. The Duke must know his escapade would eventually be related to his wife. "Verbena and ageratum?" he repeated. "Am I to assume that Vivien *does* bore you with such stuff?"

"You know he does! Not that I find it boring, precisely—it is just occasionally I would welcome a discussion of more *personal* things, or *would* have welcomed such discussions! Now the opportunity has passed." Lady Davenham's energetic perambulations about the small chamber brought her in frequent proximity to the hearth. Each time her skirts brushed by him, Nimrod snarled. "Never have I been so mistaken in anyone. I mean to say: fleshpots!"

Fleshpots? This simple declaration snagged Sir Malcolm's attention, which had begun to stray. Not surprisingly, he assumed Lady Davenham had used the term in conjunction with himself. "You've been around Vivien too long, my Thea; you are beginning to talk like him! I told you I would not be reformed, moreover, so you have only yourself to blame."

"Not *you!*" Frowning ferociously, Lady Davenham regarded one of her silver sconces. "Although I still wish you would overcome your aversion to respectable females. Rather, I was—"

"I don't *like* respectable females!" Sir Malcolm explained, unnecessarily. "Except for you! At all events, I thought you envied me my adventures. Not long past you indicated a wish that you might share in them."

"I did?" Thea's frown transferred itself from the silver sconce to Sir Malcolm's face. He looked very exotic in his *banjan* and slippers and tasseled cap, she decided. He also looked, in so mundane a setting, a trifle absurd. "I did not. It is Vivien who has that aspiration. You need not look so skeptical; he told me so himself! Marriage, according to my husband, does not suit the Davenants. Indeed, so *little* does it suit Vivien that I am no higher in his opinion than an insect!"

"An *insect?*" echoed Sir Malcolm, in tones so startled that Nimrod twitched in response. "You must have mistaken his meaning. Surely Vivien was talking about his garden."

"No," retorted Lady Davenham, "Vivien was *not!* He very distinctly told me that I am lower in his opinion than a caterpillar. That is not *all* he intimated—and the rest of it, Malcolm, you will not like one bit!"

If Lord Davenham's further sentiments were of the order that had compared his wife to a caterpillar, Sir Malcolm wished he might be spared an account. Judging from Thea's determined expression, however, his wishes were not to be fulfilled. "Come out of the mops!" he hastily advised. "It cannot be so *very* bad!"

"Can it not?" inquired Lady Davenham. "When I recall that Madame le Best *promised* me that gown would cause his eyes to start out of his head—at least now I *know* why he doesn't find me desirable!" Having delivered herself of this pronouncement, she burst into tears.

Although, and to his great dissatisfaction, Sir Malcolm had already realized he was in the presence of a lady verging on an emotional outlay, it was some seconds before he recovered sufficiently from his astonishment to try and succor her. Meanwhile, Nimrod manipulated his arthritic bones into a sitting position, the better to observe the bookroom's occupants. On his dewlapped countenance was an expression of canine glee.

"This is very bad of you, Thea!" soothed Sir Malcolm, as he cradled Lady Davenham in his arms. "First I must contend with my valet's sulks, and now you are water-spotting my silk *banjan*. Come, do not take on so! Tell me what is behind this farrago of nonsense."

"Nonsense!" Thea withdrew her head from Sir Malcolm's chest, a very comfortable position spoiled only by the knowledge that countless other females had enjoyed it before. "You'd be in the mops yourself, Malcolm, were you destined to become a fubsy-faced old maid!"

Had the lady fast in the grip of an emotional outburst been other than his Cousin Thea, Sir Malcolm would have long before withdrawn. Once more he reminded himself of the selfless energy she'd expended on his account. "You can't be left on the shelf when you are already married!" he sensibly pointed out.

"No?" Lady Davenham's dark eyes sparkled with mingled tears and rage. "But Vivien does not *wish* to be married—I suppose he never did, but he is a model of good breeding, and has always had a general wish of doing right. He would not have wanted me to realize

I was being forced on him against his will. Then *you* came home, and put Vivien in mind of what he had *missed!*"

Perhaps Thea *did* know of the damsel who had set the recent meeting of the Horticultural Society at naught. "What *has* Vivien missed?" Sir Malcolm cautiously inquired.

Thea's glance was impatient. "*You* know! Bachelor's fare!"

"She *isn't* bachelor's fare." The reverence in which Sir Malcolm held womankind forbade that he allowed one to be unjustly maligned. "At least she isn't *yet*. I have it on the chit's own word, although she admits she is destined to eventually toss her bonnet over the windmill. The Bagshots, I am informed, have Wild Blood."

"The Bagshots must!" Lady Davenham was not certain how or why Miss Bagshot had suddenly intruded on the conversation. "If that chit is a paragon of virtue, what about Captain Birmingham, pray? Perhaps she failed to mention Brighton to you, or that this is not the first time she has been turned off without a character. And *this* is the sort of female you prefer? I wash my hands of you, Malcolm. Or I *would,* had not Vivien decided I have a *tendre.*"

"A *tendre.*" Sir Malcolm removed his hands from his cousin's shoulders as abruptly as if he'd grasped hot coals. "May one inquire for whom?"

Between her head cold and her marital difficulties, Thea had no time to indulge in maidenly reticence. Irritably, she retorted: "Who else but you? Vivien even offered to free you from your entanglement with Miss Bagshot, because if I hadn't been betrothed to him from the cradle, I'd have had you in the first place—or so he thinks."

Thus was Miss Bagshot's presence at the meeting of the Horticultural Society explained. Lord Davenham had gone to the milliner's shop to expostulate and had instead been ensnared. "What do *you* think, my Thea? I confess this question of whether you do or do not have a *tendre* interests me very much—not that I wish to appear impertinent!"

The amusing aspect of this conversation struck Thea —it was not commonplace to engage in such plain speaking with a gentleman for whom one might nourish a fatal passion, after all—and she managed a faint smile. "I don't know!" she confessed. "I was never used to think such things. There was always Vivien and we rubbed on together tolerably well. I had interesting things with which to occupy myself. Then we came to London"—she made a despairing gesture—"and nothing has gone right since! Some days I think I have lost control of my own life."

Sir Malcolm was not pleased to discover that he was, if inadvertently, the cause of Thea's distress. He must somehow make it up to her, he thought. But how? The manner in which he made restitution must be decided by the lady. In an attempt to settle this question of whether his cousin did or did not nourish a *tendre,* Sir Malcolm grasped her expressive hands and drew her once more into his arms. This time he offered no solace, but an ardent embrace. It was an endeavor in which he had no little expertise. Conversation did not move forward for a lengthy interval, during which time Nimrod slavered, snarled, and wheezed.

At length Sir Malcolm released Lady Davenham. "I thought we should discover for ourselves whether or not you have a *tendre,*" he explained.

Thea backed away, fingers pressed to her bruised lips. "Yes, well—I don't!" she said.

Though Sir Malcolm had spent the interval thinking of the enterprising Miss Bagshot, he was startled to discover Thea similarly unmoved. Females did not generally respond so coolly to his advances. He wondered if perhaps he was losing his touch.

Nonsense! he decided. One did not alter so radically overnight—and Sir Malcolm's experiences of the previous eve, passed in the gallery of the Argyll Rooms in Great Windmill Street, had left him in no doubt whatsoever of his continued good standing with the opposite sex. Some other cause existed, then, for Thea's lack of response.

Sir Malcolm could think of only one such explanation. "The devil!" he ejaculated. "You're in love with Vivien!"

"Of course I am in love with Vivien!" Thea retorted crossly. Having backed into the hearth, she was now struggling with Nimrod. The hound had not yet forgot the scrap of blue sarcenet which he had retained and treasured as a symbol of battle fairly joined and won— and of which, upon her ladyship's command, he had been forcibly deprived. In retaliation he clamped his remaining teeth into the fabric of her skirt. Thea sought to free herself. With—to Nimrod—a very satisfying sound, the spotted sarcenet tore.

Lady Davenham was too unhappy to overly concern herself with a ruined skirt, especially the skirt of a dress she privately considered dull. (In point of fact, Lady Davenham had come to adjudge all her dresses dull, in comparison with the gown Malcolm had insisted she wear for her rout.) After aiming a half-hearted kick at Nimrod, which the hound evaded, she moved away. "I have always been in love with Vivien! Much good it has done me. I merely wondered if I might love you, *too!*" She realized the import of her latter statement. "Gracious God! I *am* a Davenant! And so is Vivien, apparently, or he would not yearn to kick over the traces. Oh, Malcolm, this is such a dreadful tangle! What am I to do?"

Though he was more accustomed to contributing to tangles than resolving them, Sir Malcolm couldn't refuse the pleas of a lady in distress, especially when the lady was his cousin, who had just absolved him of the necessity of mollycoddling her by admitting she did not have a *tendre*. "It is your own fault!" he said bluntly. "Even Davenants don't go out looking for adventure when it's awaiting them at home. You have let Vivien

Bachelor's Fare

get in the habit of taking you for granted. You haven't even tried to keep his interest sparked."

There was little she *could* do to spark her husband's interest, Thea thought morosely, other than invent a new thrashing machine or sprout branches like the rhododendron so recently cut back. "I will concede you are the expert in such matters!" she retorted waspishly. "Very well! What must I do?"

Sir Malcolm ran a knowledgeable eye over his cousin's gown, the dullness of which was not relieved by the piece torn from her skirt. "First you must stop dressing like a dowd! Have Madame le Best provide you with some new dresses—or, rather, *I* will! She doubtless kept your measurements, and can bring the garments here to you, so you need not even go near the shop." And thus would be spared further encounters with the garrulous Melly, he thought. "And then— I think you must flirt very desperately with me."

Lady Davenham exhibited no great excitement in response to this invitation to embark upon a flirtation with the gentleman that a Princess had nicknamed Le Roué. "I would much rather try and flirt with Vivien!" said she. "In case you haven't noticed, I *did* flirt with you at my rout. Vivien didn't even notice, any more than he noticed that gown."

"My dear Thea, *everyone* noticed that gown." Wearied by his cousin's continued perambulations, Sir Malcolm sat down at her writing desk. "Vivien was no exception, I assure you—and so you would realize, were you not so naïve."

Definitely, Thea must be naïve; she did not understand how flirting with her cousin would inspire her husband to revise his opinion of their marriage. Still, she supposed Malcolm must know best. "Perhaps I was not *obvious* enough," she said doubtfully. "I did not want the whole world to say I had thrown myself at your head."

"But that is what the world *must* say!" chided Sir Malcolm, remembering his own wish that Vivien might

144

be inspired to demand he leave the house. Were he sufficiently clever, Malcolm might kill several birds with one stone. "And when have Davenants cared about what the world says, anyway? You must make a dead-set at me, Thea, and cast out lures; in response, I will dance attendance on you and make you my compliments at every opportunity. If Vivien does not notice us, you may be sure that some interfering busybody will point out that we are engaged in an open intrigue."

So fascinated was Lady Davenham by this strategy that she ventured once more too close to the hearth. With a burst of vigor amazing in a hound of such advanced years, Nimrod leaped. Hastily, Thea moved aside. Nimrod landed flat on his arthritic leg. So unhappy was he at this miscalculation that he howled. As he did so, the spotted sarcenet fell from his opened jaws. Thea snatched it up. "And *then* what?" she inquired, beating a prudent retreat.

Sir Malcolm rose from the writing desk and advanced upon the door. "Then you must seduce him!" he announced, as he passed into the hallway.

Seduce her own husband? Thea stared at the door, wondering if her cousin had gone quite mad. She thought he must have done so. None but a madman would conceive of the serene Lord Davenham displaying a dog-in-the-manger attitude.

But Thea would indulge Malcolm, all the same. While he danced attendance on her, however uselessly, he at least would be prevented from further foraging among the fleshpots.

Chapter Fifteen

Alas for Lady Davenham's convictions; even as he left her bookroom Sir Malcolm was contemplating the flesh-pots, in particular the young fleshpot who had set the recent meeting of the Horticultural Society at naught. No gentleman to waste time in speculation when action would better serve, Sir Malcolm had soon exchanged his *banjan* for coat and pantaloons, Hessian boots and beaver hat, a transition accompanied by his valet's laments. Leaving Hopgood deep in mourning for the lost delights of the Continent, Sir Malcolm departed Davenant House.

Madame le Best did not seem especially delighted to witness Sir Malcolm's arrival in her Oxford Street shop. Once he had explained his errand, however, her attitude altered drastically. "Oh, *là,!*" exulted Madame, and hastened into her atelier. Immediately, Sir Malcolm turned his attention to Miss Bagshot, seated sedately upon one of the japanned chairs. Melly returned the regard.

"So many dresses!" said that damsel, with a reproachful face. "And you said Lady Davenham was your *cousin!* But that ain't *my* business, and my aunt would be cross as a cat if she knew I was quizzing you. Not that she ain't cross as a cat, anyway!" She heaved a great sigh. "Sometimes I think my aunt is *worse* than Lady Birmingham."

"You are in a pickle again, Melly?" Sir Malcolm inspected the lace Miss Bagshot was tatting, and found it very fine. "I wonder if it might have to do with the recent meeting of the Horticultural Society? You see I know all about it. My cousin came here to persuade you that you must not take up with me, and so you took up with him, instead."

"Was *that* what he was after?" Miss Bagshot looked amazed. "Bless my soul! He *said* he only wanted a look at me, and then we got to talking about growing things —you need not look so skeptical; I *have* grown things! Snowdrops and hyacinths, and though there wasn't room to grow a rhododendron, I'll wager I *could!* Yes, and even without soil!"

Sir Malcolm, who had not been privileged to hear Lord Davenham hold forth, wondered whether Miss Bagshot was in complete possession of her wits. "This is fair and far off! I did not come here to talk about plants, but *why* you accompanied my cousin to the meeting. You know you should not have done so, Melly! I am very disappointed in you."

Sir Malcolm was fated to experience stronger emotions than disappointment, Miss Bagshot feared. She hoped she would not be around to witness his expression when he was taken into custody by Bow Street. "If I did nothing but what I *should* do," she retorted archly, "I'd never do nothing at all! If you was kept a virtual prisoner in a milliner's shop, you'd leap at the chance to go *any*where. And I thought there wasn't no harm in it, because what larks could I get up to amidst a group of people talking about plants and the like? But Aunt Hel don't see it that way."

"Monsieur!" uttered Madame le Best, emerging from

her atelier, laden down with swatches and samples and snippets of ribbon and lace, perfectly on cue. *"Regardez!"* Soon she was engrossed with Sir Malcolm in a discussion of the relative advantages of a sprigged poplin and the patriotic Spitalfields silk, white flower-bordered China crepe scarves, India muslin at thirteen shillings a yard, and silk gloves at four and sixpence. Interesting as was that conversation to Madame and Sir Malcolm—especially to Madame; if business continued in this exhilarating manner, she could soon expand her operation—it left Miss Bagshot feeling very hipped.

"Lady Davenham is very lucky!" she remarked, when her aunt withdrew again into the atelier. "She will cut a nacky dash! I have always wanted to, but my aunt don't like the notion. She even took away the gown I made myself—in the highest kick of fashion, it was, with a *very* narrow skirt. As if my leaving the shop and going to the Horti-what's-is Society with Lord Davenham had anything to do with my skirts!"

A discussion of Miss Bagshot's skirts was the last thing Sir Malcolm wanted to embark upon, at least in this particular moment. "Don't try and play off your airs on me," he said, though not unkindly. "I know you and Vivien are embarked on a May-game."

"We *are?*" Melly's brown eyes widened. "Fancy that!"

"You're barking up the wrong tree, my girl!" Sir Malcolm continued. "Vivien is no pigeon for your plucking. Do not pretend that you do not know he is rich as Croesus!"

"Croesus?" Miss Bagshot looked adorably confused.

"Minx!" responded Malcolm, appreciatively, as Madame le Best once more demanded his attention, and shot a darkling glance at her niece. Chastened and abandoned, Miss Bagshot bent once more over her lace.

But Melly was not of a temperament that remained long subdued, and she was very soon congratulating herself on the progress of her schemes. Perhaps there was a place for this wealthy Croesus person in her plans. As she ruminated, Melly continued with her tatting, and listened to her aunt extol the virtues of a toque of Ionian cork intermixed with fawn satin, finished with tassels and plumes. Then she set aside her tatting and hastily rose from her chair because Sir Malcolm was preparing to take his leave. Deftly, she interrupted his progress, exactly as he had intended she should. "If you do not mind, who *is* this Croesus person, sir?"

Sir Malcolm was not put off by this indication that Miss Bagshot was on the dangle for a fortune. He derived considerable amusement from the hopeful expression on her elfin face. "There is no such person," he confessed.

"Bless my soul!" ejaculated Melly, disappointed. "And you accused *me* of playing a May-game."

Sir Malcolm grasped Miss Bagshot's elbow and urged her away from the doorway, where they had very effectively prevented three fashionably clad females from entering the showroom. "Shame, Melly! You must not tarnish others with your own brush. And you must not set your cap at my cousin, even if he *is* as rich as— er, very rich!"

"That's easy enough for *you* to say!" Her aunt being occupied with the recently arrived customers, Melly could enjoy a comfortable prose. "*Your* pockets ain't to let! I'll wager if you hadn't a feather to fly with, you wouldn't have any scruples about feathering your nest!" She strove for innocence. "But surely Lord Davenham ain't as rich as all *that,* or he wouldn't be letting you buy his wife gowns! Not that it's any bread-and-butter of mine! I like Lady Davenham, even if she *did* call me bachelor's fare!"

Sir Malcolm did not explain that Lady Davenham had called Miss Bagshot much worse. "Let us put our cards on the table!" he said bluntly. "You have made a dead-set at my cousin, knowing he is well heeled. But Vivien is not one for the ladies, as you no doubt have already discovered. If you are smart, you will give him up."

Miss Bagshot glanced cautiously at her aunt, who with the newcomers was absorbed in the *Gallery of Fashion*. "Yes, but I *ain't* smart!" she retorted. "Anyone will tell you I am bird-witted—you need only ask my aunt! However, I ain't so bird-witted I don't know you're trying to persuade me to cut my losses, and I *can't*. Much as I would like to oblige you, sir! As you would understand, had you ever been short of the Ready-and-Rhino!"

The fact that he was well supplied with that commodity so inelegantly referred to by Miss Bagshot inspired Sir Malcolm to attempt a different approach. "*I* have a fortune!" he suggested craftily.

Enchantingly, Melly giggled. "As if I didn't know the minute I first clapped my eyes on you that you was a well-breeched swell! And I'm sure if I was to toss my bonnet over the windmill for anyone, I'd rather it was you! But *you* wouldn't make a settlement on a girl— and why should you, the way females are always casting you out lures? They *are* always casting you out lures, ain't they? That's what I thought!"

Whatever else might be said of her, Miss Bagshot was an original; never had Sir Malcolm's advances been repulsed in so regretful a way. In fact, Sir Malcolm's advances had never before been repulsed at all, save by Lady Davenham, and since Thea was his cousin, she didn't really count. "What if I *did* offer you a settlement, Melly?" he inquired.

"*Are* you offering me one?" Miss Bagshot responded skeptically. "You must be one of the warmest coves in England if you can stand all this nonsense of settlements and gowns! Yes, and that puts me in mind of something else: you ain't a fitting person to rake me over the coals. All *I* did is give my aunt the slip. Though I ain't one to cast aspersions—it *is* aspersions? Grand!—you should be very grateful that Davenham ain't horn-mad." She frowned. "He is such a *nice* person. Anyone else would be fit to murder you. I don't know how you can be a party to planting the antlers on his brow."

It occurred to Sir Malcolm that this discussion was best not overheard. Madame le Best was still engrossed in her *Gallery of Fashion* and thus made no outcry when her niece slipped out the shop door. "I have not given you a rake-down *yet,*" said Sir Malcolm, when they had achieved the noisy confusion of Oxford Street. "But I shall at any moment if you don't cut line! You seem to have forgotten it is *your* misconduct I came here to discuss."

"How was I to know that? You never *said!* I thought you were wishful of refurbishing Lady Davenham's wardrobe." Melly contemplated Sir Malcolm's stern expression and decided that his temper had been sufficiently strained. "I hope you don't mean to get to dagger-drawing, because I wouldn't like for us to be at daggers' points! I have a great regard for you, sir, and I would *like* to oblige you, except that I am in the basket, and I ain't wishful of finding myself leg-shackled to some nodcock, like my aunt means to arrange." She sighed. "We are at point nonplus! I had better go back inside."

Twice in one day, Sir Malcolm had failed to charm. He hoped anew that this was no ominous portent. "Not just yet! In other words, you seek the means by which to be independent of your aunt. And you have discovered that Vivien could easily provide those means. But my cousin is no fool! How did you think you may persuade him to finance your independence?" A memory of the papers strewn across Lady Davenham's writing desk struck him; he smiled. "Especially when, unless I am very much mistaken, it is *Thea* who handles the accounts!"

"That makes it even better!" Melly clapped her hands together, then raised them to her pretty chin. "I don't see why I shouldn't tell you—I mean to make a nuisance of myself!"

"A nuisance?" So that they might not be parted by the throng of pedestrians, Sir Malcolm drew Miss Bagshot back into the shadow of an alleyway.

"Oh, yes!" Melly was delighted by the speed with which their friendship had advanced. "You hope I won't take up with Lord Davenham, and he hopes I won't take up with you, or so you say—well! It's clear as noonday that neither of you would care a rush about *who* I took up with if you wasn't afraid of being dipped in the scandal-broth!"

"And therefore you mean to make a nuisance of yourself until one of us buys you off?" Here was a novel resolution of financial difficulties! Sir Malcolm was so entertained by Melly's strategy that he hated to tell her it would not serve. "But the Davenants do not care for scandal-broth."

"Davenants?" Melly looked suspicious. "I thought you was a Calveley! You ain't trying to hoax me, are you, sir? I wish you would not! Because whatever you call yourself, you're pitching it too rum. Though *you* might not mind, and Lord Davenham would probably never even know the difference, I'll wager anything you like that *Lady* Davenham would dislike the scandal-broth very much!"

That wager, Sir Malcolm was not prepared to take. "You will wager *anything,* Miss Bagshot?" he wickedly asked.

"Not *that!*" Bewitchingly, Melly dimpled and blushed. "Do not change the subject! I wouldn't care a rush if the gabble-grinders washed all my dirty linen in public, nor would you, but Lady Davenham is *different!* Was you a gentleman, you'd make certain she was spared."

With a careless finger, Sir Malcolm flicked Melly's rosy cheek. "But I am *not* a gentleman!" he said. "Give up this foolishness; there's a good girl!"

In her desire to further Sir Malcolm's education, Miss Bagshot had not considered that her own might be broadened apace. Hastily, lest he be tempted to further transgressions, and consequently further muddle up her thoughts, Melly stepped back into the alleyway.

Here was no damsel who had to be told how to get up a flirtation, thought Sir Malcolm, interpreting Miss Bagshot's retreat in the light of the considerable education he already possessed. He followed her into the alleyway, caught her by the shoulders. Melly gasped. Sir Malcolm needed no further invitation; he kissed her. When he had concluded that highly pleasant undertaking—during which, for the record, he thought of no one, save Miss Bagshot—it was his turn to gasp. Melly slapped him, hard, across the cheek.

"I have just got through telling you I must have a settlement!" she wailed. "It is very bad of you to *tempt* me!"

With no little wonder, Sir Malcolm touched his stinging cheek. "*Did* I tempt you, Melly? You have a queer way of showing it!"

By the intelligence that she had injured her victim's self-esteem as well as his cheek, Miss Bagshot was aghast. "Bless my soul, of course you tempted me! Any female who ain't tempted by you ain't worth her salt. *If* I had a competence, I wouldn't have to worry about being offered false coin, or played fast and loose with—but I ain't got a groat with which to bless myself, and you *do* have a, er, cousin—and so I think we should get out of this alleyway, sir!"

Sir Malcolm was amenable; continued seclusion with Miss Bagshot would doubtless result in further injury to himself. He wanted nothing more than to embrace her again, conduct of which she had already made her opinion painfully clear. At that opinion, Malcolm marveled. No female had ever struck him before. "We are at a stalemate," he observed. "Permit me to escort you back to your aunt's shop."

"Now *you* are out of frame." With the natural perversity of her species, Melly took Sir Malcolm's arm. "I wish you wasn't! Mayhap you'd understand better if you'd never had a garden of your own. Lord Davenham was telling me about a cove who had five hundred *acres* of gardens with Temples of Venus and Virtue and Concord, and bridges and pavilions and pyramids. When I think of that, it don't seem at all unreasonable that I should want to grow my own rhododendrons!"

"What you *want* is not the rub, but how you are going about *getting* it." Sir Malcolm suffered an impulse to present Miss Bagshot with one of Lord Davenham's rhododendrons, potted in a terracotta *jardinière*. "I am curious, Melly: *Were* you possessed of a competence, and *if* I kissed you again, would you react any differently?"

Here was an encouraging conversational gambit; Melly fluttered her long lashes and looked unutterably coy. "That is a very silly question!" she reproved. "Ain't I just got through telling you that very thing? Although you shouldn't be wishful of kissing me, what with Lady Davenham—but I ain't one to scold! Some people don't like to put all their eggs in one basket! It takes all kinds, *I* say, to make up a world."

Sir Malcolm almost explained to Miss Bagshot the reason for his highly compromising interest in Lady Davenham's wardrobe. Recalling the damsel's garrulous nature, and her acquaintance with Lord Davenham, however, he refrained. No purpose would be served by alerting Vivien. "Then you do not hold me in dislike," he murmured ironically.

"Bless my heart!" By this arrant misconstruction of her sentiments, Melly was shocked—so shocked that she stopped dead in her tracks, causing in the pedestrians crowded behind her a chain reaction that ran the entire block. "Nothing of the sort! I'll prove it if you like."

Sir Malcolm drew Miss Bagshot out of the general flow of traffic, and away from the pedestrians who wished to seek personal redress for bumped elbows and bruised toes. "I daresay, *ma chérie,* that I would like it excessively."

"Your *what?*" inquired Melly curiously. "Oh, you

was speaking French! And I daresay I would like it, too, but that ain't what I'm talking about. You mustn't laugh at me; this is *serious!* Sir Malcolm, I *know!*"

"You do?" Sir Malcolm was intrigued less by the ominous tone of Melly's voice than by her rosy cheeks and big brown eyes and tenderly fashioned mouth. "Upon my word."

Melly would have liked to move closer, the better to conduct this conversation with the confidentiality it deserved, but for several reasons she could not. Melly did not believe a girl should cuddle with a gentleman in the midst of a public thoroughfare in broad daylight, and especially not outside the plateglass window of her own aunt's shop. Furthermore, in this instance, she did not believe the gentleman should be made aware that she wished to cuddle with him at all.

"You need not fear I'll ride grub!" she therefore said, in ordinary conversational tones. *"You* know, lay an information against you with the magistrates! Although Bow Street is already on to you, so you must take care. I know I should not warn you, but it only seems fair— and if I did not need the money, I wouldn't have any part of it, because I like you very much, no matter *what* you've done!"

Bow Street's interest in him was of less pressing concern to Sir Malcolm than Miss Bagshot's sentiments, so charmingly expressed. Alas, he could not pursue this matter just then. Madame le Best stood in the doorway of her shop. "Ah, Madame!" said Sir Malcolm, who had during his adventures learned to extricate himself from tight spots. "Miss Bagshot has just persuaded me that my cousin must also have a new carriage dress. It must be the color of that building across the street! I will leave her to explain to you the details." Treasuring the memory of Miss Bagshot's last grateful, merry glance, Sir Malcolm strolled away.

Chapter Sixteen

The glance cast Sir Malcolm Calveley by Miss Bagshot was also very much on the mind of Samson Puddiphat, as was the conversation overheard between them in an Oxford Street alleyway. What to make of these developments, Puddiphat was not certain. Was Miss Bagshot attempting to lull the suspicions of Sir Malcolm, thereby luring him to indiscreet confidences which she would then relate to Bow Street? Or was she playing some sinister deep game? These matters Puddiphat mulled over as he made his way to Bow Street Public Office. For several days he had seen neither hide nor hair of Mr. Crump.

Nor did he do so that day; inquiry solicited the intelligence that Mr. Crump had departed London on confidential inquiry work. A less responsible person than Puddiphat might have interpreted this circumstance as an invitation to relax his own diligence. But Puddiphat saw clearly where his duty lay. After only the slightest hesitation he approached the office of the Chief Magistrate.

Thus it came about that Sir John's cogitations concerning his most recent encounter with the Home Secretary were interrupted by an earnest brown-haired young man whose unremarkable figure was enlivened by the uniform of the Horse Patrol, and whose nondescript features had something of the aspect of an anxious racoon. Sir John was not intimately acquainted with this individual, though as an adjunct of Bow Street, he had seen Puddiphat before. He did not think the occasion of that prior acquaintance had been especially auspicious. "What the devil do *you* want?" Sir John wearily inquired.

What Puddiphat wanted was to immediately flee the august presence of this supreme official of Bow Street, but Puddiphat was no coward, no matter how numerous his faults. "Want to become a Runner!" he confided. "Like Townsend and Sayer! Armstrong and Keys!" He struggled with his saber, which had gotten stuck. "And Crump."

Somewhat uncharitably, Sir John surveyed the member of the Horse Patrol wedged in his narrow doorway. Puddiphat's cheeks were pink with exertion, and his leather hat had fallen to the floor. "It is not quite so easy as all that, I'm afraid."

Easy? Who had ever said it was easy? Puddiphat manipulated his saber in the proper direction and popped out of the doorway like a cork from a bottle of champagne. The impetus of his entry sent him barreling straight into the side of the Chief Magistrate's desk. The Chief Magistrate swore.

"Beg pardon!" Impervious by long usage to catastrophe, Puddiphat righted himself and retrieved his hat from the floor. "Thing is, I *know* it isn't easy! Milliners don't take kindly to questioning by Bow Street!"

If Sir John had heard aright, a member of the Horse Patrol had for some as yet unstated reason been interrogating the city's milliners. Scant wonder they did not appreciate that fact, especially if Bow Street's emissary habitually got stuck in doorways. "Milliners?" he echoed, rubbing the skin bruised by Puddiphat's assault upon his desk.

"Milliners!" confirmed Puddiphat, who had withdrawn to the window. "Armenian Divorce Corsets, Invisible Petticoats, and Bosom Shields!" he added, as proof of his claim.

The Chief Magistrate left off rubbing his bruised shin to instead massage his brow. "I do not doubt your word! What I want to know is *why?*"

Puddiphat wanted very much to please Sir John, for without the Chief Magistrate's approval, he would never be made a Runner. It was a desire in which he was achieving no marked success. "Why what?" he inquired.

"Why have you been questioning milliners?" Sir John's tones were distinctly grim. "What maggot have you taken into your head?"

Maggots? Though Puddiphat was not precisely needle-witted, once he properly understood a question, he could answer it very well. "Crump!" he responded, with a relieved smile.

"Crump." Sir John recalled the favor he had asked. He anticipated having several sharp words to say to Crump when that genial individual had returned from his current private commission. "You had better tell me about it! From the beginning, if you please."

In considerably more detail than Sir John had anticipated, or welcomed, Puddiphat obliged. The Chief Magistrate learned of Puddiphat's encounter with Crump in the tavern near Bow Street Public Office, and of the opportunity thus offered for Puddiphat to better himself. The Chief Magistrate also learned of every shop visited by Puddiphat.

"Enough!" he said abruptly, as Puddiphat digressed upon an explanation of various of the more arcane aspects of the millinery trade. "How much did Crump tell you about *why* these investigations are being made?"

Puddiphat screwed up his features in an effort to

recall. "Said I was to find a milliner who had some connection with a rum customer—one who came afoul of Bow Street!"

The sheer inanity of this utterance caused Sir John to cease massaging his brow. "Do you have any idea," he grimly inquired, "how many milliners that description fits? At least I must be grateful Crump didn't mention Blood-and-Thunder to you, I suppose!"

Blood-and-thunder? Puddiphat wondered why the conversation had switched so abruptly to liquid refreshment. "Only found one such milliner myself!"

Sir John was so incensed by Crump's negligence that he failed at first to grasp the significance of Puddiphat's remark. "I *should* make you a Runner!" he said bitterly. "Yes, and put you in Crump's place!" Then his heavy brows lowered. "You found *what?*"

Addressed in such exasperated tones, Puddiphat started, and at first could not recall. "One milliner connected with a rum customer!" he finally remembered. " 'Twas her brother! He sloped off."

What Puddiphat had found, suspected Sir John, was one milliner who would admit to such a connection, which was not to say that countless of the city's other milliners didn't have a brother or a father or a lover who had been brought before the magistrates—if not all three. "You had better tell me about it," he repeated, without any hope that the Blood-and-Thunder would be so easily tracked down. Indeed, Sir John was tempted to forget the whole business. No recent robberies had been reported. If Blood-and-Thunder *had* returned to England, he'd not resumed his old habits. Yet.

Puddiphat, meanwhile, launched into an explanation of Madame le Best's refusal to discuss That Man. "Sloped off!" he wound up. "Took French leave! But Bow Street isn't interested in such things!"

Only the fact that Puddiphat had undertaken these inquiries in addition to his regular duties prevented Sir John from issuing remarks that were very unkind.

"*When* did this person slope off?" he inquired, though without any real curiosity. "Bow Street might be very interested in that."

Puddiphat looked chagrined. "Dashed if I know! Didn't think to ask. Crump didn't tell me the particulars of the business. And Madame le Best doesn't like to talk about her brother. Won't have his name spoken beneath her roof."

"What *was* his name?" persisted the Chief Magistrate.

Puddiphat was disappointed by Sir John's lack of quick-wittedness. "Told you, sir! Madame le Best won't have his name spoken! So how could I find out?"

Perhaps Puddiphat might be subtly made aware of how unsuited he was to detective work, thought Sir John. "French, is she—this Madame le Best?"

"French?" Puddiphat fidgeted with his leather hat. "Shouldn't think so myself. That is, Miss Bagshot!"

"Who the devil is Miss Bagshot? I thought we were talking about a milliner called le Best!"

Puddiphat was not surprised that the Chief Magistrate experienced a degree of confusion; the mere thought of Miss Bagshot affected Puddiphat that way. "*Says* her name is le Best!" he explained. "Don't believe it myself! Miss Bagshot is her niece, recently arrived from Brighton, where she was in service until she lost her place." Lest Sir John be put off by this circumstance, he added: "A taking little thing! Fine as fivepence!"

The Chief Magistrate had in the pursuit of his profession met many fine damsels, and had scant interest in the taking Miss Bagshot. "I begin to comprehend why you are so fascinated by this particular milliner!" he said ironically. "But it is Blood-and-Thunder you are supposed to be tracking down."

Blood-and-thunder? Again that queer reference to liquid refreshment. Could the Chief Magistrate of Bow Street be addicted to the bottle? Puddiphat politely offered to nip into the nearby tavern and fetch Sir John a drink.

"Not me, you ninnyhammer!" thundered that sorely tried gentleman. "The cracksman!"

Eager as he was to please, Puddiphat was not without pride. *"Not* a ninnyhammer!" he protested. "Even if I *don't* understand why you wish me to fetch a cracksman a drink! *What* cracksman? Moreover, I worked very hard on this business—yes, and on studying, too. Have *you* read Lavatar's *Physiognomical Fragments?* All four volumes? Can *you* look at a corpse and tell the nature of his crime? Dashed if I *want* to be a Runner if this is all the thanks I get!"

"Very well; I apologize." Sir John was conscious of having been unfair. "Perhaps we will go on better if I fill you in on the background of this affair. Blood-and-Thunder was a cracksman who eluded us several years back—in point of fact, he eluded Crump. We had reason to believe he fled the country. Recently, there have been rumors of his return."

This was the stuff of which careers were made. "Zounds!" breathed Puddiphat.

Sir John overlooked this interruption. "We have no description of the scoundrel, so are groping in the dark. All we do know is that he was connected with a milliner. How, we are not certain. Perhaps he was a member of her family. Perhaps she was his *petite amie.* Such liaisons are not unusual among young bloods."

"Young bloods!" Puddiphat was thrilled to discover that he was in truth on the trail of something big. "You mean this Blood-and-Thunder might be *Quality?*"

"I mean I don't know *what* he is!" Sir John's tone was short. "Or even *if* he is! There is no real proof that he has returned to England—as your inquiries have borne out. We may consider the matter closed, I think."

"No!" Puddiphat saw his chances of advancement vanish. "Dashed smokey, sir!"

By these utterances, Sir John was given to understand that Puddiphat's suspicions had been aroused. Much as he would have liked, the Chief Magistrate was in no position to ignore those suspicions. "Why is it I anticipate I will not like what you have to say? Do not stand there gaping, man! Out with it!"

Relieved that he was not expected to explain the Chief Magistrate's anticipations, Puddiphat leaned over the battered desk. "There *should* be penalties for trying to hoodwink officers of the law, just as I said!"

Almost Sir John longed for the return of Crump. Though that genial individual might frequently exasperate, one did not need to concentrate so hard to understand what he was trying to say. In the absence of Crump, however, Sir John concentrated. "Who has been trying to hoodwink you, Puddiphat?"

Puddiphat thought Sir John was not paying proper attention, or he would not have to ask. But the Chief Magistrate of Bow Street, Puddiphat reminded himself, was a very busy man. Puddiphat strove to make his explanations simple and concise. "Miss Bagshot!" he explained.

"Miss Bagshot?" So tense was Puddiphat's posture, so reminiscent of a racoon prepared to attack, that Sir John instinctively leaned back in his chair. "You think her father is our man?"

"I do?" Puddiphat looked blank.

Sir John realized his concentrated efforts had not served. "Thunder, man! *I* don't know what you think!"

"Oh." Puddiphat backed away from the desk. What had they been talking about before Sir John had flown into a temper? "I have it! Not her papa, but Sir Malcolm Calveley, sir! He admitted he was a fugitive from justice, and *she* admitted he was dangerous enough. *And* he's just returned to England after having left it under a cloud."

"Sir Malcolm Calveley," repeated the Chief Magistrate, his mood not improved by this indication that Blood-and-Thunder might well be a well-born young buck. Not that the circumstance of Sir Malcolm's mysterious departure was conclusive; young bucks were prone to quick departures, with irate parents or bailiffs at their heels. "I think you had better tell me everything you've found out." Before he had finished issuing the invitation, Puddiphat had launched into his explanation. It was a highly colorful account, in which Miss Bagshot figured largely, as well as her sightseeing expedition in the company of Sir Malcolm, and her visit to the Horticultural Society with Lord Davenham as escort.

"Davenham?" Sir John roused his head, which Puddiphat's style of narration had caused him to drop to his desktop. Trying, indeed, was the lot of a Chief Magistrate, what with Quakeresses determined to reform the women prisoners, and the Regent alternately receiving snuffboxes engraved with ominous verses, and getting his carriage windows shot out. As if those woes were not sufficient, Puddiphat must bring Bow Street into what promised to be the scandal of the year. "What has Davenham to do with this business? I hope you do not mean to tell me that the Duke is also in it."

Puddiphat had no intention of telling the Chief Magistrate anything he did not want to hear. "No, no! It's Calveley who is the desperate and suspicious character, sir! *There's* your Blood-and-Thunder! *Now* may I become a Runner?"

Sir John would have liked to deliver a very graphic pronouncement of what Puddiphat might become, but he was prevented by awareness of the hours of effort the man had put forth. Sir John disliked Puddiphat's allegation that Sir Malcolm Calveley was their quarry, but the charge could not be ignored.

Nor, at all events, must it be made public. "Puddiphat, I must warn you to be circumspect. We don't wish to set the cat among the pigeons. This is a very awkward business."

"Yes, sir." Puddiphat basked in what he interpreted

as approval of a job well done. "I'll just go and fetch him, shall I? So that you may clap him into jail."

"You'll do no such thing!" Sir John propped his elbows on his desk for emphasis. "Where is your proof, man? We have only your word for it that Sir Malcolm has done anything exceptionable."

Perhaps he had failed to convey the basic perfidy of Sir Malcolm's character, mused Puddiphat, as to mask his disappointment he turned away from the Chief Magistrate's desk. So briskly did Puddiphat turn that his saber struck the desk a mighty blow, causing Sir John to bite his lip. Unaware of this disaster, Puddiphat walked to the window. He wondered if the Chief Magistrate would appreciate an explanation of Sir Malcolm's perfidy, as demonstrated by his adverse effect upon Miss Bagshot. Once Miss Bagshot had professed herself eager to assist Bow Street—yet she had turned right around and warned Sir. Malcolm, as Puddiphat had heard with his own two ears. Yes, and she had also vowed she liked the scoundrel very well, no matter what he'd done. Though Puddiphat could not help feeling a little wounded that Miss Bagshot had abused his confidence, he did not judge her too harshly. Obviously, Sir Malcolm had on Miss Bagshot an effect similar to Miss Bagshot's effect on Puddiphat, rendering her not mute, but bereft of principle. Poor girl! If only Puddiphat might determine which Melly meant to diddle—Sir Malcolm, or Bow Street.

Behind his back, Puddiphat realized, the Chief Magistrate was making some very queer sounds. Puddiphat charitably overlooked this lapse. "Tell you what, I'll *get* the proof! *Then* I'll fetch the fellow so you may clap him in jail!"

"You'll do nothing of the sort!" thundered Sir John, in tones that were very garbled by the handkerchief he'd pressed to his wounded lip. "*If* you find proof, you will present it to Crump, who'll know what to do!" In a very un-Christian manner, Sir John added a silent wish that Crump might be stricken with a resultant apoplexy.

Crump was to earn the credit for his own ceaseless work? Stung by the unfairness of this development, Puddiphat swung sharply around. His saber struck the window with a sharp crack. The glass shattered. Not trusting himself to speak, Sir John grimly indicated the doorway with his free hand.

Chapter Seventeen

"Gracious God!" ejaculated Lady Davenham, then discreetly lowered her voice. "I don't believe a word of it! Vivien and that chit? Malcolm, this is some monstrous hoax!"

"I wish it were," responded Sir Malcolm softly, with a warning glance. "Remember you are mad for me, my Thea! I am telling you this only because someone eventually must, and I thought it would come better from me."

The intelligence that her husband had lost little time in carrying out his stated intention of foraging among the fleshpots left Lady Davenham feeling very hipped. She turned her head and gazed upon her spouse. A twinkle lit his dark eyes; a smile played around his mouth. No wonder Miss Bagshot was intrigued by him, thought Thea—and no wonder he appeared in such good spirits. Of the three occupants of the Davenant box at Drury Lane Theatre, only Lord Davenham's attention was fixed upon the stage. Thus far he had sat rapt through the several acts of a grand melodramatic spectacle in which the magnificence of the scenery and costume atoned for the indifferent acting. Lady Davenham turned back to Sir Malcolm, her discontentment no whit diminished by the spectacle of her perfidious spouse enjoying himself. "Tell me more!" she demanded, *sotto voce*.

Sir Malcolm began to regret his introduction of the subject. "Perhaps," he suggested, "it might be wiser to wait."

Lady Davenham glowered. "I am not feeling especially wise! If you did not intend to discuss the matter, you should not have brought it up. How on earth did Vivien ever encounter the chit?" She looked appalled. "Oh, no!"

"Oh, *yes,* my Thea, and I must point out that you are supposed to be absolutely enraptured with me. If you cannot look ardent, at least try to appear a little fond." Personally, Sir Malcolm was finding this pseudo-flirtation very dull work. "Vivien went to persuade Melly that she must not take up with me, and so she took up with *him,* instead. The scheming little minx!"

It seemed to Lady Davenham that her cousin didn't regard this situation with sufficient solemnity, a conclusion prompted by his reminiscent smile. "Why do you say that she is scheming? Has it not occurred to you that she may *like* Vivien? Or perhaps you cannot credit that he has cut you out!"

Sir Malcolm glanced over Thea's head at Vivien, who was as usual looking serene and elusive and vague. Sir Malcolm wondered what thoughts seethed behind that calm façade. "You're right; I *do* find it difficult to credit! And I'm afraid I made matters worse by telling Melly Vivien is rich as Croesus." He smiled. "She would have given up Vivien for this Croesus fellow, she intimated, and was very sorry to learn he is long dead."

"So!" Thea was queerly disappointed to discover that the enterprising Miss Bagshot was motivated by avarice. "The chit is on the dangle for a fortune, after all. I am surprised you did not offer her yours, you like her so well."

"I did." Sir Malcolm continued to smile. "I wish you would not look so cross, my Thea; it is *not* the way one goes about exhibiting a *tendre!* Miss Bagshot turned me down. She requires that a competence be settled on her so that she may be financially independent, after which she may toss her bonnet over the windmill for whomever she pleases—yes, and grow rhododendrons without soil."

Lady Davenham, considerably better versed than Sir Malcolm in the science of hydroponics, realized that her spouse had been baring his soul. She was no longer a sufficiently stimulating audience, it seemed. "Surely the girl cannot think *Vivien* will provide her with a competence!" she murmured. "Miss Bagshot must be mad."

"Not *mad,* precisely." It was obvious from the expression on Sir Malcolm's swarthy features that he was deriving inordinate amusement from these recent developments. "Recall the wild blood of the Bagshots! It is not Vivien the minx means to persuade to finance her break for independence—her aunt virtually holds her prisoner, you will recall—but *you!*"

"*Me!*" Thea, who had been trying very hard to look like a lady deep in the throes of infatuation, looked dumbfounded, instead. "And you claim she *doesn't* have windmills in her head? I'm beginning to wonder if you *both* do not! What makes her think I'll pay?"

"It is not so absurd a notion as you may believe." Sir Malcolm throughout this conversation had presented the guise of a man conducting a serious flirtation; currently, he was leaning so close to Lady Davenham that his breath caressed her cheek. "Melly is convinced that you would not wish to be plunged into the scandal-broth, as you would be if she took up with Vivien—as you already *have* been, in fact, due to her disruption of the recent meeting of the Horticultural Society."

So shocked was Thea by this disclosure that she

drew back to stare, first at her cousin, then her spouse. "The Horticultural Society!" she echoed, quite forgetting to lower her voice, thus attracting the notice of several theater-goers in adjacent boxes, and diverting Lord Davenham briefly from watching the stage.

Was Thea cross because he had presented Miss Bagshot to the Horticultural Society? wondered Vivien. But had not Thea and their dashing cousin been racketting about together everywhere? Somewhat perversely, his lordship murmured: "Would *you* like to see the gardens, my dear? The Society had the first experimental gardens in London, you know: strawberries as large as apples, masses of flowers, red and green Providence pines—I will arrange for you to visit it." He glanced back at the stage and added vaguely: "First Astley's, and now this. How social you are become!"

"Astley's?" murmured Sir Malcolm.

Responded Thea: "Never mind!"

In all the years of their acquaintance, Vivien had not once offered to take her to the Horticultural Gardens, she thought to herself.

No, and never had he flirted with her or offered her unsolicited compliments. Thea didn't imagine for an instant that the mischievous Miss Bagshot would tolerate similar neglect. How the *deuce* had Melly accomplished miracles? Thea could dress in a style designed to create scandal—this evening it was a gown of crepe trimmed with needlepointed lace which left nothing at all to the imagination, and a white China crepe shawl bordered with flowers—without earning from her husband a single second glance. Thea had no notion of how to bring herself to Vivien's attention. Indeed, she had seen little of her husband of late. For all she knew, he was sleeping in his potting shed.

Thea did not care to discuss that aspect of the situation with Malcolm. She had not forgotten her dashing cousin stood next in line. Few men, in such a position, could fail to secretly wish to inherit a dukedom. Malcolm could not be trusted to render impartial advice on the topic of acquiring offspring. Yet Thea needed desperately to talk to someone. It was a pity circumstance prohibited her from asking Miss Bagshot's advice!

"The chit *admitted* her intentions?"" she murmured to Sir Malcolm. "What was your reply?"

Sir Malcolm did not mind being distracted from the performance, in which Braham as first singer was exhibiting the great power of his voice. "When Melly admitted she meant to put you to the touch? Nothing. I kissed her, instead."

"You *kissed* her?" echoed Thea, appalled. She had meant to settle her cousin respectably. Instead, she had inadvertently driven him—as well as her husband—straight into the arms of a designing minx.

"My Thea, I have kissed a lot of females." Sir Malcolm looked both reminiscent and self-satisfied. "You make too much of it. Some of us don't care to put all our eggs in one basket! Which reminds me—you are to have a carriage dress designed by Melly, in a fashionable new shade called London Soot."

Lady Davenham's imagination boggled at contemplation of what manner of dress might be designed for her by the damsel engaged in leading the male members of her family down the garden path. "London *Soot?* If this is the sort of adventure you usually have, Cousin, I don't care for it much!"

"But this is not the usual sort! This is even better." With his usual faculty to enjoy each moment, Sir Malcolm settled back, in an academic manner, to savor his cousin's magnificent bosom. "If Melly does try and put you to the touch, you must immediately tell me. Otherwise you must let this *affaire* run its course." He elevated his eyes from Lady Davenham's décolletage to her unhappy face. "You will ruin my reputation if you go on in this manner; your expression will convince the ladies that intriguing with me has *not* been the most delightful experience. Which I promise you it *would* be if we actually were." He looked thoughtful. "I suppose I had better tell you that Miss Bagshot thinks we are. Lest she alert Vivien, I could not inform her otherwise."

Lady Davenham had not been paying proper heed to her cousin's conversation, had instead been pondering her inability to spark the ardor of her spouse. Here she sat, clad in the most revealing gown ever worn by any woman, and Vivien's sole reaction had been an absentmindedly murmured "Fine feathers make fine birds." Thea consoled herself that birds were preferable to caterpillars, as comparisons went. "Miss Bagshot thinks we are *what?*" she asked.

Sir Malcolm suspected he was losing not only his touch with the ladies, but also his taste for flirtation. "Planting the antlers on Vivien's brow!" he explained frankly. "Which may explain why she slapped my face."

Miss Bagshot had *slapped* Malcolm? Lady Davenham began to question whether, as regarded mending fences, her dashing cousin was the most proper person for the task.

Sir Malcolm quitted the box at the interval, to throng with other hopeful gentlemen into the Green Room opposite the royal box, there to chat backstage with the cast. Lord Davenham made no move to follow his adventurous cousin. Lady Davenham supposed she should be grateful that his hankering after fleshpots was not so overpowering as to lead him to visit actresses in the dressing room. "Such a charming evening!" she observed brightly. "Do you not agree?"

With every indication of giving the question his serious consideration, Lord Davenham glanced around the theater. "Apollo's Head!" said he.

At this evidence that her spouse was in one of his more exasperating moods, Lady Davenham almost despaired. And then she thought that Miss Bagshot, in a similar situation, would surely persevere. "This is not a classical entertainment!" she protested. "What has put you in mind of the Greeks? Or was Apollo Roman? Oh, it is all the same thing!"

"I doubt the Greeks and Romans think so," Lord Davenham responded drily. "At all events, I was referring to the Catherine-wheel."

"The Catherine-wheel." Thea plucked at the fragile fabric of her gown. "I say it is a pleasant evening and you refer to Catherine-wheels. If you do not wish to talk to me, Vivien, you need only *say* so."

"Poppycock, my dear!" Though he was both annoyed with her and anxious about her, Lord Davenham still enjoyed his wife's company very well. *Too* well, in fact, for his own peace of mind. He placed his hand over Thea's. "Of course I want to talk to you; there is no need to shred your pretty dress. *You* said it was a pleasant evening and I was agreeing with you. I am enjoying it very well. One of the reasons I am enjoying it is because the theater has an excellent system of water-sprinklers! We need not fear that the performance will be cut short because the theater has gone up in flames."

Lady Davenham contemplated her husband's hand, which he appeared to have forgotten, and which rested with her own upon her knee. She would not remind him of its presence there, she thought. "But Apollo's Head?" she protested. "And Catherine-wheels?"

"Did I not explain?" Lady Davenham, it appeared, had since their arrival in London become accustomed to having gentlemen's hands rest upon her knee. Not long ago, in the country, such an act would have offended her modesty. "I tend to take it for granted, my dear, that you will know what I mean. You usually *do*, when you put your mind to it—although it is unfair of me to expect you to always be making an effort, I suppose! The sprinkler fitting in the decoration of the pit ceiling is called an Apollo's Head. It works upon the same principle as the Catherine-wheel. The system was evolved by Benjamin Wyatt and Colonel Congreve several years ago. But that puts me in mind of something I especially wished to ask you."

Perhaps he meant to speak sternly to her about her

blatant flirtation with their cousin, or scold her for her shocking dress; perhaps even to suggest that they amend their differences and settle down to this matter of an heir. Breathlessly, Lady Davenham awaited explanations. They were not forthcoming. "Yes?" urged Lady Davenham, with an encouraging glance. "Speak your mind, Vivien; I'm sure I will agree."

"You are a good girl, Thea." And so she was; Vivien could not blame her for falling under Malcolm's spell. Most females did. Lord Davenham surveyed the hand which still rested upon his wife's knee.

Lord Davenham looked as if he were not sure how his hand had gotten there, his wife thought; lest he be inspired to remove it, Lady Davenham placed her other hand atop it and held on tight.

Here was boldness! reflected Lord Davenham, who— except for where his wife had learned it—did not mind in the least. Could she mean—but he knew better. Malcolm's absence had merely left her feeling a little lonely. Vivien sought to divert himself from such unwelcome reflections. "Not that there is any reason to quibble about installing a Rumford fireplace in the potting shed."

So different was his lordship's request from what she had anticipated that Lady Davenham stared. "A Rumford fireplace," she echoed, bemused.

"Doubtless you are wondering why I want a fireplace in my potting shed," concluded Lord Davenham, as result of his wife's blank stare. "It gets very cold out there! And it *is* a large potting shed! A Rumford fireplace with a solid, angled, fireclay surround is much more efficient than a huge chimney, don't you think? Of course, if you do not like the notion—"

Drastic measures were called for; the Duke could think only of fireplaces, even while clutching—though not of his own volition—his Duchess's knee. With an exasperated exclamation she released him. "My dear, are you quite all right?" inquired his lordship, massaging his hand.

As must be apparent to all but her spouse, Lady Davenham was very far from all right, but she did not feel competent to render up explanations of that fact. That Vivien had grown discontented with their marriage was her fault, as Malcolm had explained. She should have made their homelife more adventurous, and failure to realize that Vivien craved adventure did not excuse her negligence, or free her from abiding the consequence. "Vivien," she said abruptly, with an irritable shrug. "I hope you do not think our cousin is paying me attentions that are a little too pointed."

"*Is* he?" inquired Lord Davenham, who privately thought exactly that. However, any gentleman must thus respond bemusedly to the exuberance of his wife's movements in a gown which invited speculation upon whether a careless movement might prove disastrous. "I see nothing objectionable in it if you don't, my dear."

Did Malcolm intend Vivien to display a dog-in-the-manger attitude? Thea decided there was little chance the even-tempered Duke would ever exhibit any of the signs of an enraged spouse. Vivien was not selfish. Having discovered his own source of amusement, he would not deny Thea the same opportunity.

Knowledge of that amusement rankled. "I hear that you have struck up an acquaintance with Miss Bagshot," she bluntly observed.

"Eh?" inquired Lord Davenham, whose hearing was as keen as his other senses, all of which were focused uncomfortably on his errant wife. "Oh, yes! She is a taking little puss, and moreover likes growing things. You need not look so unhappy, my dear! Did I not promise to extricate Malcolm?"

So he had, and Thea lacked the energy to even try and explain that she had been much better pleased when it was only Malcolm who was ensnared. Vivien's attitude clearly indicated that, as regarded their marriage, he had suffered no change of heart. Having indicated his discontentment, he trusted Thea to deal with it. She wondered what he expected her to do.

One thing was certain: Thea could no longer bear this strained silence. She initiated a conversation concerning cultivators and barrows, a very appropriate topic for a gentleman belatedly embarked upon sowing his wild oats.

Chapter Eighteen

Madame le Best paced around her showroom, tidied the magazines which lay upon the table, stared at the walls papered with imaginative Oriental motifs. On Madame's shrewd, sharp features was a disgruntled look. That displeasure was directed not at her showroom, but at her harum-scarum niece, currently banished to stitch seams in the atelier. What was to be done with Melly? Madame wondered. The child was incorrigible. Despite her threats, Madame did not think she had the heart to cast her own niece out into the streets. As she was reflecting that Melly would doubtless turn even that catastrophe to advantage, the shop door opened. Madame turned, with the obsequious expression she habitually bestowed upon her customers. When she noted the identity of this customer, however, her obsequious look changed to genuine enthusiasm. "Welcome, milady! *Entrez!*"

The lady—a tall and superbly fashioned female clad in gown and pelisse of white muslin, with a delicious concoction of ribbon and ostrich plumes perched atop bright scarlet curls—had not waited for an invitation. She strode briskly across the floor and firmly closed the door to the atelier. "There! We will wish to be private. You see before you, Helen—yes, I know you do not like me to call you that, but we are quite alone!—*not* the Baroness Dulcie Bligh, but an ace up the sleeve!"

What Madame le Best saw before her was her most influential patron, and she lost no time in ushering Lady Bligh to a chair and bringing forth the latest fashion plates. Some little time passed in a discussion of such weighty matters as the alternate virtues of "French work," embroidery inserted into a gown's bodice, and the "lozenge-front," with strips of net and satin let in slant-wise, for day use. The Baroness expressed a disinclination to purchase a *zona,* a popular corset made of silk-covered bands which wrapped around the upper part of the body and supported the lower part of the bosom. The Baroness's philosophy of fashion was that it should charm by revealing everything it concealed. And though they were not universally popular—they were indeed considered by many to smack of depravity —she was highly in favor of flesh-colored drawers.

These important matters settled, Lady Bligh pushed aside the fashion plates, expressed a disinclination to purchase a Prussian helmet cap carried out in canary-colored silk, and appreciation of a hat made of diagonally striped taffeta with a crown of hinged pleats. Then she leaned back in her chair. "This is not an official visit," she announced, somewhat cryptically. "Puddiphat is next to useless, and Crump is out of town, which leaves John without an emissary whose discretion he can trust. However reluctantly employed, I am therefore an agent of Bow Street. And you needn't think you may put me off, Helen, because I promise you may not."

Abruptly, Madame le Best sat down upon one of the japanned chairs. She had forgotten that Lady Bligh— who was as eccentric as she was beautiful, and very intuitive to boot—numbered among her many admirers not only the Prince Regent, but also the Chief Magistrate of Bow Street. "Oh, *la vache!*" she muttered.

On the Baroness's aristocratic face—the individual components of which included an inquisitive nose, lively black eyes, elegant sculpted cheekbones, generous mouth, and determined chin—an enigmatic look appeared. "Exactly so! *I* recall your ne'er-do-well brother very well. The question that most concerns Bow Street is *when* he sloped off, and why."

Madame le Best looked startled. "Sloped off?" she queried.

Roguishly, Lady Bligh smiled. "I am acquiring a very colorful vocabulary, am I not? Sloped off, took French leave, showed us a clean pair of heels! You might as well tell me, Helen! You must realize that if you don't, I will still find out."

The Baroness's ability to ferret out just the sort of thing one would have wished to remain secret was very widely known, and also her unscrupulous employment of said information to further her own ends. Wondering what possible use Lady Bligh could have for information concerning her own ne'er-do-well brother, Madame le Best gazed unhappily upon her most influential patron. Perhaps the Baroness might yet be put off the scent. Madame launched into a description of a carriage dress to which she was putting the finishing touches, made up in a fashionable shade of her own creation, London Soot.

The Baroness straightened her delicious bonnet, which had a tendency to slip to one side, due to the refusal of her heavy hair to stay pinned. Even now scarlet tendrils escaped the bonnet's confines. "You think I am being vulgarly inquisitive, and so I am. But you should be used to my little ways by now, Helen. I take my oath I will use any information you give me in the most discreet manner. Come now, explain to me the circumstances of your brother's disappearance." She frowned. "Or perhaps I may guess."

Madame le Best longingly gazed upon her plateglass window, as if by sheer force of will she could lure some customers in from the street, and put an end to this distressing interval. Her efforts were for naught. Unbeknownst to Madame, Lady Bligh had upon her entry locked the street door.

"What was the rascal's name?" mused the Baroness, tapping long and slender fingers on the mock-bamboo table. "William, was it not? As I recall William—"

"William's daughter is here with me," hastily interrupted Madame. Lady Bligh's memory was all too acute. "The child cannot benefit from this. Let sleeping dogs lie."

The Baroness's voice was plaintive. "But *are* they sleeping? That seems to be the point. Bow Street is convinced there should be severe penalties for trying to hoodwink emissaries of the law, I should warn you— although if there *were* such penalties, I would doubtless be in a pickle myself." Her dark eyes glittered. "Apropos of pickles, Helen, where is this niece?"

Madame le Best glanced in a very guilty manner at the door of her atelier, then back at her guest, who was looking very shrewd. "You are an excellent creature, Helen," remarked Lady Bligh, before the milliner could speak. "Save for this tendency of yours to try and humbug me. Perhaps it runs in the family! I believe there is some question as to whether your niece seeks to diddle Calveley or Bow Street."

"Calveley?" Madame le Best forgot all about her ne'er-do-well brother in the face of this new potential catastrophe. "The cabbage-head!"

Lady Bligh quirked a roguish brow. "Is it *Calveley* you are calling a cabbage-head, Helen? If so, you are very wide of the mark. Sir Malcolm is very much relished by those who know him, especially if they are female." Her piquant features were contemplative. "I think that I must meet him!" she concluded, in tones that were roguish, indeed.

Madame le Best was not beyond being shocked by her most influential patron. Privately, she thought that the Baroness was a great deal less sedate and decorous than befit a lady who could claim at least fifty years. Not that the Baroness looked decades near that age. Madame wondered how Dulcie maintained her youthful appearance. It was doubly incongruous in conjunction with her distinctly worldly air.

"You are so *stuffy,* Helen!" complained Lady Bligh. "I will not tease you further. I collect it is because of her preference for Sir Malcolm that you call your niece a cabbage-head—oh, yes, I know all about the Temple and Astley's and London Bridge. Puddiphat followed the chit. He also followed her to the Horticultural Gardens. Your face is turning an alarming shade of purple, Helen! You should have known."

This intimation that she had been negligent did not sit well with Madame le Best, who considered that she had made superhuman efforts to keep track of her thankless niece. Since it was not her habit to rip up at her customers, Madame picked up an issue of Mr. Ackerman's *The Repository to the Arts* and held it tightly on her lap. "I knew about the Horticultural Society well enough!" she said bitterly. "Ever since Melly has talked about nothing but growing rhododendrons without soil! As for the other—Sir Malcolm fetched Melly back here with a tale about finding her wandering lost in the streets. Now you tell me she was at Astley's." Madame threw up her hands, and the *Repository* thudded to the floor. "You must not think Melly is a *bad* girl, just a trifle indiscreet!"

Gracefully, the Baroness bent and retrieved the *Repository* and restored it to Madame's lap. "I'm not interested in your niece's morals!" she retorted. "No, and there's no place for her in my household, as you're getting ready to suggest."

Madame abandoned that faint hope. "And she *knows* Sir Malcolm has a *petite amie,*" she said aloud. "Gentlemen don't lavish money on their cousins like Calveley does on Lady Davenham!"

Once more the Baroness adjusted her bonnet, with

special attention to the ostrich plume which was tickling her aristocratic nose. "Calveley and Lady Davenham *are* cousins!" she remarked. "I know it for a fact."

"Vraiment?" Briefly, Madame was distracted from her own woes. *"Scandaleux!"*

Upon receipt of this pronouncement, Lady Bligh winced. "I wish you would not try to speak French! So Calveley and the Davenhams are engaged in a *ménage à trois?* How original of them—and how typical of the family. But I am not interested in Calveley's morals, either." Her dark-eyed glance was speculative. "Although a man capable of seducing his own cousin under his other cousin's nose must be capable of anything! No wonder Puddiphat calls him a dangerous and suspicious character."

It occurred to Madame le Best that Puddiphat was very likely responsible for Lady Bligh's current mission. "That puppy!" she muttered.

"Is he?" The Baroness looked interested. "I have not met Puddiphat. Are you aware, Helen, that your niece has been conniving with Puddiphat to send Calveley to jail? She requires a share of the reward money to purchase her independence. Puddiphat is on the trail of a cracksman who departed England in a very great hurry several years past. He was a very clever fellow known only to the authorities as Blood-and-Thunder, after his preference for that drink."

Upon Madame le Best these confidences had a startling effect. She turned ashen, loosened her grip on the *Repository,* and moaned.

"Precisely," said the Baroness, once more retrieving the *Repository,* which was not benefiting from its abrupt descents to the floor. "Wouldn't it be ironic if your niece connived to send Calveley to jail in her own father's place?"

"You don't know that!" Madame's sharp features were frantic. "This is only guesswork!"

This time the Baroness deposited the *Repository* on the table, instead of Madame's lap. "I have told you not to try and humbug me!" she said severely. "The law is not to be trifled with—or if the law may be, because I have done it, *I* am not! Since when have you become so devoted to that rascal William, by the by?"

Deprived of Mr. Ackerman's *Repository,* Madame grasped a current edition of *The Ladies' Monthly Magazine* and vigorously fanned herself. "Devoted? I wouldn't shed a tear if I was to see him hang! But what would my ladies say to *that,* do you think?"

In a ruminative manner, the Baroness again tapped her long, elegant fingers, this time against her delicately tinted cheek. *"I* should think it vastly diverting if my milliner's brother was hanged as a cracksman, but I admit that not everyone might feel similarly," she allowed. "It was precisely for that reason that I did *not* tell John that your brother had done worse than abandon his wife and child—and no sooner did he mention milliners with relatives who'd run afoul of Bow Street than I thought of you. And when he mentioned to me Blood-and-Thunder—" She shrugged her elegant shoulders. *"Voilà!* I recalled your brother's fondness for that drink."

Madame gripped the *Ladies' Magazine* so tightly that the pages tore. "What are you going to do?"

"Do?" Lady Bligh continued to look contemplative. "I have not quite decided. There is no real reason to think that William has returned to England, save Dame Gossip—yet, for some odd reason, I feel that in this instance rumor does not lie. How refreshing! I must know everything you can tell me about your brother, Helen—yes, I know you would prefer not to speak of him, but wishing will not dissolve the connection! There are several members of my own family I would dispose of, if only I could."

Faced with this ultimatum, Madame le Best fell back on her usual excuse. "I am vowed never to mention That Man's name under this roof."

"Twaddle! You have already done so," the Baroness pointed out. Madame continued to look obdurate. Immediately, Dulcie's patrician features took on a melancholy cast. "What resolution you exhibit, Helen! I am inspired by your example. I, too, will nurture self-discipline. Where shall I begin, I wonder? I have it! Long have I deplored my extravagance."

Warily, Madame le Best eyed her most influential customer, from whose extravagance Madame had reaped considerable benefit. "What a pity," mused the Baroness, "that you who inspired my reformation will suffer for it most."

Not surprisingly, in light of this remark, Madame le Best lost no time in attempting to cajole Lady Bligh into a resumption of her extravagant ways. "I've changed my mind! I'll tell you all you want to know!" she hastily amended, and did so. At all events, there was little enough she *could* tell, having always turned blind eyes and deaf ears toward her feckless brother, of whom she had never been fond.

"Humph!" remarked the Baroness, when Madame had done. "I had hoped for more. You have had no hint, then, that William might have returned."

Becoming belatedly aware that she was shredding it, Madame returned the *Ladies' Magazine* to the table-top. "None. But William isn't likely to get in touch with me, knowing there's no love lost." Her sharp features contorted. "He *might* attempt to contact Melly, though I never saw in him any spark of paternal feeling." And then she flung herself onto the floor at Dulcie's feet. "I beg you, Lady Bligh, don't betray us to Bow Street!"

The Baroness surveyed her milliner, who was clutching her calves, and weeping upon her knees. "Pray do not enact me a Cheltenham tragedy, Helen! *Were* I going to blow the gaff, I would have already done so— not that John is such an ogre as all that!"

Mortified by her lack of self-control, Madame le Best untangled herself from Lady Bligh's knees. "John?" she echoed.

"The Chief Magistrate of Bow Street." Dulcie's roguish smile flashed. "And an old friend. You must trust me, Helen! Now, I would like to speak with your niece."

Madame le Best had scant choice but to trust the Baroness, she reflected, as she climbed to her feet and crossed slowly to the atelier. One glance within revealed that Melly was not there. With this fact, she acquainted Lady Bligh.

Prior to departure, the Baroness adjusted her bonnet one last time. "Has it occurred to you that your niece has inherited her father's tendency toward stealth and guile, as well as his enterprising nature?" There was neither warmth nor humor, now, in Lady Bligh's dark glance. "We must trust that the chit benefited from her glimpse of Newgate."

Chapter Nineteen

"This is *better* than the Tower and London Bridge!" sighed Miss Bagshot, who was this day spreading sunshine in St. James's Park. "Yes, and Newgate, too! You are a first-rate hand, sir! Dashed if I *don't* have a knack for being in the right place at the right time! But you was telling me about your cousins before I interrupted you, and I wish you would go on!"

Lord Davenham did not do so immediately, but drew up his carriage and set down his groom with vague instructions to enjoy some gentle exercise. That worthy—whose corpulent person exercise could not fail to benefit—looked offended, but voiced no outright protest. The Duke gathered up his reins. He drove a vehicle as whimsical as himself, a sprung whiskey perched upon two great wheels, painted in shades of violet and blue and old rose, and sporting the family crest. "Now we may be private!" he remarked to his companion as they drove away.

"Bless my soul! Who'd've ever thought I'd be private with a Duke?" giggled Miss Bagshot. "I am very glad I gave my aunt the slip, though I expect she'll be mad as toads over it. But there ain't the least use borrowing trouble, because it comes soon enough, anyway. Here I go again, jawing on like a regular rasher-of-wind!"

Upon Miss Bagshot's inelegant description of her style of conversation, Lord Davenham roused sufficiently from his habitual preoccupation to cast his companion a quizzical glance. She looked very charming in a simple sprigged muslin gown with blue trimmings and a blue spencer, worn with a bonnet composed of thousands of pieces of fine Ionian cork pieced together in a mosaic pattern.

Melly responded to his lordship's attention with fluttering lashes and a dimpled smile. "You saw a grand melodramatic spectacle at Drury Lane!" she prompted.

"So we did." Lord Davenham was at his most vague. "Did I tell you that James I introduced mulberry trees into the park?"

"Yes, and you explained to me how St. James's Palace was built on the site of a leper hospital, and how it's haunted by the Duchess of Mazarin!" Miss Bagshot's voice was stern. "I hope I ain't ungrateful, but I don't care a fig for palaces and mulberry trees. Tell me how you liked the play!"

"The play? At Drury Lane?" Lord Davenham's hands were deft upon the reins. "It was very well if you like that sort of thing."

Melly had no notion whether or not she would find such entertainment to her taste. Personally, she suspected that greater melodrama had been enacted in the Davenant family box. "Does *Lady* Davenham enjoy the theater?" she slyly inquired.

"I suppose she must. She said it was a charming evening." Lord Davenham gestured. "You will notice the canal, Miss Bagshot. Charles the Second added it to the park. It runs from the mulberry garden to Whitehall."

Melly's interest in canals was little keener than her

interest in palaces and mulberry trees; but she was not to be gifted with a description of the adventurous Davenant *ménage à trois* at play. She fidgeted with her bonnet, which she had appropriated from her aunt's atelier, and tried a different approach. "Sir Malcolm wants me to give you up! He told me so himself. He said we was playing a May-game, and talked a great deal of nonsense about a person named Croesus who isn't even alive!" Her tone was wistful. *"What* an out-and-outer Sir Malcolm is! A regular hand."

Lord Davenham bestowed upon his companion a whimsical smile. "You seem to be quite taken with my cousin, Miss Bagshot."

"Taken with him?" echoed Melly. "What female *ain't?* Sir Malcolm needs only walk into a room to set hearts fluttering, you know—or perhaps you *didn't!* It don't signify. I'm not going to be played fast and loose with."

"Fast and loose?" The Duke looked intrigued.

"Fast and loose!" Miss Bagshot was firm. "I'll make book on it. Of course you must take up the cudgels on Sir Malcolm's behalf, because you're a gentleman and he's your relative, even if you *don't* like him above half!"

Lord Davenham arched a brow. "I don't?" he said.

"How *could* you?" In a sympathetic manner, Miss Bagshot patted the Duke's arm. "You of all people must realize Sir Malcolm is depraved—after all, it's your wife he's being depraved *with!* As I told Sir Malcolm, he's dashed lucky you ain't horn-mad."

"Ah." Lord Davenham's second eyebrow joined its fellow. "And what was his reply?"

Melly frowned. "I don't recall, exactly. That may've been when he followed me into the alleyway and kissed me—you look startled, sir! It's the truth, I swear it! Sir Malcolm *did* kiss me, and I slapped his face for it, even if I did like it *prodigious* well. A girl must look out for her future." Her frown gave way to dimples. "Now, if *you* was to try and kiss me, sir—"

Lord Davenham's brows lowered, simultaneously. "I hope you will not take offense, Miss Bagshot, but I am not in the habit of such things."

"No?" Melly looked arch. "Then it ain't no wonder Lady Davenham has allowed herself to be trifled with! Kissing is all very well in its place, I vow!"

"You misunderstand, Miss Bagshot," responded the Duke, as the sprung whiskey approached the trees that lined Birdcage Walk. "I have nothing against, er, kissing. I merely think that to do so in the middle of St. James's Park is not the thing."

"Bless my soul!" This hint that Lord Davenham might yet be persuaded to set aside his scruples inspired Melly to snuggle closer on the carriage seat. "Wondrous great together, are we not?"

Lord Davenham gazed serenely down the length of Birdcage Walk. "Have I told you about Jethro Tull's seed drill?" he inquired.

Seed drills! Though Melly might be bird-witted, she could take a hint. "I can take a hint!" she said, as she undraped herself from Lord Davenham's arm. "You think that to get up a flirtation with me would be the most improper thing. It seems to me that you have an excessively high regard for propriety, sir! Which is very hard on a girl. That is to say, you *look* so adventurous. Oh, I know you can't help it, any more than *I* can help falling into pickles and cutting larks." She was very thoughtful. "Mayhap that is why Lady Davenham has tossed her handkerchief in Sir Malcolm's direction. One shouldn't pretend to be something one ain't!"

"I shouldn't think so," Lord Davenham responded vaguely. "We were betrothed in the cradle. If you will direct your attention over *there,* you will see Duck Island, Miss Bagshot."

Poor Lady Davenham! thought Melly, even as she expressed her admiration for some distant pelicans. Married to someone she'd known all her life—naturally the Duchess was flirting with her cousin; the Duke would have few surprises left. In such a situation, Melly would be flirting, also. To own the truth, Melly would have flirted in *any* situation, but that is quite beside the point.

From waterfowl and pelicans, Lord Davenham had progressed to wheat. Reluctantly, Melly abandoned her intention of diddling the Duke in lieu of Sir Malcolm and Bow Street. "Sir Malcolm warned me you wasn't a pigeon for my plucking!" she sighed. "But a girl has to *try!* I have decided that I don't *wish* to see Sir Malcolm taken into custody by Bow Street, no matter how much reward money is involved. And so I warned him that Bow Street is on his trail."

"Did you, Miss Bagshot?" Lord Davenham was quickly enough diverted from seed plows and turnip drills once one had discovered how to set about it. "And what was my cousin's reply?"

"Oh, I didn't tell him about *you!*" Miss Bagshot was rendered indignant by the inference that she was untrustworthy. "I just meant to put him on his guard against Puddiphat. It ain't pleasant to be imprisoned, sir, as I should know, due to my aunt. What a hobble! I have had to positively cudgel my brain."

This graphic description of Miss Bagshot's thought processes caused Lord Davenham to smile. "Surely the situation is not so serious as all that."

"In a pig's whisker, it ain't!" Melly responded bluntly. "That shows all *you* know. But then you ain't dwelling under the hen's thumb! Or do I mean foot? I *am* going to get clear of this pickle, no matter how much of a kickup Aunt Hel may make. Yes, and I even know *how* to do it."

Miss Bagshot's pregnant pause clearly invited comment. Lord Davenhad halted his sprung whiskey in a leafy copse. "And how is that, my dear?"

Delighted to have at last received his lordship's full attention, Melly nonetheless was severe. "You shouldn't call people 'my dear' unless you mean to flirt with them," she scolded, "and you've already said you *don't* want to flirt with me—although I'm sure as check you'd have liked it excessively! But I ain't one to flog a dead horse." Her escort gave vent to a strangled noise, and she frowned. "It ain't a laughing matter! Since I'll have no reward money from either you or Bow Street, I've had to think of some other way to get out from under my Aunt Hel's thumb, and after puzzling my head very hard over it, I've hit on the very thing: you must buy me off, before I make a nuisance of myself!"

To this ominous pronouncement, the author of which looked inordinately pleased with herself, Lord Davenham responded with an ironic expression. "You cannot seriously think that I will allow you to blackmail me, Miss Bagshot."

Melly had not expected his lordship to be thrilled by the prospect, had indeed anticipated something much stronger than this lukewarm response. "Not you *precisely,* sir; you ain't done anything to be blackmailed *for.*"

"Ah." Lord Davenham drew forth his snuffbox. "But other members of my family have been less prudent."

Fascinated, Melly watched the Duke take snuff. "You know they have! And you *wouldn't* have known if I hadn't told you, so I'd think you might show a girl some gratitude. Why is it that people who *have* the Ready-and-Rhino are so relucant to share it with those of us who *don't?* Not that I mean to call you a nip-farthing, sir! Though it stands to reason that if you *wasn't* clutch-fisted, I wouldn't have to put Lady Davenham to the touch!"

The Duke tucked away his snuffbox. "Just what is it you mean to blackmail my wife about, Miss Bagshot?"

"If that don't beat all!" Enchantingly, Melly chuckled. "Now you're trying to pull the wool over *my* eyes! Not that I hold it against you, sir! But *I* know *you* know about Lady Davenham and Sir Malcolm, because I told you myself!" Anxiously, she nibbled at her lower lip. *"Would* Lady Davenham dislike scandal, do you think? Sir Malcolm hinted she might not—not that a girl can trust the rogue!"

Lord Davenham was rueful. "You harbor a great animosity toward my family, Miss Bagshot."

"Poppycock! Not a bit of it!" In her eagerness to refute this allegation, Melly clutched his lordship's sleeve. "Oh, *why* is everyone so reluctant to part with their blunt? You are being positively cheese-paring, and Sir Malcolm accused me of trying to feather my nest. I would not act so shabby, was *I* snugly placed." Sadly, she watched Lord Davenham remove her hand from his sleeve. "As for disliking you—why, I even offered to fix it up all right and tight. I'll admit I ain't figured out how to go about it yet, but I've had other things on my mind!"

"Such as how to, er, put the screws to my wife. I am very disappointed in you, Miss Bagshot." Lord Davenham maneuvered his sprung whiskey out of the leafy copse.

"Everyone is disappointed in me!" muttered Melly. "I don't know what people expect. Yes, and I don't want to make anyone unhappy, but I don't want to be made unhappy myself, either! I *like* Lady Davenham, even if she *did* call me bachelor's fare! I even designed her a first-rate carriage dress! But I don't know anyone else who I *can* blackmail." She sighed "Now I suppose you'll threaten to clap me in jail, which would be all of a piece with everything else."

The elusive Lord Davenham was not so predictable. "No," he said. "You must do as you please, Miss Bagshot."

"The deuce!" ejaculated Melly, rearing back on the carriage seat, the better to gaze dumbfounded upon her escort. "Don't you *mind?*"

As usual, nothing in his lordship's features gave a clue to his thoughts, which in this instance beggared description anyway. "The Davenants have survived other scandals," he said coolly. "It is a matter of principle. Nor would I be so high-handed as to try and dictate to you. I did point out, did I not, the mulberry trees?"

Silently, Miss Bagshot consigned all mulberry trees to the nether regions, and his lordship with them. "Sir Malcolm ain't the only one who don't know all there is to know about females!" she said aloud. "If that's the way you talk to your wife, it's no wonder you've had the antlers planted on your brow! You've as good as said she *could!* What you *should* do is put your foot down—it's only when you don't care a rush for someone that it don't matter what they do. Or maybe you *don't* care. Because if you *did,* you wouldn't let me make Lady Davenham food for scandal, even if you wasn't plump in the pocket, which Sir Malcolm assured me you are!"

As Lord Davenham recalled, it was Miss Bagshot who had urged him to adopt an indifferent air—not that his lordship had followed her advice—or any other. Unaided by anybody, he had arrived at point non plus. He guided his horse back through the park. "Have you ever seen an opium-eater, Miss Bagshot? Once started on that course, it is difficult to stop. The same is true with anything one *shouldn't* do, because it generally turns out to be a great deal more pleasurable than what one *should.*" The same could be applied to his own policy of non-involvement, he supposed. Not that the consequences of said policy had proven the least bit pleasant. Ruefully, he smiled. "What a high stickler I sound. What I mean, my dear, is that I trust your better nature to prohibit you from embarking upon so disastrous a course."

Miss Bagshot was not altogether certain she *possessed* a better nature, or that she wholly grasped his lordship's high-flown sentiments. These things she freely admitted, adding: "It becomes clearer and clearer to me why Lady Davenham took up with her cousin; you neglected her, sir! She *deserves* to have a flirt! And the most wicked thing I have *ever* done is set my cap at Sir Malcolm and try to cut her out!"

"Was that your intention, Miss Bagshot?" In the distance Lord Davenham's groom waited impatiently. "A gentleman is not expected to prose on about his wife, but it would not be easy to steal a march on Thea. She is a diamond of the first water, you must realize."

This suggestion of inferior quality caused Melly to bridle—and then stare. There was an abstracted expression on Lord Davenham's unmeritedly adventurous features, a wry twist to his lips. The significance of this expression was not lost on Miss Bagshot, thorough flirt that she was; and she did not for an instant suspect that she was its inspiration. "Bless my heart! I thought *I* got into dreadful pickles, but this is worse than any of my scrapes!"

Lord Davenham's abstracted expression turned to puzzlement, which he enacted with curved mouth and arched brow. "*I* have merely got turned off without a character," Melly gently explained. "*You,* sir, are in love with your own wife!"

Chapter Twenty

Lord Davenham retired to his club after picking up his
groom and setting down Miss Bagshot in Oxford Street.
By the time he returned to Davenant House, the hour
was considerably advanced, and the majority of the
servants asleep. The Duke repaired to his dressing
room, dismissed his valet, and prepared to similarly end
a long and thought-provoking day. Then he noticed the
candlelight issuing from the bedchamber next door.
Even so aloof a gentleman as Lord Davenham must
experience some curiosity as to why his wife remained
awake at so belated an hour—especially after being
made privy to repeated statements regarding horns
planted on ducal brows. He opened the connecting
door.

It was a large chamber, dominated by the ancestral
four-post bedstead, the wood canopy of which was
carved with all manner of scrolls and moldings of classical form. The headboard, treated in a similar style,
included a coronet of rank; the summit was ornamented
with panaches of flowers. The enveloping curtain and

frill were of chintz edged with tassels and fringe. Upon hearing the door open, Lady Davenham thrust her head through the curtains. "Hah!" she said. And then she glanced back behind her into the shadows. "Oh, do be still!"

Upon this indication that his Duchess was not alone in the ancestral four-poster, Lord Davenham hesitated. "Perhaps I should leave," he suggested, in polite tones that were very hard achieved.

"The deuce you will!" snapped Lady Davenham, who, after considerable thrashing about, had arranged herself in a not-quite-decorous position on the edge of the bed. "I have a crow to pluck with you—or have you forgot you were engaged with me this evening? You put me all out of patience, Vivien!"

It occurred to Lord Davenham that ladies surprised in compromising situations were less likely to attack than to cajole. He strolled across the room and peered into the four-poster's depths. Arranged upon the pillows, in a position of maximum comfort, was Nimrod. Upon espying his dilatory master, the dog snarled.

"I *did* forget our engagement," admitted Lord Davenham, as he plucked his loyal hound from off his pillows, deftly avoiding Nimrod's teeth. "And I am very sorry for it. But, Thea, it is not the first time."

Lady Davenham, already sunk in a brown study, did not take kindly to this remark. She watched her husband stroll about the chamber, inspecting the black Jacobean cabinet, the wardrobe, the dressing stand, and stool. Any other man would have looked absurd, she thought, clad in a nightshirt, cradling a wheezing hound. Sight of Vivien instead made her pulses pound erratically, and her heart leap straight up in her throat. That buccaneer face, with the lock of hair so endearingly tumbled forward on his handsome brow; the overall impression of passions held strongly in leash—

Too strongly in leash, at least as concerned herself. By no means did Lady Davenham intend her husband to discover she found him damnably attractive. "Vivien!" she snapped, as he twitched away the window hangings and peered behind the cheval glass. *"What* are you about?"

Lord Davenham did not imagine that a confession of his suspicions would improve his strained relationship with his wife, especially since he was not convinced that his suspicions were wholly without merit. Solicitously he settled Nimrod near the cozy fire that blazed upon the hearth, then arranged himself upon a chair. "I dined at my club," he offered. "William Huskisson was there —Liverpool's Minister of Woods and Forest—and we had a very interesting conversation about currency depreciation. But you are used to enjoying yourself without me, my dear!"

Thea, who interpreted this last statement as a gentle reminder of her husband's marital discontent, emerged wholly from the four-post bedstead and crossed to the dressing stand, on which stood a bottle of ratafia and a glass. Of this gentle stimulant, she availed herself, not for the first time this night. Because the floor was cold, she then joined Nimrod on the hearth. "Minister!" she muttered into her glass. "Depreciation!"

It occurred to Lord Davenham that his wife, if not precisely cast away, was distinctly in her cups. "It is an important subject!" he reproved. "Thea, you are scowling! What has put you in a tweak?"

"I am *not* in a tweak!" retorted Thea, in tones so acerbated that Nimrod wakened and snapped at her skirts. Hastily, she moved aside. "I am in a passion! Vivien, I Know All! And it makes me *very* cross to learn that you have been tooling the ribbons in St. James's Park, with Miss Bagshot beside you on the carriage seat. Oh, I know that you do not wish to be married, and that I am lower in your estimation than a caterpillar—or was it a snail? But you were supposed to extricate Malcolm from Miss Bagshot's clutches, *not* to cut him out!"

As result of this somewhat inebriated outburst, Lord Davenham contemplated his wife, who was lounging in a disgraceful and highly provocative manner against the wall near the hearth. Thea looked ravishing *en déshabillé,* clad in a froth of muslin and lace, her hair loosened from its tight braid to curl wildly around her face and cascade down her back—so very ravishing that, lest he embarrass her with unwelcome advances, Vivien abruptly transferred his gaze to Nimrod. *"Caterpillars?"* he said.

Lady Davenham was too well accustomed to her husband's vagaries to be so easily sidetracked. "As if it is not bad enough you must suddenly decide to kick over the traces, you must do so with a chit whom Malcolm has been kissing!" she continued. "Although I daresay Miss Bagshot didn't tell you about *that!*"

"Ah, but she did." Thea was less angered by the fact that he had supposedly strayed than by the fact that he had thereby interfered with Malcolm's romance —or one of Malcolm's romances, amended Lord Davenham. Rather than jealousy of Miss Bagshot, Lady Davenham's primary reaction seemed to be irritation with her spouse. Lord Davenham wondered if a hitherto undetected strain of madness tainted the Davenants. His own current overriding emotion was not outrage at his wife's various perfidies, but a wish to take her to bed.

Looking very wry, Lord Davenham clasped his hands upon his knee. "I have it on Miss Bagshot's authority that Malcolm sets feminine hearts aflutter without the slightest effort. However, Miss Bagshot doesn't mean to be played fast and loose with, she promises, so you need not concern yourself."

That Thea didn't care a button whether or not Miss Bagshot was thus abused, she didn't point out, lest she be tempted to similarly confess her ardent desire to abuse the minx herself. "Good God, Vivien, the girl is on the dangle for a fortune! Something to do with a wish to grow rhododendrons without soil, I believe. I warn you, if you try and settle a competence upon her

—well, much as you may dislike the circumstance, I am still your wife!"

During this outburst, Nimrod had waddled from the hearth to collapse at his master's feet, which gave Lord Davenham an excellent excuse to avert his face, a very necessary act, lest he give way to his overwhelming impulse. Few ladies appeared to advantage in a state of undress. Thea, unfortunately for Vivien's peace of mind, was one of them. "But I do *not* dislike the circumstance that you are my wife!" he protested. "Nor do I intend to provide Miss Bagshot with a competence, as I have informed her. I could not similarly vouch for you."

"For me?" Bored with holding up the wall, and feeling left out of the snug family scene presented by the Duke and his hound, Lady Davenham collapsed onto another chair. "What *are* you talking about, Vivien? I wish you would explain."

Promptly, Lord Davenham did so, and not entirely without malice; he was only human, after all. Succinctly, he said, as he pulled Nimrod's ears, "Blackmail."

"Blackmail?" Lady Davenham contemplated her ratafia. "Oh, dear."

"Exactly so." The Duke straightened, his handsome features flushed. Even a gentleman determined to withstand the temptations of an inebriated, wrong-headed, ravishing wife can remain bent over only so long. "Until someone buys her off, Miss Bagshot means to make a nuisance of herself."

"Miss Bagshot already *has* made a nuisance of herself!" Thea responded bitterly. "Oh, I wish Malcolm had never come home. We rubbed on well enough until he started making sheep's eyes at a wretched little minx. And now *this* imbroglio—it is more than flesh and blood can stand!"

"Poor Thea!" Noting that his wife was fairly gnashing her teeth, Lord Davenham took her hand. "I warned you, did I not, that it would not be the *beau monde* Malcolm wished to embrace?"

Lady Davenham gazed upon the hand which clasped hers and experienced a most untimely impulse to burst into tears. "If you say you told me so, Vivien, I think I will *scream!*"

"I would not say that, my dear; I, too, was wide of the mark. Though Miss Bagshot may not be of the *beau monde,* you are." Since his friendly overture had only increased his wife's irritability, Lord Davenham released her and rose from his chair.

Here, an altercation ensued: his lordship had forgotten the hound sprawled across his feet. Vivien tripped, Nimrod snarled, Thea burst into nervous laughter. "But, Vivien!" she gasped, as she tucked up her feet to avoid Nimrod's angry teeth. "Malcolm does not wish to embrace *me!*"

Lord Davenham picked up his snarling hound, carried him at arm's length across the chamber, and shut him in the dressing room. "You must not," he said, as he turned back to his Duchess, "try and pull the wool over my eyes. What was I saying? Ah, yes! Miss Bagshot doesn't think you would care to be plunged in the scandal-broth, and therefore trusts you may be persuaded to buy her off. But you must not take it personally! She bears us no animus." He smiled. "Indeed, she would much rather blackmail Croesus—but she *knows* us."

Ratafia consumption had not elevated Thea's spirits, and Vivien's obvious lack of concern for her dilemma had an equally adverse effect. She was nothing to her husband, Thea thought sadly; no man who cared a fig for his wife could be amused by her prospective blackmailer. Vivien hadn't even expressed interest in what she was to be blackmailed *about*. Thea raised her chin. Very well, then, let him think the worst!

It had not escaped Lord Davenham's notice that his Duchess was looking very belligerent. "My dear, you are making a piece of work about nothing!" he soothed. "Miss Bagshot will not carry through her threats."

"Hah!" ejaculated Lady Davenham, further annoyed

by the conviction with which her husband predicted Miss Bagshot's actions. Clearly, Vivien was quite *épris* in that direction. "I hope you may not be disappointed in the minx, because *I* have not the slightest intention of financing her bid for independence!" Sadly, she contemplated her spouse. "Can you not understand it is *Malcolm* whom she wants?"

Though Lord Davenham could hardly be thrilled by his wife's obsession with their cousin, he was prone neither to displays of temper nor blunt speech. "Yes, I think it is!" he said, as he sat down on the edge of the four-post bedstead. "I hope you do not mind too much."

Why should she mind? wondered Thea, and opened her mouth to ask. Then she remembered that she was embarked upon a blatant flirtation with Malcolm. Did Vivien look the least bit dog-in-the-mangerish? Thea looked at him with narrowed eyes and decided he did not.

"I shall not wear the willow!" she said, upon a hiccough. "I hope that you may be equally sanguine."

Lord Davenham leaned back against a bedpost and looked whimsical. If Miss Bagshot were to attach Malcolm, his own problems would be partly solved. "I think I might."

In despair, Thea threw up her expressive hands. "I vow I shall never understand you!" she cried. "Miss Bagshot signifies little to you, you claim—yet you took her with you to the Horticultural Society, and driving in St. James's Park. I wish you would tell me what the chit has that I do *not*."

This hint that his wife did not hold him in total disinterest sparked a distinct glitter in his lordship's dark eye. Then he checked himself. Thea did not realize the significance of her own words—or the effect they would have upon a gentleman whose amorous inclinations had been too long restrained. "That settles it! First caterpillars and now Miss Bagshot—you have had too much ratafia, my dear."

Lady Davenham was not accustomed to being dictated to. As she approached the ratafia decanter, there was a glitter in her own eyes. Lord Davenham reached the dressing stand first, and deftly moved the decanter aside. "I think that we must talk seriously, Thea," he said ruefully. "I have it on very good authority that, though I do not wish to appear high-minded, it is time I put my foot down."

"Your foot?" Lady Davenham glanced down at that appendage, and consequently discovered that the ratafia had had more effect than she'd realized, because her head swam. She clutched at Vivien. Taken off guard, Lord Davenham stepped backward and both the Duke and his Duchess tumbled on the ancestral bedstead. "What *about* your foot?" persisted Thea, when she had caught her breath, the loss of which had not resulted from her exertions, but from the memory of her cousin's advice regarding the seduction of her spouse.

"Ummm?" responded his lordship, who was currently a great deal more interested in various lush portions of his wife's anatomy.

Now that she had, if inadvertently, accomplished the first step in the seduction of her husband, to wit his presence in the ancestral bed, Thea decided that his interest must next be gained. Though the interior of the four-poster was shadowed and she could not clearly make out his expression, Thea suspected that Vivien's mind was not on her words. How to wake him from his air-dreams, focus his attention on herself? She must introduce one of his enthusiasms into the conversation. "I have been thinking about reaping machines!" she said. If only she had asked Malcolm about practical details.

"Reaping machines?" Lord Davenham was disconcerted to discover how far his wife's thoughts were from romance. Resolved to be amiable, the Duke propped himself comfortably among the pillows so recently adorned by Nimrod. "Have you figured out how to put the cart before the horse?"

Since his lordship had made himself comfortable, her ladyship felt free to do likewise, and arranged herself amid the pillows by his side. Foolish, after several years of marriage, and a lifelong acquaintance, to feel so giddy, she scolded herself. "It seems to me that if you arranged your cutting knives on one side of the horse, the machine could be drawn with greater comfort," she remarked. "If a pully at one side of the road-driving wheel was connected to another pulley above—"

"I have not the least distant interest in pulleys," interrupted Lord Davenham, thereby delaying the invention of the first efficient reaper for fifteen years. "You must not change the subject, Thea."

So much for seductions, Lady Davenham thought glumly; she had lured her husband only into reading her a scold. "I don't know why I bother!" she said bitterly. "Doubtless you would be happier in your potting shed! You need not deny it; you have already told me Davenants are not suited to marriage. I was used to think we dealt well together, Vivien. *Now* I think I must not know you at all." Her voice quivered. "And if you hankered after adventure, you should have told me, instead of foraging for it among the fleshpots!"

So startled was Lord Davenham by these accusations —and so rapt in contemplation of what fleshly activities his wife envisioned him embarked upon in his potting shed, with caterpillars and moles and snails— that he was briefly silent. His cogitations were interrupted by Thea's sniffles and Nimrod's distant howls. "But it was *you* who hankered after adventure, my dear."

He had not denied her accusations, Thea noted sadly; not that in good conscience he *could*. Still, one would have appreciated a consideration of one's feelings, however vain. "That was before I knew what it was *like* to have adventures!" she retorted. "I may be enough of a Davenant to relish the idea, but I'm *not* enough of one to enjoy the thing itself. You and Malcolm may find blackmail amusing; *I* do not." Especially, she added silently, when she had done nothing of which to be ashamed. "Talking won't pay toll! Vivien, I will not mince words. We have both been going on in a very bad way."

With this sentiment, at least, his lordship was in accord. "So we have! My dear, about those fleshpots—"

"The devil with your fleshpots!" snapped Thea. "Can't you for an instant put them from your mind?" It occurred to her that seductions were not hastened by cross words. "Never mind that. I do not wish to introduce a topic that is repugnant to you—but have you forgotten that Malcolm will inherit if you do not make a push to get an heir?" The shadows hid her blush. *"Legitimate,* that is!"

In response to this intimation that he was so far sunk in depravity as to be peppering the countryside with illegitimate Davenants, Lord Davenham grinned. In point of fact, his lordship had been heroically restraining mirth for the past several moments. "Oh, no! I haven't forgotten!" he gasped.

Clearly, she had grown repugnant; the simplest mention of an heir caused her husband strain, as indicated by his voice. Abandoning all notions of seduction, Lady Davenham sat up, hugged her knees, and hiccoughed. She looked altogether bewitching in that posture, as the firelight revealed; her dark hair was all atangle, her big dark eyes pensive, her lower lip swollen from where she had nervously bitten it.

She did not remain long in that position. Lord Davenham reached out, caught her arm and pulled her back down amid the pillows. Then he propped himself up on one elbow and looked down into her face. His own features had nothing in them now of whimsy or vagueness.

Lady Davenham had the odd impression of lying with a stranger, so very unlike himself did Vivien look. "What are you going to do?" she whispered shyly, around the constriction that had risen in her throat.

His lordship smiled. Thea blushed at her own foolishness.

"Has it been so long that you must ask me?" With that intentness so unlike him, Lord Davenham tangled his fingers in the curls at the nape of his wife's neck. "I had thought to explore this matter of tardy offspring."

Blushing furiously, she reached up and shyly clasped her husband's shoulders and drew him toward her. As he caught her up against him, Lord Davenham laughed aloud.

Had there been a note of triumph in that laughter? Thea thought there might. And for that matter, who was seducing whom, and why?

But tomorrow was soon enough for questions. Lady Davenham surrendered herself to her husband's caress, with a happy little sigh.

Chapter Twenty-one

The matter of offspring also concerned Madame le Best, in the sense that she wished her ne'er-do-well brother had had none. These sentiments she was explaining to the damsel whom she had come to regard as a mill-stone around her neck. "You have tried me too far!" hissed Madame, in tones that were angry, if pitched low so that the customers would not hear. "You gave me your promise that you would do only as I told you and keep a still tongue in your head!"

Miss Bagshot looked up from the issue of *La Belle Assemblée,* which she had been laboriously perusing, in particular the advertisements. Obviously, her aunt was once again in a pelter. "But I didn't *truly* promise!" said Melly in her own defense. "I had my fingers crossed!"

Madame glanced at her customers, who were carrying on a spirited discussion of the relative merits of a spencer of rose-colored satin and another of cream-colored broché silk, both with cord trimming to match. The ladies appeared perfectly content. Madame envied them that peace of mind. She scowled upon the niece in whose conduct she found so much for which to blush.

"You seem to think you are having a holiday!" Madame said bitterly. "Driving all around London in company with peers. Sometimes I despair of ever marrying you off. When I present you to someone suitable, you're either rude or pushing, or you aren't here at all!"

"I *thought* that was your lay!" Melly also frowned. "What if I ain't ready to be married, Aunt Hel? Because I don't mind admitting that I ain't!"

"Not ready to be married?" repeated Madame le Best, in awful tones. "What nonsense is this? I suppose you would rather go on headlong to your ruin!"

The sunny-tempered Miss Bagshot marveled that a member of her family could be habitually sulky as a bear. "Stuff! I ain't doing anything of the sort."

"Oh, no!" retorted Madame, more bitterly yet. "You are only determined to make a byword of yourself, racketing about with Baronets and Dukes. Don't deny it! I know all about the Tower and Astley's and St. James's Park. You were seen."

"Bless my soul!" Miss Bagshot craned her lovely neck to observe the customers. "Who's the prattle-box? Not that *I* care about tale-pitching, nor should you, Aunt Hel! It don't hurt a girl's credit to be seen with a Duke."

"*Credit!*" Madame fairly shrieked the word, then with belated discretion lowered her tone. "You're a fine one to talk of credit. Every time my back is turned, you blot your copybook. There'll be no more of it, do you understand?"

Certainly Miss Bagshot understood; she was not a feather-head. Her aunt was bent on acting as her jailer. "For someone who is so wishful of seeing me tied up, you choose a queer way to go about it! If I was to do as you wished, I'd never go anywhere—I'd dwindle into a fubsy-faced old maid." That unflattering description perfectly fit her aunt, Melly realized. "There's nothing *wrong* with being an old maid, mind! Marriage ain't for everyone. Look at Mama! *She* was used to rue the day she stepped into parson's mousetrap!"

That day Madame had also rued, and seldom more than at this moment. "Oh, *la vache!*" she muttered. "And now I learn you are conniving with that—that Bow Street puppy—to send Calveley to jail. How *could* you, Melly? One of my best customers! Cabbage-head!"

Much as Melly disliked brangles, she could not let this injustice pass. "Sir Malcolm," she said sternly, *"ain't* a cabbage-head! He is a regular out-and-outer! Just the sort of gentleman who makes a girl wish she *was* one to toss her bonnet over windmills. Don't fly into alt, Aunt Hel; I ain't going to! No, and I ain't going to hand Sir Malcolm over to Bow Street, either." She looked very pleased with herself. "I have other fish to fry."

Other fish? To Madame, those words had an ominous ring. But she had neglected her customers too long. Pondering what larks her sly-boots niece might next get up to, a topic which filled her with the utmost apprehension, she shepherded the ladies into the atelier, there to view masterpieces in progress.

In her aunt's absence, Miss Bagshot returned her attention to *La Belle Assemblée.* As she contemplated the latest fashions, her elfin face was glum. Even a girl so sunny-natured as Melly could not help but be adversely affected by repeated exposure to an aunt who was forever kicking up a dust over trifles, and always cursedly provoked.

Having settled her customers in the atelier, there to exclaim rapturously over works in progress, Madame le Best returned to the attack. Hands on her hips, she towered over her niece. "What other fish?" she said. Miss Bagshot, who had progressed from advertisements for beauty aids to instructions on care of the feet and bosom, looked blank. "You said you had other fish to fry," Madame repeated. "I want to know what you meant."

"Yes, so that you may throw a rub in my way,"

sighed Melly. "What has come over you, Aunt Hel? You wasn't used to cut up so stiff. The way you carry on, I might as *well* be bachelor's fare!"

"Bachelor's fare!" Madame le Best sank down onto one of her chairs. "Melly!"

Miss Bagshot giggled at her aunt's horrified expression. "Don't put yourself in a taking; I ain't put my foot wrong yet. Though if that Croesus fellow was alive now, I might have! But that is far and far off."

Madame gazed upon her Oriental wallpaper and sought to compose herself. Perhaps her niece might be less prone to larks and frolics if she understood the danger in which they stood. "You will recall when that person from Bow Street came around asking questions," she remarked.

"Samson!" Melly responded promptly, delighted to be presented a topic on which she need not equivocate. "Samson wishes to become a Bow Street Runner. But I will not help him bring Sir Malcolm to justice, no matter *how* large the reward."

By this proof of Sir Malcolm's charm, Madame's apprehensions were not eased. "Bow Street is on the trail of a cracksman who left England in a great hurry several years ago."

"A cracksman!" Melly was not disenchanted by this new light shed, as she thought, on Sir Malcolm's character. "Fancy that!"

What Madame le Best fancied, however ignoble, was the casting of her niece out into the street. "A cracksman known to the authorities as Blood-and-Thunder," she persevered. "Melly, you must realize what this means."

Melly, alas, realized nothing of the sort. "Means?" she echoed, her big brown eyes opened wide.

As if by considered movement she might contain her frustration, Madame carefully folded her hands in her lap. "There is a rumor that this cracksman has returned to England after an absence of many years. Bow

Street seeks to find him before he resumes a life of crime."

"Yes, but he don't *need* to resume it!" Melly pointed out. "He's plump enough in the pocket to buy his cousin any number of new gowns, and at the same time he ain't open-fisted, as I can vouch! Unless that's how he comes by his blunt? Bless my soul!"

It was not blessings that Madame currently called down upon her niece. "I am not speaking of Calveley," she said, with clenched jaw. "And no matter how distinguishing the attentions he has paid you, Miss, you may not aim so high. The same is true of Lord Davenham. Both are a great deal above your touch. *Think,* Melly! What did your father do?"

What Miss Bagshot thought was that her aunt was a candidate for Bedlam, being victim of a demonstrable affliction of bats in the cock-loft. "What he did was break my mama's heart!" she responded. "As you should know very well, Aunt Hel, since it was you as took care of us. Which is why I ain't wishful of being leg-shackled! When they don't have to be polite to one another, people *change!* Or so they must, because Mama surely wouldn't have married a curst loose fish, like she was used to say Papa was." Melly looked suspicious. "I thought you said his name wasn't to be spoke under your roof!"

In a nostalgic manner, Madame le Best gazed about her elegantly appointed showroom, allowed her glance to linger upon each japanned chair, each example of imitation bamboo and Oriental lacquer-work. At the rate matters were deteriorating, she would not long enjoy these luxurious surroundings, would more likely be incarcerated with the remaining members of her family in Newgate. "I meant, what did he do for a *living?*" she explained.

Melly wrinkled up her pretty little nose. "Dashed if *I* know! But I wasn't more than a child when Papa sloped off. I ain't wishful of getting into another brangle with you, Aunt Hel, but it seems to me *you* should know what your own brother was about."

Madame was very much afraid that her niece's opinion would be shared by Bow Street. She wondered if one could be clapped in jail for failing to air a suspicion that one's brother had been up to no good. "What would you do, Melly, if your papa tried to get in touch with you?"

"Papa?" Definitely her aunt had fallen prey to bats, or such a nonsensical question would never have been posed. Kind-heartedly, Melly did not express this sentiment. "I'd give him a rare trimming for behaving so scaly to us! Why? It ain't likely he'd try to see me after this many years."

"It may not be as unlikely as you think—if he has been out of the country and only recently returned." Guiding her niece toward comprehension, reflected Madame, was an exhausting business.

Though Melly was not prone to rumination, she occasionally achieved revelation in one incredible bound. "Zounds!" she cried, one of those moments being upon her. "It's not Sir Malcolm, but *Papa,* who Samson is after!"

Nervously, Madame le Best glanced at her atelier. "Keep your voice down, Melly! We must be *very* discreet."

Because her aunt was suffering from an overheated brain—for which she had sufficient reason; Melly was herself feeling a trifle flushed—Miss Bagshot did not point out that discretion was not compatible with wild blood. "Just think!" she murmured. "I almost saw Sir Malcolm put in prison for my own papa's crimes."

"We do not know that your papa committed any crimes," Madame le Best responded severely, "or that Sir Malcolm has *not*. I only wished to put you on your guard in case William did approach you. You must speak of this to no one."

Miss Bagshot looked astounded. "Not even Samson? But it ain't right to let Sir Malcolm take the blame."

Already Madame regretted the impulse that had led her to confide in her bird-witted niece—but what else could she have done? Melly could not be allowed to connive at placing one of Madame's most generous patrons behind bars. "Calveley will be blamed for nothing," she said firmly, hoping it was true. "Do you understand me, Melly? I must have your promise that you will not repeat what I have told you—no crossed fingers this time, my girl!"

"Must I?" muttered Miss Bagshot. Her aunt nodded. "Oh, very well!"

That those grudging words were not precisely an oath of silence, Madame failed to realize. "One more lark, Melly," she added for good measure, "and I *will* turn you out into the street." With this dire pronouncement, she rose. As she did so, there came a commotion at the street door. Through that portal came a workman, carrying before him a young rhododendron plant in a terracotta tub. Madame stared open-mouthed.

"Oh!" Miss Bagshot flew to embrace the shrub. "Looked too far above myself, did I, Aunt Hel? That shows all *you* know! I wonder if it was Sir Malcolm who sent it, or Lord Davenham? Prodigious kind it was, *whoever* did it!" She looked sad. *"Not* that it will cause me to change my mind."

"Change your mind about *what?*" inquired Madame, gazing without appreciation upon the rhododendron, which looked distinctly odd in that Oriental setting. "I have warned you about getting into further mischief."

Melly did not doubt that her aunt would consider blackmail under the general heading of frolics, mischief, and larks; yet Melly was not prepared to abandon her visions of financial security. Clearly, Madame le Best and Miss Bagshot had reached a parting of the ways. "I know that you have warned me!" Melly responded. "Wasn't I right here when you did it? There ain't nothing wrong with my hearing, Aunt!" And then she reminded Madame of the customers abandoned in the atelier.

Madame had totally forgotten about the ladies; with a little shriek, she darted toward the atelier. In so doing she brushed very close to the rhododendron. *"That,"* she said severely, "will have to go!"

"Never mind!" murmured Miss Bagshot to the rhododendron; Miss Bagshot saw nothing untoward in talking to plants. "Aunt Hel don't mean it personally, she is just as cross as crabs. It's my fault, I suppose, because I ain't the sort of niece she would like to have—but she ain't the sort of aunt I'd prefer, either, so it all evens out!" She paused to stroke the rhododendron leaves. To own the truth, Miss Bagshot was sick to death of the way her aunt sought to dictate to her, first decreeing that she must not attempt to haul Sir Malcolm's coals out of the fire, and now announcing that Melly could not keep her rhododendron.

"And it is very bad of her!" said Melly, as she bent and took firm hold of the terracotta tub. "I have *always* wanted to grow a rhododendron! And now that I have been given one, she means to make me give it up. Well, I shan't! And I shan't get married, either!" As she spoke, she dragged the tub across the floor.

It was a very heavy tub, Melly quickly learned, a circumstance that caused her a temporary setback. She intended to depart the Oxford Street shop before her aunt literally locked her away; and she had no intention of leaving the precious rhododendron behind to receive the brunt of her aunt's wrath. Yet she could not drag the plant through the streets. Melly stared out the door, beyond which lay freedom, almost in despair. And then her elfin face brightened, and her long lashes fluttered, and her dimples reappeared. Near the plateglass window, trying to look casual, lurked Samson Puddiphat.

Chapter Twenty-two

"Pauline Bonaparte!" exclaimed Lady Bligh, who, having dealt most effectively with her milliner, had next sallied forth on behalf of Bow Street to Davenant House. "The Princess Borghese. She is the beauty of the family, of course, but mean. I believe she used to stick out her tongue behind Josephine's back, poor soul."

Whether the soul thus sympathetically referred to was in the possession of Napoleon's first Empress or his amoral sister, none of the Baroness's audience was prepared to guess. That audience consisted of Lord and Lady Davenham and Sir Malcolm Calveley. They were in the drawing room of Davenant House.

Nor was Lady Bligh in the habit of explaining her more cryptic remarks. As she adjusted the turban which sat atop her scarlet curls, the Baroness awarded Sir Malcolm a roguish glance. "Le Roué!" she murmured speculatively. In recognition of a kindred spirit, that gentleman grinned.

From her position on the straight-legged sofa, Lady

Davenham witnessed this byplay. She supposed she should be glad that some members of this impromptu gathering were enjoying themselves. She wondered again at the purpose for Lady Bligh's unprecedented visit. Surreptitiously, Thea studied the Baroness, who, in addition to her turban, wore a gown of cinnamon jaconet, its sleeves tightly buttoned at the wrist, its hem embellished with a broad embroidered flounce. But she found no answers there. Nor did explanations await Lady Davenham in the person of her husband, who stood in his habitual position at the window, looking down upon his garden. Before he could become aware of her attention, Thea looked away. What was their visitor saying? Something about people who emigrated and changed their names?

"But Malcolm has not changed his name," Thea pointed out, since it was at her cousin that Lady Bligh's remarks were directed. "And if he emigrated, it was only temporarily, because he has come home. I do not understand what all this is about."

Neither did Sir Malcolm understand, but he was enjoying it very well. "I have returned home only temporarily, my Thea," he confessed, as he concentrated on dazzling the Baroness with his smile. "It was never my intention to settle down."

Lady Davenham was neither disarmed nor-diverted by the spectacle of her adventurous cousin making sheep's eyes at their flamboyant guest. "I could wish that you had told me sooner!" she said reproachfully. "I have gone to some effort on your behalf."

"So you have, and I am grateful to you for it," Malcolm responded cordially. "Or I *would* be, were I desirous of becoming leg-shackled, which I'm not!" Briefly, he glanced away from Lady Bligh, seated beside him on the carved gilt settee. First he contemplated Vivien, gazing somberly out the window, then at Thea, seated despondently on the sofa. "I've done my best for you, and it hasn't served—which is yet another reason to avoid parson's mousetrap."

Thea had grown very tired of hearing the male members of her family express adverse viewpoints of the venerable institution of matrimony, which she had once liked very well. Once more she glanced shyly at her spouse, with whom she had had no opportunity for private speech since she had brazenly lured him into her bed. As result of that episode, Thea had sworn off ratafia. Not that the interval had been unpleasant; quite the opposite, if memory served correctly—and one of the things it served her was a distinct impression of her own shocking abandonment. Had Vivien taken her in disgust for that display of unladylike enthusiasm, as she had been brought up to believe any gentleman must? He had said nothing to indicate the opposite, or to suggest any lessening of marital discontent.

"Air-dreaming, Cousin?" inquired Sir Malcolm. Suddenly made aware that she was the cynosure of all eyes, Lady Davenham bit her lip. "I do not think I care to hear marriage compared to a mousetrap!" she said ungraciously, wondering what the commotion in the hallway was about. As she spoke, the door was violently flung open. Miss Bagshot darted across the threshold, scant steps ahead of several servants.

"Mousetraps!" gasped that damsel, flushed and panting from her exertions and looking altogether adorable. "I ain't wishful of stepping into one myself! No, and I ain't wishful of becoming a fubsy-faced old maid, either. And I am *prodigious* tired of people kicking up a dust over trifles!" Recalling her manners, she dropped a curtsy. "Hullo, all! I'm sorry for bursting in on you this way."

"That is quite all right, Miss Bagshot." Lady Bligh waved away the servants, the Davenants apparently for their various reasons being all bereft of movement and speech. "I assume you *are* the young woman who tried to diddle Bow Street?"

Miss Bagshot looked mournful. "Why is it that when a girl tries to look out for herself everyone assumes the worst? I suppose *you* are rich as this Croesus fellow, too, ma'am. It ain't fair. All *I* wanted was a competence!"

Recovered from the shock of receiving in her drawing room the damsel who had recently received distinguishing attentions from the male members of her family, Lady Davenham sat up very erect. "I refuse to pay one penny!" she grimly announced. "Do your worst, Miss Bagshot!"

Melly dragged her big brown eyes away from Sir Malcolm's handsome face. "I was afraid you'd feel like that. Are *all* the nobs so clutch-fisted? It is very hard! But if you want your dirty linen aired in public, it's no skin off *my* nose!"

Vivien had been mistaken in Miss Bagshot, after all; Thea cast him a swift glance. The Duke still stood gazing out the window, as if eschewing all part in the scene. "I do not *have* any dirty linen!" she snapped.

"And I thought *I* told clankers!" responded Melly, shocked. "I ain't never told a taradiddle as whopping as *that!* Yes, and you shouldn't be calling *me* names. I may be a dreadful flirt, but I ain't planted the antlers on anybody's brow!"

"Antlers!" gasped Lady Davenham, aghast.

Though Sir Malcolm was enjoying this exchange mightily, he suspected his cousin was not. "No antlers, Melly," he said kindly. "It was all a hum."

"A *hum?*" In response to Sir Malcolm's brilliant smile, Miss Bagshot clutched herself in the vicinity of her fluttering heart. "I'll wager I couldn't have gone through with it, anyway."

Lord Davenham had understood Miss Bagshot better than the damsel understood herself, thought Thea, further depressed by this evidence of her husband's acumen. Vivien did not want a wife, certainly not one who wore her heart upon her sleeve. Thea sought to restrain her tears.

In her efforts at self-control, the Duchess was assisted by yet another diversion: an anxious-looking person wearing a blue greatcoat and scarlet waistcoat, blue trousers and saber and boots with steel spurs, appeared in her drawing room doorway. "Ah!" said Lady Bligh, who had keenly observed the recent proceedings. "Enter Bow Street."

"Bow Street!" At last Lord Davenham stirred. "You've come about my rhododendron. Good man!"

"*Your* rhododendron?" Miss Bagshot's elfin features were indignant. "I like that! I wouldn't have thought you was the sort of gentleman who gave a girl a present and then took it back!"

Not only had her husband never invited her to a meeting of the Horticultural Society, but he had never on his wife's behalf uprooted one of his precious plants. "Oh, Vivien!" Thea softly cried.

By this indication that she had distressed Lady Davenham, Miss Bagshot was herself upset. "You must not take it so much to heart!" advised Melly, as she sank down beside Thea on the settee. "No gentleman who'd do such a shabby thing is worth a fig! He *knows* how much that rhododendron means to me because I told him myself that I've always been wishful of growing one. Yes, and I told him also you deserved to have a flirt because he neglected you so shockingly!"

"*Did* you?" echoed Thea, faintly.

"Yes, and she told me also that she would fix it up all right and tight." Lord Davenham appeared to find nothing remarkable in the spectacle of Miss Bagshot patting his wife's hands. "Now, about my rhododendron."

"Yes, sir." Puddiphat closed the drawing room door and clasped both hands upon his saber, terrified of inflicting damage on his surroundings, which were the grandest he'd ever seen. "Tell me about it."

"It was a relatively young rhododendron." His lordship vaguely gestured. "About so wide and so tall——" He broke off as the door again opened and two of his footmen, profusely perspiring, hauled the terracotta tub into the drawing room. "My man, you are the best of good fellows! When I awoke to find it gone, I thought I would never see this rhododendron again."

"Gone." Laboriously, Puddiphat strove to make sense of the bizarre situation in which he found himself. "Stolen, sir?"

Lord Davenham inclined his head. "Stolen. In the dead of night. When I was otherwise engaged."

"Bless my heart!" cried Melly, wondering what in the Duke's simple statements had caused his Duchess to blush. "Then it was Sir Malcolm who was the thief!"

In response to this accusation, that gentleman winced. "Let us say instead that I had overindulged slightly in the grape. You wanted a rhododendron, and Vivien had several. It seemed like a good idea at the time."

"And so it was!" Miss Bagshot released Lady Davenham, the better to clasp her own hands to her breast. "A perfectly *nacky* notion! Dashed if you *don't* tempt a girl to toss her bonnet over the windmill!"

Though the exalted company in which he found himself might not blink an eyelid in response to a damsel's declaration that she hovered on the brink of ruin, Puddiphat was not so sanguine. He recalled he had a duty to perform. "Sir Malcolm," he studiously intoned, "I hereby take you in charge and notify you that you will be taken into the safe-keeping of—"

"Poppycock!" Brutally, Lady Bligh shattered the moment of which Puddiphat had so long dreamed. "You haven't a particle of evidence against the man."

Lord Davenham strolled across the room and took up a position behind the settee which held Miss Bagshot and his wife. Though he did not understand her attitude, which seemingly swung from wild enthusiasm to a marked disinclination to look at himself, he would defend his wife. "I do not like to argue with a guest in my home, but I must point that a very *large* particle of evidence is existent." He indicated the terracotta tub. "Not that I mean to make an issue of the business, since the rhododendron has been returned."

"You are very good, Cousin!" responded Sir Malcolm, in ironic tones.

"Oh no, he ain't!" interrupted Miss Bagshot, gazing wistfully upon the tub. "Because if I ain't allowed to keep the thing, I'd as lief not have had it in the first place! Nor would I have had poor Samson haul it all the way across town lest my aunt toss it out!" And then Melly remembered why she had done so. "Like she has *me!*" she wailed.

Now it was Lady Davenham's turn to pat Miss Bagshot's hands. "There, there!" she said. "Do you mean your aunt has cast *you* out? What a shocking thing!"

"She ain't cast me out *yet!*" sniffled Melly, who saw nothing exceptionable in accepting comfort from this source. "But she promised that she *will* if I cut one more lark—and I ain't capable of *not* cutting larks, you see! And so I came here thinking I'd put you to the touch, but then I couldn't go through with it—and now I don't know *what* to do!" She dissolved in tears.

Puddiphat alone remained unaffected by this touching scene, perhaps because he had previously discovered the only route to coherence lay in ignoring Miss Bagshot. He fixed his gaze on the Brussels carpeting. "*Ample* ground for suspicion!" he observed, to the room at large. "Sir Malcolm Calveley, I take you in charge—"

"Have you a warrant?" sternly inquired Lady Bligh.

"I have *said* I do not wish to make an issue of the business!" Lord Davenham added plaintively. "If I were to take offense at all of my cousin's mischief, he would spend the remainder of his life in jail."

"Vivien!" said Sir Malcolm, greatly moved by this unexpected defense. "I did not know you held me in such high esteem."

Lord Davenham wore his most whimsical expression. "I don't. But you *are* my heir."

"And you think I wish to step into your shoes?" Sir Malcolm's shrewd eyes moved from Lord Davenham to his Duchess. "Set your mind at rest, Cousin: I don't!"

"You mistook my meaning, Malcolm." Of one thing was Lord Davenham certain, amid all this confusion: he would no longer stand idly by while his vacillating wife flirted with other gentlemen. In a very absent-minded manner, the Duke touched Thea's dark hair. "You shall not, whether you *want* to or no."

"Sets the wind in *that* quarter?" So intrigued was Melly by this exchange that she forgot her tears. "Fancy that! And I was going to ask you, ma'am, just whose chest you prefer I cast myself *on!*" She removed herself from Lady Davenham's bosom, which had made an excellent stopgap. "Dashed if that gown don't look *splendid* on you! Did you know I designed it myself? Though it was Sir Malcolm as named it London Soot."

Puddiphat was growing very frustrated, as result of his recognition of a plot that had thickened, and his failure to make a subsequent arrest. "There are severe penalties for interfering with Bow Street!" he roared.

Into the sudden silence came Lady Bligh's voice. "Oh no there aren't!" she said.

As result of their acquaintance, Melly was not long impressed by Puddiphat's rage. "I must cast myself on *someone*'s chest!" she explained to Thea. "There is nothing else to do, now that I have run away from my aunt—sloped off! Just like my papa, I've shown Aunt Hel a clean pair of heels—though I ain't supposed to talk of that!"

Not without good benefit had Puddiphat read *Physiognomical Fragments* and other related works; he knew very well the physical characteristics of individuals inclined toward burglary. Small ears and sharp vision and slender fingers—unfortunately, that description applied to several of the people in the room. Puddiphat could only trust to his instinct. "Sir Malcolm Calveley, I take you into custody—"

"Bless my soul but you're deuced persistent, Samson!" observed Miss Bagshot. She turned to Lady Davenham, whom she was beginning to look upon as a bosom bow. "Samson wishes to become a Bow Street

Runner, and that is why he's so determined to clap someone in jail. I shan't help you, Samson! No matter *what* Sir Malcolm may have done!"

"I do not *think* I have done anything more criminal," said Sir Malcolm, though not with a great deal of conviction, "than digging up my cousin's rhododendron."

Puddiphat had not needed Miss Bagshot's announcement to alert him she was set on leading Bow Street down the garden path. "—on suspicion of being a cracksman known commonly as Blood-and-Thunder!" he concluded triumphantly.

For a moment, the fact of Sir Malcolm's arrest was not absorbed by the assorted company. This oversight occurred as result of Miss Bagshot's failure to accord the proper respect to the official emissary of Bow Street. "I'll wager you've done a great deal worse than dig up rhododendrons!" she said sternly, before being stricken by the impact of Puddiphat's words. "But Sir Malcolm *ain't* Blood-and-Thunder! It's my papa as was a cracksman—I think. I ain't seen him in years, and neither has my aunt. And no matter what Aunt Hel says, I won't let Sir Malcolm take the blame, so you may *un*arrest him immediately!"

"Your papa?" echoed Puddiphat, stunned.

"You are surprised!" Melly said wisely. "I was myself. I ain't even thought of him in years; it was a long time ago that he hopped the twig. And a good job he did of it, too, for my mama could never trace him one step. She always thought he'd gone to the Continent." Melly sighed. "I promised Aunt Hel I wouldn't let the cat out of the bag, and here I'm doing that very thing— which just goes to show what promises are worth, which is why I wanted a competence."

Sir Malcolm was looking very thoughtful. "The deuce!" he said.

"Precisely," murmured Lady Bligh, as she gracefully rose. "It is a singular stroke of good fortune that I am here, you know. Since Puddiphat has no warrant for your apprehension, I think we may safely assume that you need *not* consider yourself in custody."

Puddiphat took serious exception to this blithe assumption. Sir Malcolm Calveley was to appear before the Chief Magistrate of Bow Street, he insisted, and have his deposition taken there. Lady Bligh glanced back at him, her hand on the drawing room door.

Through that door, which now stood slightly ajar, waddled Nimrod. The ancient hound was in no good humor, having been excluded from proceedings that had sounded from the hallway to be highly emotional. In search of a fitting object on which to vent his outrage, Nimrod settled on the nearest candidate. He waddled and wheezed his way toward that object, then joyfully sank his remaining teeth into Puddiphat's boot. Though sparse, the hound's teeth were sharp. Puddiphat howled and clutched his wounded member. Lady Bligh was not one to bypass such an opportunity. Deftly, she plucked the saber from its scabbard and with it prodded Puddiphat.

"As I was saying, Calveley," she continued, adjusting her turban, "you need not present yourself in Bow Street before resuming your travels. You *are* going to resume your travels? I thought you might. No, Puddiphat, Sir Malcolm is *not* Blood-and-Thunder." She flourished the saber. "But you may take *me* to Bow Street and explain to John how I have prevented you making a Jack-pudding of yourself."

Chapter Twenty-three

As Lady Bligh escorted Puddiphat back to Bow Street Public Office—and a highly diverting spectacle they made, the Baroness prodding her unhappy companion along and scolding all the way—Sir Malcolm Calveley escorted Miss Bagshot into the gardens behind Davenant House, there to watch the rhododendron being restored to its rightful place.

"I don't understand!" sighed Melly, in lament not for her lack of comprehension, but for the loss of the rhododendron. "If you ain't Blood-and-Thunder—and you *can't* be Blood-and-Thunder if my papa is—why are you leaving the country? Come to think on it, why did you leave the country in the first place? Wasn't you under a cloud? It was that what set Puddiphat on to you."

Sir Malcolm looked rueful. "I am *generally* under a cloud!" he confessed. "That particular episode concerned a woman, as I recall. I was no more anxious then than now to step into parson's mousetrap."

Miss Bagshot transferred her mournful gaze from the

rhododendron, which several busy gardeners were hovering solicitously about, to Sir Malcolm's handsome sun-bronzed face. Her big brown eyes lingered upon his unruly black curls and curly side-whiskers, his dark eyes and flyaway brows, his adventurous nose and sensual mouth. "No, and you ain't anxious to do other things, either! If you had a grain of proper feeling, you'd flirt with me just a little, because I'm feeling very *hipped!*"

With vast appreciation, Sir Malcolm contemplated his companion, paying particular attention to her enchanting little face, her blonde curls and pretty nose, big brown eyes and merry lips. "I think I may have lost my taste for flirtation," he admitted, as he took Melly's arm and guided her away from the scene of his crime. "My last such venture was not a success."

Melly looked anxious, then puzzled; then her dimples appeared. "Bless my soul! You're talking about your cousin! I thought at first you was talking about *me.* And I was going to accuse you of telling clankers, because I ain't ever met anybody I'd rather have lead me down the primrose path! But I still don't understand, sir, why you pretended to be planting antlers if you *wasn't.* Lord Davenham wanted your head on a platter, you know—or if he didn't, he *should* have! Which reminds me that I ain't thanked you properly for the rhododendron, even though I wasn't allowed to keep it, and was very wishful to—" Sadly, she glanced over her shoulder at the busy gardeners. "It was such a *nice* rhododendron, too!"

Sir Malcolm led Miss Bagshot along the romantic graveled pathway that led through picturesque vistas enhanced by weeping willows from China and tulippoplars from America, and into the rustic garden shelter fashioned from tree roots and branches. "My darling, I will plant you a rhododendron on every one of my estates—oh, yes, I have several."

"That is very nice," said Melly, as she sank down on a rustic bench, "but I'd much liefer have a rhododendron I can *see*. It won't do *me* a particle of good for *you* to grow rhododendrons, though I thank you for the thought."

"I intended that you see them." Wearing a very fond expression, Sir Malcolm joined Miss Bagshot on the bench. "I'd assumed you'd be with me."

"*With* you, sir?" Melly's brown eyes were watchful and huge.

For the first time in his lengthy career, Sir Malcolm felt inept. "What am I saying?" he groaned.

Solemnly, Miss Bagshot pondered this question. "I *think* you was desirous of offering me a slip on the shoulder, sir. And I wish you would go on!"

But Sir Malcolm was discovering in himself the vestiges of a conscience, and that highly inconvenient appendage dictated he could not casually make this darling minx his light o' love. "I shouldn't!" he temporized. "You can aim a great deal higher, Melly."

This latter piece of nonsense, Miss Bagshot ignored, only abjured Sir Malcolm to cease talking like a nodcock. "If you *don't*, someone else will!" she additionally pointed out. "And I'd much rather it was you! You *do* make a girl's heart flutter, sir! And I'll wager you wouldn't cut up stiff about trifles or forbid me from cutting a dash. Oh, I know you promised not to presume upon our friendship, but I've been wishing for the longest time you *would!*"

Sir Malcolm gazed upon Melly's hopeful countenance and in several languages roundly cursed his newborn conscience. Never, among all the females by whom he had been favored, had he met a maiden whom he wanted quite so much.

"You don't want me!" sighed Melly, apt if less than acute. "I've made a rare mull of it, ain't I? My intentions were the best. I thought I was the properest person to fix everything up shipshape. There ain't nothing else for it: I *will* have to go upon the stage."

Sir Malcolm's newfound conscience was no match for his long-standing dislike of causing distress. He grasped

Miss Bagshot's shoulders and turned her toward him. Melly fluttered her long lashes and looked enchantingly coy. Sir Malcolm could not help but smile. "You are a designing baggage, Miss Bagshot."

Melly dimpled. "Ain't I just? But I ain't cutting a wheedle with you, on my honor. You mustn't think I make it my habit to diddle everyone—and, anyway, you are as bad! That is one of the things I like about you, because I know exactly how it is. Or not *exactly*, because I truly ain't bachelor's fare—yet! Though I've always known *some*one would lead me astray—it's in the blood!" She paused for breath. Sir Malcolm still made no move to avail himself of her generous offer. Melly took hold of his lapels and gave him a little shake. "Sir, I do not *want* to go upon the stage!"

Sir Malcolm's conscience decreed that he should posthaste remove Miss Bagshot's hands from his lapels, lest she thereby sound the death knell for his self-control. He equivocated by placing his hands over hers. "I'm sure you can persuade your aunt to forgive you this latest start. There are other things that a beautiful young lady may do with herself beside treading the boards."

"Yes, like step into parson's mousetrap!" Had not Sir Malcolm admitted that he liked her looks, Melly might have given up. She achieved a sorry little sniffle, and a mournful glance. "And I *ain't* a young lady!"

Refraining from seduction, decided Sir Malcolm, was far more difficult than seduction itself. "You are a darling!" he informed the inspiration of his considerable inner turmoil. "But I am used to, er, variety. I would not wish to mislead you, Melly. I do not know that it is in me to be constant to any one female."

"Pooh!" By the discovery that Sir Malcolm's shilly-shallying was inspired by nothing more serious than scruples, Miss Bagshot's dimples were restored. "I never thought I'd hear *you* talking such skimble-skamble stuff. You wouldn't keep a girl without money for common necessaries, or pull a long face over her every time she tumbled into a pickle—and, anyway, we are *both* dreadful flirts!" Still he hesitated. Miss Bagshot therefore took matters into her own capable hands. She tugged so hard on Sir Malcolm's lapels that he leaned forward. Promptly, and enthusiastically, Melly kissed him. Sir Malcolm bid his conscience go and be damned.

Some little time elapsed in this very pleasant manner, at the end of which Miss Bagshot was seated on Sir Malcolm's lap, her head resting very comfortably on his shoulder, and her pretty cheeks pink. "Bless my heart!" she gasped. "If I had known how much I'd like it, I'd have tossed my bonnet over the windmill long ago!"

"Then I must be glad you *didn't* know, else you would have done so with someone other than me." Sir Malcolm gazed down upon his armful of bird-witted femininity, thinking in a distinctly besotted manner that constancy might not be all that difficult to achieve. "You seem to have forgotten your concern for the future, Melly. I have not promised you a competency."

Miss Bagshot turned up her elfin face. Huskily, she consigned the future to that infernal region whence Sir Malcolm's conscience had already flown. Naturally, Sir Malcolm kissed her again in consequence. Had they not been interrupted, Melly and Sir Malcolm might well have continued in this manner all the afternoon.

That interruption was provided by Sir Malcolm's valet. Upon discovering his master engaged in ardent embrace, Hopgood discreetly cleared his throat. "You wished to see me, sir."

"So I did." In a leisurely manner, Sir Malcolm concluded his embrace, and smiled down upon Miss Bagshot. "My darling, this is my man. He will be traveling with us."

Melly had not the slightest interest in valets or travel at that moment, or in anything under God's blue heavens but the man who held her so tenderly in his arms. What frolics they would have! she thought. And if Sir

Malcolm eventually grew tired of her and turned her off—well, the future could take care of itself, and, anyway, she meant to ensure that he did not.

Sir Malcolm, who was feeling a trifle bemused himself, gave Miss Bagshot a little shake. "If you keep looking at me like *that*," he said with mock severity, "we shall remain forever in the garden, and I think my cousins would rather be shut of the pair of us! Yes, I *know* it is very ungrateful of them, after all the trouble we have gone to on their behalf!" he added, as she frowned. Then he looked at his valet. "You have packed?"

"Yes, sir!" Hopgood inclined his head. "And may I say, sir, that it ain't a minute too soon!"

Clearly, she was to have no more kisses for the moment, decided Melly, and she transferred her attention to Sir Malcolm's valet. He stood in the doorway, his features indistinct in the pale sunlight.

"It was almost several moments too late," retorted Sir Malcolm, at his most saturnine. "You have been remiss, Hopgood! I may not remember precisely where we met, but I *would* remember had you told me you departed England only paces ahead of Bow Street." He glanced down at Melly as Hopgood moaned. "Now you understand why I have so suddenly decided to resume my travels. Hopgood may be a trifle devious, but he is a damned good servant. My need is greater than Bow Street's."

"Oh, yes, sir! Thank you, sir!" babbled Hopgood, in an excess of relief. "I don't want to go to prison, sir! And, anyway, I have reformed!"

Sir Malcolm gazed upon his anxious valet, who was literally wringing his hands. "Blood-and-Thunder!" he marveled. "Egad!"

"I *still* don't understand!" lamented Melly, as she slid off Sir Malcolm's lap and approached the stricken valet. "How can this person be Blood-and-Thunder? My Aunt Helen said——" She paused, speechless, as her vision adjusted to the sunlight.

"Your Aunt *Helen?*" echoed the valet.

"*Papa!*" Melly shrieked.

"Allow me to introduce you to one another!" suggested Sir Malcolm, from the bench. "Melly, say hello to my valet. Hopgood, make your bow to my, er, *petite amie.*" And then he fell into whoops.

Sir Malcolm's valet and *petite amie* looked without especial appreciation upon their chortling patron, and then upon each other. In this latter glance was even less delight. "You *abandoned* us!" said Melly.

And at the same moment Hopgood muttered, "I knew his weakness for fancy-pieces would land us in the suds! I felt it in my bones!"

Fancy-pieces? This from a cracksman! Miss Bagshot was not reluctant to make her indignation known. "Bless my soul, here's my own papa calling the kettle black!" she observed. "I *ain't* a fancy-piece, and even if I *was,* it'd be better than *stealing* things!" She looked very stern. "And you'd better never steal from Sir Malcolm, because I won't stand for it—and I mean to keep a very close eye on you!"

Hopgood's bones had misled him; it was not Sir Malcolm who had landed in the suds. Moreover, Hopgood knew not how to extricate himself. "And I you, Miss!" he retorted. "You needn't think the master is a pigeon for your plucking, because I mean to see he *ain't!*"

No damsel to take offense at plain speaking, Melly thoughtfully regarded the subject of this conversation, who was chuckling still. "I shouldn't think anyone *could!*" she said. "Since we are going to be living in one another's pockets, P—— Do you mind if I do *not* call you Papa? I ain't seen you for so long, and it sounds very queer!"

Hopgood was relieved to discover he had sired a sensible offspring. Promptly he agreed.

Melly nibbled contemplatively on her lower lip. "I can't call you Bagshot because that's *my* name, so it will have to be Hopgood. That's a very clever name, sir, because it is exactly what you did! But here I am, jawing on again! I meant to say that we should call a truce, Hopgood. I shan't scold you for abandoning Mama and me—to say the truth, I sometimes thought of abandoning her myself!—so long as you don't scold me about my frolics and larks." She shook a cautionary finger under the valet's nose. "Providing that you don't steal anything!"

Frolics and larks? Hopgood was each moment growing more reconciled to his daughter. He was not delighted about this reunion, but if Sir Malcolm had to take up with some female, Melly was doubtless better than most. In a rare moment of paternal excess—so rare, in fact, that he only ever experienced one other such—that second moment being the occasion when Sir Malcolm and Melly, after sharing many frolicsome adventures, overcame their mutual antipathy to marriage and stepped together into parson's mousetrap during a small and private ceremony witnessed by London's most fashionable milliner, and Lord and Lady Davenham and their numerous tardy offspring—he said, "The master has a nasty temper, Miss."

"Sir Malcolm?" That individual looked anything but tempersome, sitting on the bench clutching his sides and gasping for breath. Melly shrugged. "I don't care a straw for *that*. But maybe you don't know what it's like, Papa—I mean Hopgood!—to have a decided partiality."

Lest Miss Bagshot explain to her parent just how it felt to nourish a *tendre*—only one of countless bizarre contingencies that he anticipated with great glee—Sir Malcolm overcame his mirth. "Hopgood, you doubtless have some last-minute details to attend to. We shall go to Paris by way of Calais. Melly, you will like Paris. Calais is only a little fishing village, but Dessein's hotel is unrivaled throughout Europe."

"It sounds even *better* than Brighton!" Thus did Miss Bagshot bestow the supreme accolade. "Have you *always* known my papa was a thief, sir?"

Obviously, Miss Bagshot had not derived from her reunion with her papa an enjoyment equal to his own. Sir Malcolm arose from the bench and drew her into his arms. "I realized it only today. You must not fret, my darling. Hopgood *has* reformed."

"Oh, I don't give a fig for Hopgood." Melly gazed up at Sir Malcolm, looking demure and adorably misty-eyed. "I was just afraid that stealing might be in the blood. But I don't think Aunt Hel's ever stolen anything, and I know *I* ain't——"

Sir Malcolm's tone was very serious. "But you *have* stolen something. Melly: my heart."

"Zounds!" enthused Miss Bagshot, when she was allowed to draw breath. *"Now* are we going to toss my bonnet over the windmill?"

In a nigh-miraculous burst of self-control, Sir Malcolm set her away. "No, my darling. We are not going to go near that accursed windmill again until a settlement has been drawn up. Not all of us are nipfarthings, Melly."

"Bless my heart!" cried Miss Bagshot, pressing her hands to her palpitating breast. "If you don't know everything there is to know about women, sir, you know more than anyone *should!"* And then—alas for Sir Malcolm's self-control and good intentions—she blushed and giggled and cast herself upon his chest.

Chapter Twenty-four

"Slowtop! Muttonhead! Pea-brain!" uttered the Chief Magistrate of Bow Street. Having thoroughly demoralized Puddiphat, he turned his acerbic gaze on Crump. "You are little better. Stolen rhododendrons and attempted blackmail and antlers planted on ducal brows!"

By this somewhat cryptic utterance, Crump understood that he was to be held responsible for Puddiphat's errors of judgment. Due to long experience with his Chief Magistrate, Crump understood also that it was pointless to try and put forth a defense until Sir John's wrath had ebbed. The Runner withdrew to the window, in which the broken glass had been replaced, and brought forth his pipe. Profitable as had been his private inquiry work, it had apparently prevented his involvement in rare shenanigans.

Bow Street's emissaries in those shenanigans were disposed about Sir John's scarred desk. Puddiphat stood before it, in receipt of strict orders not even to breathe, let alone move, lest he wreak further havoc. His posture was as rigid as if he were indeed a member of a military organization. Lady Bligh, perched on a corner of the old desk, was considerably more relaxed.

"Do not be so *stuffy,* John!" The Baroness awarded the Chief Magistrate her roguish glance. "I have already read poor Puddiphat a severe scold. He has tried to do a good job for you, even if he did manage to only make a Jack-pudding of himself." She flourished the saber which she still held.

Anxious as Puddiphat might be to please, he had his sticking point, and he still smarted from the ignominious spectacle he had presented, being marched at saber's point through the London streets. "Dashed if it's *fair!*" he muttered. "All I did was look for proof, like I was told to do—was even going to turn it over to Crump, and let him take credit for my work!" He craned his head to cast the Runner a hostile glare.

"Ah, no, laddie!" responded Crump, around the pipe clamped between his teeth. "I'll take none of the credit for you making a cake of yourself."

"Tsk-tsk, Crump!" Lady Bligh laid the saber across her lap and applied herself with gusto to the hot chestnuts she'd purchased en route. "You were responsible for drawing Puddiphat into this business— although it was Miss Bagshot who set him to rainbow-chasing. Have a chestnut, John! You would have liked the minx."

What Sir John would have liked was to clear his office of irresponsible Runners and inept bunglers wheedled into carrying out their tasks, and devote his full attention to a certain irrepressibly nosy Baroness. But the Chief Magistrate of Bow Street was a serious and dedicated man. He kept his peace and helped himself to hot chestnuts.

Despite Sir John's forbearance, the peace was not long kept. Footsteps pounded up the stairs. In the doorway appeared a sharp-faced, fashionably clad female with heaving bosom and a lace cornette atop her faded hair. "Ah!" said Lady Bligh, through a mouthful of hot chestnuts. "Helen. John, this is my milliner, Madame le Best."

"*Your* milliner?" suspiciously inquired the Chief Magistrate, swallowing his own hot chestnuts a trifle too fast. Solicitously, the Baroness pounded him on the back.

Madame le Best had known Lady Bligh far too long to be especially surprised to find her dangling her elegant ankles from a desktop, eating chestnuts and cradling a saber. That latter item, Madame darted across the room and snatched, then brandished under Puddiphat's nose. "What have you done with my niece, you —you *puppy?* Don't deny it! I know she left with you!"

Puddiphat concentrated so hard on the menacing saber that his eyes crossed. "The rhododendron!" he gasped.

"You'd clap the child in jail because someone gave her a rhododendron she should not have?" Madame recalled various other reasons why members of her immediate family might be clapped in jail, and additionally that she claimed to be French. "*Ma foil Mon Dieu! La vache!* I won't stand for it, you hear!"

To fail to hear Madame would have required a state of deafness, thought Sir John, who had never heard the French language so uniquely pronounced, or in tones that were quite so shrill. "Compose yourself, Helen!" said the Baroness. "Your niece has not been imprisoned, despite her propensity toward attempted blackmail. Give me back that saber, if you please! Before poor Puddiphat swoons from shock." Having recovered the weapon, Lady Bligh removed the last chestnut from Sir John's fingers and popped it into her mouth. "Why are you in such a pucker, by the by? You threatened to turn the chit out."

"Only if she cut another lark!" Madame protested quickly; there was something in the Baroness's dark glance that prompted her to self-defense. "I never seriously meant to turn Melly out, although I vow I do not know what to do with the child!"

Dulcie wiped her fingers on her jaconet gown in a very vulgar manner. "I fancy," she said serenely, "that matter has been taken out of your hands. At least you need no longer worry about the chit tossing her bonnet over the windmill now that she has already done so."

"Bonnet?" gasped Madame, so faintly that Crump abandoned his window long enough to push forward a wooden chair. "Windmill? *Hélas!*"

"It is nothing so bad as all that." The Baroness remained unmoved by her milliner's histrionics, which included eyes rolled heavenward, and a rigidity of the extremities, and culminated in collapse upon the wooden chair. "Calveley is in very easy circumstances— and I do not think he has ever traveled with a female companion before. You must realize by now that your niece is incapable of *not* cutting larks, Helen! At least this way she may cut them as far away from you as is possible."

Although Madame keenly felt the force of this argument, she did not wish to appear heartless. "Heartshorn! Vinaigrette!" she moaned.

"Moonshine!" retorted Dulcie, and leaned forward to thwack her milliner with the saber, an act which caused the Chief Magistrate to reflect wistfully upon her superb physique. The Baroness sighed in a manner that would have done justice to Miss Bagshot. "Ah, La Roué."

Puddiphat had listened to this dialogue with a rapidly burgeoning sense of injustice done himself. Everyone was devilishly tolerant, he thought, of a damsel who'd done her utmost to diddle Bow Street. Puddiphat wasn't entirely convinced, moreover, that the damsel hadn't succeeded. In the whole miserable time he'd spent in this office, Blood-and-Thunder hadn't once been named.

"Blood-and-Thunder!" ejaculated Puddiphat, thus remedying that oversight and casting a very effective damper on the conversation under way. "Aye, and what *about* Blood-and-Thunder?" inquired Crump, from the window. Due to the discomforts Blood-and-Thunder had caused him one way and another, Crump was beginning to take a distinctly proprietorial interest in the rogue.

"That's what *I'd* like to know!" Puddiphat craned his head to look again at the one sympathetic person in the room. And then he launched into a long and garbled expostulation, the main contentions of which were that Sir Malcolm Calveley had indeed been Blood-and-Thunder, and that Miss Bagshot had been his accomplice, and that corruption must be rife in high places, else so dangerous a duo would not be allowed to go free. "A suspicious and dangerous character!" he said in conclusion. "Miss Bagshot herself said he should languish behind bars."

"Miss Bagshot is an incurable humbugger," Lady Bligh retorted dismissively. "You must take my word for it that Calveley is not the man you seek."

Puddiphat saw no reason why he should do anything of the sort. *"Physiognomical Fragments!"* he protested. "Calveley left the country under a cloud!"

Sir John had all this time been raptly—and most improperly—reflecting upon the bounty inadequately concealed by Dulcie's jaconet morning dress. That he roused now was due only to the sharp pinch she bestowed upon his arm. Repressively, he inquired, "Do *you* remember that old scandal?"

"I *always* remember a rogue." The Baroness smiled, leaned across the desk, and whispered a name in the Chief Magistrate's ear. "Thunder!" said he.

"Blood-and-Thunder!" supplied Puddiphat helpfully. "Told you so! Yes, and that blasted dog bit my boot!" He extended his mangled footwear for all to see. Alas, as might have been anticipated, this act caused Puddiphat to lose his balance. He stumbled across the room and fetched up at last on the lap of Madame le Best. "Young man, you are a perfect *block!*" she snapped.

"No such thing!" Ludicrous as may have been his

position, Puddiphat glowered. "I know what I know, even if nobody wants credit given where it's due. Tell you what; I don't think I *want* to become a Runner after all this."

"Take my word for it, laddie!" observed Crump, from the window. "You *don't!*" Genially, he met his Chief Magistrate's unappreciative stare. "If that's all, guv'nor, I'll be off."

"Do!" responded Sir John, testily. "And take this precious pair with you!" He indicated the wooden chair, whereupon Puddiphat was informing Madame le Best that they were partners in misfortune, both having been thoroughly diddled by a sad romp.

"Never mind, Helen!" soothed Lady Bligh, as the milliner forcibly evicted Puddiphat from her lap. "You shall provide me *several* new gowns. One, I think, must be made up in London Soot."

London Soot? It was not the first time Crump had wondered if perhaps the Baroness was quite mad. He shepherded his charges out of the office and into the nearby tavern, where he did his utmost to persuade Puddiphat against a career as a Runner, and Puddiphat alternately bewailed his ruined boots and the wriggling of Sir Malcolm Calveley off the hook of justice, and Madame le Best silently congratulated herself on a similar escape.

Meanwhile, in Sir John's office, a brief silence reigned. The Chief Magistrate contemplated Lady Bligh, who in her turn looked pensively down upon Puddiphat's saber, which she still held. Then she put aside the saber, tucked her feet beneath her, and rested her elbows on her knees. "Now we may be comfortable, John!"

Comfortable the Baroness may have been, but Bow Street's Chief Magistrate was not. Hastily, he pushed his chair back from his desk. "A pretty to-do this has been!" he said, crossing to the window where Crump had so recently stood. "And furthermore, I'm very much aware that you know more than you've told."

Dulcie's glance was wicked. *"Dearest* John, you have only yourself to blame for this muddle. Puddiphat would not have had occasion to leap to so many erroneous conclusions had you enlisted my aid in the first place—not that you ever had any real cause to get the wind up." She untangled herself from her highly provocative position and slid off the desk. "I have told you before that you work too hard, John! If you allowed yourself some recreation, you would not be so prone to fashion mountains from molehills."

"What sort of recreation?" inquired the Chief Magistrate, in most unmagisterial tones—for Dulcie had come to stand beside him, and her scent was thick and sweet in his nostrils.

"Shame on you, my friend!" Dulcie leaned against his arm. "You owe me a favor in return for my efforts on your behalf. I think you must escort me to the theater tonight. The world will be abuzz with the news of Calveley's departure, I'll warrant; and we may chuckle among ourselves because we know the truth of the tale."

The Chief Magistrate was well acquainted with Lady Bligh's talent to distract. *"Was* Calveley a cracksman?" he bluntly inquired.

Replied the Baroness, with equal bluntness: "John, you are in grave danger of growing positively *dull!* What does it matter *who* Blood-and-Thunder was, since the man has obviously reformed? Ah, I see you do not agree with my reasoning."

Sir John was at that moment far more interested in Lady Bligh's patrician face, in her heady perfume, and in the warm and lissome body so tantalizingly close to his own. Sternly, he reminded himself that she was a married woman, and he the Chief Magistrate of Bow Street Public Office, and that many years had elapsed since they had been more than friends. Those reminders having done him not the least good, he moved away.

The Baroness wrinkled her aristocratic nose and perched at the windowsill. *"Definitely* dull! I will make you a bargain, John. Providing you promise not to act on it, I will pose you a hypothesis."

"Very well." Sir John folded his arms and prepared to limit his enjoyment to Lady Bligh's keen mind.

"Suppose you had once had in your employ an excellent seamstress whose only failing in the world was that she had a brother who was a great deal less high-minded than herself," suggested Dulcie, who had the rare ability to, whilst discussing serious matters, look very roguish, indeed. "Suppose, also, that when that seamstress left your employ you assisted her in setting up her own shop. Naturally, under such circumstances, you would keep in touch, would be aware her rascally brother had left the country. Suppose, then, that it was brought to your attention that this seamstress had roused the curiosity of Bow Street."

Roguish as the Baroness might look, Sir John was not so disarmed that he failed to realize she'd been less than forthright. "Dulcie, are you telling me—"

"I am trying to *tell* you nothing!" the Baroness reproved. "Merely to offer one of many hypotheses which an intelligent person might, under these circumstances, have formed. Where was I? Ah, yes. Certain suspicions were harbored by Bow Street." She tapped a fingernail against her perfect teeth. "Suppose that there was some basis for the suspicions of Bow Street, as occasionally there are; suppose that the seamstress's rascally brother was in fact Blood-and-Thunder, and that he *had* come home."

Sir John was growing weary of all these suppositions, which were distracting him from his current main concern, which dealt not with matters of law and justice, but an intention to take the provocative Baroness into his arms, a lapse that may perhaps be forgiven him, because he had not done so for some while. "Get to the point!" he demanded.

"Patience, John!" Lady Bligh straightened her turban for the umpteenth time. "Where Puddiphat erred was in his assumption that Calveley was the cracksman, which of course he was not." Triumphantly, she smiled. "But Calveley has a very discreet and unobtrusive valet, whom he hired during his travels, and to whom he has grown quite attached."

All thoughts of dalliance flew straight out of Sir John's head. "Do you mean to tell me Calveley's *valet—*"

"I mean to tell you nothing." The Baroness departed from the windowsill. "This is merely guesswork. But you have overlooked the implications. *Were* Calveley's valet the missing Blood-and-Thunder, he would also be Miss Bagshot's father." Mischievously, she smiled.

Sir John had sat too long in his shabby office, had heard too many cases to be surprised by any of the tangled relationships indulged in by the human animal. "You seem to have gone straight from A to Z! What made you suspect the valet?" he complained, then raised his heavy brows. "Of course you knew what the milliner's brother looked like. You recognized Calveley's valet."

"I have always enjoyed skulking about," Lady Bligh said enigmatically, as she came to a halt before the Chief Magistrate and touched his wrist. "This is the purest conjecture, John! Whoever Blood-and-Thunder was, he has not resumed his criminal activities, and no one is going to pay for his prosecution after so many years. This entire business is best forgotten."

So it was, and if Sir John deplored the inadequacies of criminal justice, it was not his place to impose reform. "You make forgetting easy, Dulcie." His smile lifted the weight of years from his tired face.

"I had meant to!" admitted the Baroness, as she moved her cool fingers from the Chief Magistrate's wrist to his shoulders. "Now you may kiss me, John, and then we shall have our tea."

Chapter Twenty-five

Lady Davenham was also having her tea, albeit a great deal less cheerfully. Thea was in her bookroom, seated at her kneehole writing desk, upon which reposed the tea tray. Having given up all hope of ever achieving a condition of unobtrusive emaciation, she was munching indiscriminately upon Shrewsbury tea cakes. Opened on her lap was a very old book—*New Principles of Gardening,* by Batty Langley, of which she had not read one word. As result of recent developments, Lady Davenham was feeling very confused. Speculations chased themselves around her head like angry hornets.

"There you are, my dear!" Lord Davenham strolled into the bookroom, Nimrod wheezing at his heels. "I have been looking for you. You will be pleased to learn the rhododendron has been restored."

Deep in a fit of the blue devils, result of her various conjectures, Lady Davenham handed her husband a tea cup. "I have been wondering," she murmured, "if perhaps we should introduce the Colling brothers short-horn cattle into our own herd, and thus improve the breed. You had at one time considered doing so, I believe."

"Shorthorns." Looking very ruminative, Lord Davenham sat down upon a highbacked chair. "That calls to mind something I particularly wished to say to you, Thea. I didn't mean that you *should* plant the antlers on my brow, but that I trusted you *not* to!"

By the calmness with which her exasperating spouse uttered this sentiment, Lady Davenham was further depressed. A reasonable husband would not respond serenely to the suggestion that his wife might have made him a cuckold, she thought. Still, Thea wished that misunderstanding to be wholly cleared up. "It was all Malcolm's idea. We were to flirt desperately with one another so that you would display a dog-in-the-manger attitude," she confessed, into her tea cup.

Lord Davenham balanced his own tea cup adroitly upon one knee. "That would not have been very generous of me, especially after—or so Miss Bagshot informed me!—I had as good as *invited* you to have a bit of frolic."

Nor were Thea's spirits lightened by this reminder of the high esteem in which her husband held Miss Bagshot. It was little wonder he had exhibited none of the signs of an enraged spouse. Yet he was exhibiting none of the signs of a rejected suitor, either. Thea wondered if she would ever understand Vivien. "A bit of frolic?" she repeated absently. "You did no such thing."

"Certainly I did not *mean* to." Lord Davenham shifted positions, thereby earning a growl from Nimrod, whose liverish bulk was stretched across his boots. "But I distinctly recall saying you should do as you wished. Miss Bagshot has informed me that it's only when you don't care about someone that you don't mind what they do—which is not the case! What I meant was that I want you to be happy."

Lady Davenham wished the same fate for her husband, despite her periodic impulses to alternately throttle him and hang weeping around his neck. "Thank you!" she said gloomily. "You are very kind. I would return the compliment, but I know *your* happiness is impossible to achieve. But that is your own fault, Vivien! You *could* have cut Malcolm out, had you made the slightest push."

In a very elegant manner, the Duke drained his tea cup. "You are mistaken, my dear. I *did* make a push."

The Duchess was not awarding the conversation her full attention, being caught up in dreary remembrance of the Duke escorting Miss Bagshot to the Horticultural Society, and tooling the ribbons in St. James's Park with Melly beside him on the carriage seat. Apparently Vivien *was* incapable of strong emotion, she concluded, or he would not so calmly accept Malcolm's triumph.

Lady Davenham's abstraction had not escaped her husband's notice. "*Do* pay attention, my dear! This is not the moment to try and repay me for air-dreaming," he said ironically. "I have just told you that I *did* make a push to cut Malcolm out. And though I would not wish to sound a coxcomb, I fancy I was successful."

"Oh, Vivien." This display of wrong-headed optimism quite wrung Thea's heart. "How can you fail to see that Miss Bagshot is Malcolm's?"

Lord Davenham set down his tea cup on the floor. "But I do not *want* Miss Bagshot," he explained, with a contemplative expression. "Although I did not think of it before, perhaps I should have let them keep that rhododendron—as a gesture of appreciation."

Vivien *didn't* want Melly? Thea tried very hard to understand. "Rhododendrons? *Appreciation?*" she echoed. "Sometimes I think I am grown mad as Bedlam, Vivien—or that *you* are! First you admit that you wished to steal a march on Malcolm, and then you wonder if you should reward him for cutting you out!" She massaged her throbbing temples. "Let us end this conversation before I succumb to a fever of the brain."

Ever-amiable, the Duke indicated to his loyal hound that he wished to vacate the high-backed chair. Sulkily, Nimrod removed himself from atop his lordship's boots.

"I have been thinking about your suggestions concerning a reaping machine," remarked Lord Davenham, as he strolled to the kneehole desk and selected a Benton tea cake. "About those pulleys—"

"I have not the least distant interest in pulleys!" snapped Lady Davenham, pushing back her own chair. "Do not change the subject!"

Upon his Duchess's inconsistency, the Duke did not comment, merely caught her chair before it could crash to the floor. "Both of us have been somewhat muddle-headed, I fear. You see, my dear, *I* have no interest in the fleshpots. Nor do I wish to kick over the traces. And I certainly do not hold you in lower opinion than caterpillars and snails."

"You do not?" Doubtless it was due to the quickness of her rising that Thea felt faint. "But you said—"

"I did *not* say that all Davenants were unsuited to marriage!" Vivien caught his unsteady wife by the waist. "I, for one, have always liked it very well. It was you who hankered after adventure, Thea."

Naturally, a lady who was being clasped around the waist by a gentleman must of necessity rest her hands upon his arms. "Yes, but that was before I knew what adventure was *like*," Lady Davenham observed, briefly hopeful. Then her spirits plummeted. "And Malcolm said that if I had made our life at home more interesting, you would not have strayed. I will not play second fiddle, Vivien! Or tolerate you embracing me in another's place!"

Elusive and vague as he might be, the Duke was still very much a Davenant. "Exactly so, my dear!" he said, and promptly embraced his wife.

"Wretch!" responded Lady Davenham, as she struggled half-heartedly to free herself. "I was not issuing you an invitation."

"No? Then you should not provoke me, Thea." Lord Davenham maintained upon his wife's lush person a gentle but firm hold. "Moreover, I thought you enjoyed being embraced. You used to seem to, at any rate; only since we came to London I thought your sentiments had changed. Then the other evening, I had good cause to believe I had been mistaken—but perhaps that was the result of the ratafia. And for the record, my dear, you have never played second fiddle to anyone."

"I have not?" Had Thea heard correctly? How had Vivien taken the absurd notion that she did not enjoy— Blushing, Thea lowered her eyes, but not before she had glimpsed her husband's expression, and the very wicked twinkle in the depth of his own dark eyes. Perhaps he was not as indifferent to her as she had thought.

Lady Davenham sought relief from her giddiness by leaning back against the desk. "Oh, I wish we had never left the country! There I did not have to contend with anything more worrisome than epidemics and droughts and failed crops—no, Vivien, I do *not* wish to talk about the crops!"

Lord Davenham, at that moment, had scant interest in his estates. He elevated his gaze from his wife's delectable bosom to the pulse beating at the base of her throat. "What *do* you wish to talk about?"

"Um," responded Lady Davenham. Her husband had touched his fingers to the pulsebeat which so intrigued him, and Thea experienced a certain difficulty in concentrating her mind as a result. "If you *didn't* want Miss Bagshot, why did you take her to the Horticultural Society and drive with her in St. James's Park?"

"Because I thought you wanted me to divert her attention from Malcolm." His lordship made a mental note to provide his wife with several similar treats before they departed London. "That is what I meant by a muddle, my dear. I thought you were infatuated with Malcolm, and you thought I was infatuated with Miss Bagshot. The two of us have been going on in a very bad way."

"You truly thought I had a *tendre* for Malcolm?" Thea cried, astounded. Then she recalled that she had once thought so herself.

"What else *was* I to think?" Lord Davenham raised

his other hand and placed it against his wife's flushed cheek. Not unpleasurably, she shivered. "Malcolm's conduct was calculated to create exactly that impression. My dear, no man alive would relish the spectacle of another man paying such marked attention to his wife. It was deuced difficult to stand by and do nothing, when I would have liked no better than to wring Malcolm's blasted neck. But I wished that you should make up your own mind."

Lady Davenham relished this dog-in-the-manger attitude, however belatedly exhibited. "I did not think you had noticed. You are always so confounded *calm!* But Malcolm paid no more attention to me than he would have to any other female in my position. Until he decided you should be made jealous, that is! Never did I suspect that it was such heavy work to carry on a flirtation." She frowned. "Our cousin is a devil. And we still do not know what brought him home."

"*I* do; it was some business matter with which he had to deal personally." Lord Davenham's gentle fingers moved from Lady Davenham's throat downward. His lordship was wearied of conversation. That her ladyship felt similarly was indicated by the rapid beating of her heart. "*Must* we talk about Malcolm?" he breathed.

"No." Lady Davenham's voice was somewhat bemused, the result of Lord Davenham's current whimsies, which included unbraiding her lovely hair. One small detail still nagged at Thea, despite her rapidly growing contentment with all the world. "Any man who cared a *fig* for his wife wouldn't be amused by a chit who tried to blackmail her."

"That is not necessarily true." Lord Davenham ran his hands luxuriously through his wife's curls. "Despite all the hints and warnings given me by Miss Bagshot and James, I knew you had done nothing to be blackmailed *for.*"

"James?" Lady Davenham was puzzled by this abrupt introduction of the squire. "What has *he* to say to this business?"

"What James had to *say* was that mettlesome fillies should not be given their heads." Lord Davenham was himself looking somewhat bemused, due to the fact that his wife was absentmindedly unbuttoning his waistcoat. "What he has to do with the business is nothing at all, save that there *has* been a certain amount of talk."

"And it has been my fault!" sighed Thea, stricken. "Vivien, can you ever forgive me for being such a— a *looby?* I cannot help but think a great deal of this contretemps has been my fault."

Looking very serious, Lord Davenham clasped his wife's hands. "My dear, there is something yet to discuss. I have recently come to realize that I have neglected you shockingly. I have not meant to do so! It is just that I have so many responsibilities." A familiar expression stole across his features. "As for my potting shed—"

To this digression the Duchess responded promptly: "May the devil fly away with your potting shed! Oh, do not look so wounded, Vivien; I am as interested in your gardens as anyone can be—but I would prefer to resolve our marital difficulties before we progress to heartsease and candytuft."

It was not to heartsease and candytuft that his lordship wished to progress. "A fig for gardens!" he said bluntly. "I had *meant* to tell you that it was not due to indifference that I have not appeared especially . . . *adventurous* of late."

Lady Davenham experienced no difficulty in deciphering this somewhat cryptic comment, as result of which she stared wide-eyed at her husband's rueful face. "You thought I had taken you in adversion and I thought you were indifferent. Yes, and that you wished to sow your wild oats! We have been a couple of gudgeons, I think. But, Vivien! You know that I am not a . . . *pushing* sort of female. I did not wish to *force* myself on you. Oh, the devil with propriety! I have never truly wished to be adventurous with anyone *else!*"

Thea might push or no, as the impulse took her, and

she would still be the perfect wife for Vivien. So he explained, as he drew her close to him, and rested his cheek on her dark curls. "About the other night, my dear. I fear I took advantage—"

"Fudge!" Lady Davenham drew back, rosy-cheeked. "You refine too much on it. *Whichever* of us took advantage, I liked it very well! I see now that I should have told you so before."

"In the future you may do so." Lord Davenham's voice was very close to a caress. "As in the future you may *not* doubt that I love you, Thea. Far more than *any* of my estates."

So much as that? Thea drew a deep, shaken breath. "And I love you, Vivien. I always have. Gracious, what larks we have been involved in! Cracksmen and blackmail and Bow Street! I shall be glad to return home." One did not recover overnight from excessive dosages of propriety, but both Lady Davenham and her lordship felt she had made a very good start. In proof of this assumption was her ladyship's next action. Shyly, the Duchess fixed her gaze on her husband's unbuttoned waistcoat, the sight of which inspired her to deal similarly with his shirt. "And . . . as regards the other night—of course it is too soon to be certain—still, sometimes one just *knows!*"

Looking not the least bit abstracted, Lord Davenham once more caught his wife's hands, which made concentration extremely difficult. "Are you speaking, my dear, of our long-anticipated heir?"

"I think I must be!" responded Thea, who at this point wasn't certain *what* she was talking about, and moreover didn't care. So moved was his lordship by this intelligence that he promptly embraced his wife in a fashion that left her no doubt whatsoever that he was capable of strong emotion, indeed.

Relish as might Lord and Lady Davenham the reconciliation of their differences, the occasion was not equally enjoyed by the hound Nimrod. Jealously, he had watched the proceedings. Now that the Duke had been inspired to actively embrace his Duchess, and in a manner much more suited to ancestral bedchambers than to bookrooms, Nimrod felt compelled to intervene. Growling and snarling, he wheezed across the room, and snapped at the Duchess's heels. Thea gave a little shriek. Rising magnificently to the occasion, Vivien swept his wife up in his arms and callously shoved aside his hound with one booted foot. Vanquished, Nimrod descended to the kitchens, where he consoled himself by terrorizing the cook.

Lady Davenham simultaneously sought to smooth her hair and adjust her *décolletage,* clutch her husband's shoulders, and puzzle out why he was carrying her up the stairs. "And in case I am mistaken, there is always the *next* time!" His lordship's grip tightened, and she gasped. "What *are* you doing, Vivien?"

Lord Davenham gazed down into his wife's face. The Duke looked most engagingly rakish, "I thought we'd get on with the next time," he suggested, with a whimsical smile.